A Wound in the Earth

A Novel

A Wound in the Earth

A Novel

JASON DURANT

Book design by Maureen Cutajar
www.gopublished.com

ISBN: 978-1-7334407-2-1

Contents

One

THE ENORMOUS EGG

When an animal or plant species no longer finds earth hospitable, it ceases to live as a physical entity, but its imprint, or group spirit, survives. Around 1507, Portuguese sailors landed on Mauritius, an island in the Indian Ocean, home of the dodo. By 1681, the dodo was extinct. The dodo spirit did some traveling. It found a new home on an astral plane and spawned a new race of dodos—super dodos. In tune with their nature spirit, they experienced rapid development and near-perfect survivability. Until they began brushing with earth.

At an agreed-upon time, the three Barney children woke and raced to the windows. They tried to see everything for miles around, but the prairie that surrounded their home remained folded in the red streaks of dawn. Was there a giant bird outside? Would it break into their house? Would it carry them away?

Half-delirious, they dressed and crept downstairs.

Ralph, the youngest Barney, crawled onto one of the living-room sofas. His sister, Angela, sat beside him and began tying his shoes.

"Hold still, Ralph," she said.

Little Ralph was thrashing his feet up and down, as if he were trying to run straight up into the air. Or maybe he was trying to fly. In any case, he could not contain his excitement.

"Hurry, hurry!" said Ralph. "Let's go, let's go!" He snapped his fingers wildly as Angela continued tying his shoes.

Hubert, the oldest of the Barney children, stepped to a window and drew the curtain aside. The sun, swelling up crimson over the horizon, cast a cool glow on his face. The scent of summer fields came in on the breeze, through the screen that held back the ever-nagging insect life. Birds—normal-sized birds, presumably—sent up their morning calls, tickling the ears of the Barney children.

"I've looked all around," said Hubert, "through all the windows. Can't see hide nor feather—"

Hubert was interrupted by Ralph.

"Giant red roc!" he cried, catching a glimpse of the sun through the window.

"Hush, Ralph," said Angela. "That was just the sun." She finished tying his shoes. "You don't want Mom and Dad to know, do you?"

"Gosh, no," said Ralph in a hushed voice. He looked around. He calmed down. He knew Mom and Dad would never allow an expedition to the giant egg—if they knew. They were still asleep, in the front bedroom.

The Barney children crept to the kitchen and packed lunches. They ate breakfast then crept to the bathroom and brushed and flossed their teeth.

They filled three canteens with water and grabbed three pairs of binoculars. They put on hats—safari hats, Angela called them, but they were ordinary cowboy and cowgirl hats.

Angela got her camera, then wrote a note for their parents and put it on the kitchen table. It read: *We're out riding horses. Packed lunches. Back about 5 p.m.*

They grabbed their lunches.

Ready ... set ... go ...

The expedition was on.

They crept out the door.

The Barneys lived in a river valley graced by gentle hills. Hearing the whisper of traffic from a distant two-lane highway, they crept to the stable. Hubert saddled two horses—Pioneer and Cassandra. Angela mounted Cassandra. Hubert handed Ralph up to sit behind her, then mounted Pioneer.

The party was off.

Hubert led, picking his way, keeping the horses to well-worn trails. Normally while riding horse, he would allow himself to be thrilled by the jostle and rush, by the feel of the powerful beast beneath him, but now he had a great responsibility upon him. The giant egg and all the unknowns that went with it could be fraught with danger. Hubert carried a loaded carbine in a saddle scabbard. He was a sure shot, and he was very careful.

A heady mixture of fear and excitement came to him now—a reassuring rush that propelled him along the trail. The egg—monster that it was, shocking to the senses that it was—fit into the world somehow, in some hair-raising fashion.

He looked back. Angela and Ralph were fluid upon Cassandra; Cassandra was fluid upon the trail. Hubert faced forward and relaxed. He scanned the sky. The menu above was changing. Pink clouds were melting off. Streamers of cool blueness were emerging. Blue was Hubert's favorite color—by far. He laughed. He heard his laughter, surprising himself.

They'd found the egg yesterday, toward evening, while riding through rangeland awash in natural prairie grasses and wildflowers. Shrimpy shrubs with purplish-brown bark, wicked barbs, and startling purple leaves had choked the area. Angela had dubbed the strange shrubs purple dwarfs. She took special pride in knowing the names of native trees, shrubs, and grasses, but these purple dwarfs, which were growing in profusion in this area of the grasslands but nowhere else, had stumped her.

The egg was near a stand of bur oak that ran along a creased stretch of land, which eons ago might have been a riverbed. Now it was just a long rimple of sorts, as seen from a distance, curving off and out of sight.

"A wound in the earth," is what Angela had called it. "An ancient wound," she had added, looking at it some more.

A glint caught their eye. They moved toward it, mesmerized, maneuvering through the purple dwarfs. An egg? they thought. Dismounting and holding the reins, they walked to it.

Yes, it was an egg. About three feet high, maybe four and a half feet long, off-white, solid, somewhat rough to the touch, and ... alive!

It felt alive.

To the palms of their eager hands, it communicated a message of life, of a heart ticking. To their rapt ears, pressed against the shell, it spoke of something deep, something primeval.

They ran from it.

Hubert did a quick reconnaissance, running a ways through the stand of oak. Out again under the naked heavens, he scanned above. Frightful thoughts chugged through his mind. He checked the egg one last time, placing his palm against it, before jumping onto Pioneer. It was calmer now, but he knew something was going to hatch from it—and soon.

The Barneys had ridden away, to home, to dinner, agreeing to keep their mouths shut about the egg, except amongst themselves. On the way home, they planned their return trip the next morning. They knew they had a monster egg on their hands, but they were thinking more so of the monster that had laid it.

"Giant roc," Ralph had said, from the back of Cassandra.

Angela had not disagreed.

Hubert had been doubtful. But what? He was keeping all possibilities open.

Dinner had been swell at the Barneys'. Night fell. Bedtime. Asleep. Up at the crack of dawn, and dawn had arrived not a moment too soon—a hot egg awaited them.

Hubert screwed his hat tighter onto his head, checked the trail, and dug his heels into Pioneer, urging the horse to go faster.

The horse stretched out and ate up ground. Cassandra gave chase. Over the trails they went, flying along. They rose with the hills, raced through flowing prairieland.

After a good sprint, Hubert slowed Pioneer to a trot, then motioned to Angela. It was usual business—a water trough for range stock, fed by pump from a well, was in sight. They pointed the horses at it and Pioneer and Cassandra walked over and drank.

The three Barneys gazed at the sky. Blue was popping out all over; the pink of early morning was gone; some gray feathers remained at odd pulsing altitudes.

"I've got the willies, Hubert," said Angela. She shivered.

"I've got the willies too," said Ralph, though he sounded more excited than nervous.

Hubert took a slug of water from his canteen. It felt cool down his throat. He watched as Angela and Ralph drank from theirs. Not too much now, he willed, but they each took just a sip without having to be reminded. What they had in their canteens was the only safe water till home, barring a downpour so thick you could stick your tongue out and lap some. The water in the troughs that dotted the range was not safe enough for people—insects swam in it, among other things—though you could drink it to stay alive if necessary, otherwise leave it for the animals.

"Willies, huh?" said Hubert. "What's a willy, Ralph?"

"Uh ..." Ralph touched a hand to his chin and looked thoughtful. "Let me think."

"You've got them, you must know what they are," teased Hubert.

"Ralph," said Angela, "it's tingling up and down your spine, you dodo ..." Angela trailed off, whispering. She remembered she wasn't supposed to badmouth anyone—her self-imposed rule since last spring, when a spirit of world peace and harmony had swept over her. She'd read something—now forgotten—that ignited a passion within her. It still held her in a somewhat tenuous grip.

Darn it, she told herself.

Hubert drew in a deep breath and let out a heavy sigh, calming his nerves. He, too, had the willies.

The horses snorted and tossed their heads. It was time to move on; they'd had their fill of water.

They hit the trail again, the horses trotting side by side this time.

"Hubert," said Angela, "can't we just let the horses roam free?" They had planned to rig up a corral for them before approaching the egg. "They'll come when we call."

Sure, thought Hubert. They might come when we call. Or they might decide to run to the far corners of the earth. Then what?

He shook his head.

"Afraid not," he said. "We have to control the horses if we want to be sure of having a ride home. And with Ralph along ..." Hubert bit off his words. It went without saying: With Ralph along, they didn't want to walk home; it was several miles. Ralph was just a tyke.

The Barneys, leaving the known trails behind, sailed out over the grasslands. A kicking-up sort of wind was rising with the growing warmth of the morning; it sent the prairie grasses, shrubs, and wildflowers into sea-like flux. The Barneys tasted the turbulent swirl of colors that swept the plain, soaked in the ever-brightening blueness above, listening all the while with animated expectancy as the wind did its sweet whispering. Not a roc was to be seen or heard. But the wound in the earth and the bur oaks and purple dwarfs lay ahead, down and around some sweeps in the land. The enormous egg would be sheltered somewhere thereabouts.

Hubert heard a melodious purring. He looked at Angela. She was getting ready to sing. Uh-oh, he thought. He heard Ralph squeal in complaint. Angela *was* a singer; her voice was a kitten of delight, but of late she'd been stuck on a certain song, which both Hubert and Ralph had heard too much of. Hubert veered Pioneer away from Cassandra just as Angela's voice sprang out.

> "*A shimmering land, but no senses around*
> *To soak in the grand, quivering ground.*
> *It's alive with motion, a rollicking ocean,*
> *As if a good God had poured it a potion.*
> *A magical place, smothered with grace,*
> *All ye who pass look upon its fine face.*
> *But no one passes, and no one sees.*
> *Could it be that old-time religion, that earth disease?*
> *That crawled from ill humans long ago*
> *And still plays a death twang on its ill bow?*
> *That religion that poses and bluffs and blows*
> *Out the candles that waved promise in glows?*
> *Their command: 'Take care of your masters,*
> *The ones better than thou, or there'll be disasters*
> *Dropped from ill sacred cow; no crying, no fits,*
> *Yawn your mouth wide and we'll pour down these writs*
> *In a glide; there's no land better than what you see*
> *Under the sliding pulpit that gouges the rut for your broken*
> *knee.'*"

A hush descended upon the plain. Angela's voice and the wind, as if following the same baton, fell silent.

She called to Hubert. "That was *my* arrangement of 'Broken Knee.'"

"I know," said Hubert. "You don't have to tell me." It wasn't actually a song; it was a poem written long ago by a writer of some renown. The writer had taught reading, writing, and arithmetic to kids in a country school. Angela had fitted her own music to it.

They guided the horses to a band of paper birches and formed a corral there, using brush and old logs, tying it together with whip-like branches and creeping vines. With the horses held captive, the Barneys walked from the island of birches to the stand of bur oaks, then made their way down the line, toward the trembling egg.

Each toted a canteen, binoculars, and a lunch box, all slung around their shoulders. In addition, Hubert had his carbine—locked and loaded.

Hubert decided it was time for a drill. He filled his hands with his carbine and flattened against a tree. Angela and Ralph, following Hubert's lead, squeezed against another tree. Hubert crept forward. They followed, staying low. Hubert hugged the earth. So did they. Hubert rose, but they stayed down to give him a clear shot. They would rise only on his command.

"All clear," he said, and slung his carbine over his shoulder.

Angela and Ralph rose, and the Barneys pressed farther on down the line, treading closer to the egg.

A swarm of purple dwarfs glanced into view. Not much farther now, thought Hubert. Last evening they had approached the egg from the meadow side; now they would be approaching it from the woods side—the safe side, they figured. Trees did afford some degree of shelter and safety. Whoever laid that egg would probably find it tough going through the trees, if it had to chase after a bunch of kids.

Hubert stopped and signaled for Angela and Ralph to stay put. He crept away from the trees, using the tall grass as cover. He crept along, ever watchful, ears bent, catching the winsome songs of sailing wind.

He caught a glimpse of the egg—a smooth, curved patch of off-white, seemingly afloat in a pond of green and gold. He put his binoculars to his eyes, made a mental note as to the egg's position, then crept back to Angela and Ralph, and together the Barneys oozed down the line.

They got closer and closer, staying well within the trees—the trees now becoming a blindfold of sorts—their horror shooting skyward.

We are really here, really doing this thing, getting so close to that egg, that insane, monstrous egg.

Shockingly, a voice intruded: a cool, sharp whisper over the wind.

"All right, children, you might as well come out now."

The voice was very British, proper British, cultured British, and Hubert, jumping around, thought, *A Brit!*

Angela and Ralph each gave a screech, their willies escaping. They turned, and both laughed. They stepped toward the Brit, Angela nearly falling into a swoon. She hugged Ralph to her side and ogled the Brit, who stood about ten feet away.

Hubert took up a protective stance in front of Angela and Ralph, his hand tightening on the strap of his carbine, which was still slung over his shoulder. The Brit's eyes rolled slightly, as if to say, *I wouldn't do that if I were you.*

The Brit was a khaki-clad, clay-skinned vision, backlit by a spray of sunlight that blazed through the foliage. He was tall, broad shouldered, and muscular. He was smooth shaven, had a chiseled jaw, and steely gray eyes. A razor-edged cord of wheat-colored hair poked out from under his hat—a bush hat, thought Hubert.

He had a large-bore hunting rifle slung over a shoulder and a .45 caliber pistol in a holster at his side. He carried a canteen, binoculars, and a wealth of ammo pouches on a web belt. A machete and hunting knife in scabbards were also on the belt.

"Ah ..." The Brit drew out the syllable into a long lyrical note as he stepped toward them and smiled, showing teeth of sparkling perfection. Rocks, thought Hubert.

Little Ralph, in his odd, jesting, childlike way, called teeth rocks. The Brit had a mouthful of bright, even rocks, all in proper order, sharp canines, enamel as white as polished ivory. Rocks. Ivory. Tusks. Hubert's mind played association. Teeth were rocks.

"Let's go bird watchin'," said the Brit in his modulated voice. He walked closer. "There's a giant 'un out there waitin' for us," he said, in an exaggerated western accent.

Hubert, though still a little uncertain, stepped forward and shook hands with the Brit. Introductions were made.

The Brit's name was Malcolm Moreland—Mel was what everyone called him. The Barneys quickly learned that Mel the Brit said *ah* a lot, sliding it up and down in strapping musical tones, changing inflections as the mood struck him. His *ah* was not an *ah* of uncertainty, however; it seemed to be one of pure, unbridled pleasure—the pleasure of hearing the sound of one's own voice.

"Ah ... Hubert ... Angela ... Ralph ..." he said, pointing in a pretend officious manner, apparently memorizing their names and faces. He ran through their names again and again, faster and faster, pointing like a machine gunner, his *ahs* forgotten for the moment.

Then he stopped, becoming proper again, and said, "Ah ... I know this must be quite shocking to you." He turned and waved toward the prairie. "The egg and all."

He faced them, becoming grim, but only for a moment. He smiled. Sharp. White. Tusks. Rocks. Ivory. "Ah ..." He reined in his teeth, his lips closing tightly for an instant, thoughtful, impish.

"I'll fill you in as we go," he said. "Ah ... I'm afraid we haven't a moment to spare. Let's hightail it out of here, children, and go watch that egg. Somethin' spooky's gonna hatch, and right soon."

They half ran, half walked to the edge of the trees. Mel cautioned Hubert.

"Ah ... don't even think of taking that carbine off your shoulder, son. I'll do the shootin', if there's shootin' to be done. But I don't think it'll be necessary."

They walked through the grass, weaved through the purple dwarfs.

"There's nothing for us to hide from," said Mel. "But we'll hunch down when the hatchling breaks out. We don't want to have it run at us thinking we're its mum."

The egg came into view.

"Ah ... I first saw you kids when you were on your horses," said Mel, offhand. "Trailed you. Ah ..." He raised a hand and stopped walking. "Close enough." They settled into the grass.

The egg, approximately a hundred feet away, grew big in their eyes when they raised their binoculars.

"Decided it would be okay for you to stick around and ... ah ... observe the proceedings, maybe even spill the whole works to you, ah ... maybe."

Mel laughed, lowering his binoculars. A haunted laugh, thought Hubert, looking at him.

"What do you mean, Mel?" asked Hubert. He was uncomfortable addressing an adult by his first name. He'd never done it before. "Spill the whole ... works?"

"Ah ... fill you in as we go, Hubert, my boy." Mel raised his binoculars again. "Take a while." As tuneful as the Brit's voice was, it was also capable of some very clipped speech—clipped British style: proper, tasteful, elegant. "Take a while."

The Brit laughed again, seemingly at some inner joke this time.

"Ah ... Why not? Security's all blown to hell anyway." He looked at Hubert conspiratorially. He leaned and looked at Angela and Ralph, winking. "No one'll ever believe you, so why not?" He turned back to the egg and raised his binoculars.

"Ah ... Mel, tell us," said Angela. She became self-conscious, having used the telltale *ah*. She looked away as the Brit peered at her.

"Tell us, Mel!" cried Ralph. He bounced up and down in the grass, fingering his binoculars, a kid's model, unlike Hubert's and Angela's. "Ah ... ah ... ah ... Tell us! Tell us!"

"Ah ... such irrepressible children. Curiosity, the mother of invention. Never lose the spirit, children." Mel spoke quietly, casually, while watching the egg. "Take a while. No harm, I'm sure, in tellin' you."

Ralph bounced again, happy to be in on things. "Tell us! Tell us! Is it a giant roc?"

The Brit laughed.

"Wish that it were. Wish that it were." He turned to the children. "A giant roc? We'd have a party then, folks. No harm in it. But this ...?"

He turned back to the egg, binoculars screwed to his eyes. "This ...?" He paused, then said, "You're minin' gold with this 'un, folks. Minin' gold, you are."

A slight tremble had been in the Brit's voice, thought Hubert. It sent shivers up and down his spine—the willies. Something else had been in the Brit's voice too. What? It was hard to tell.

Then it struck Hubert—awe. A trembling awe it was.

Hubert put his attention on the egg. Binoculars up ... down ... Resting his arms ... then wearing them out again.

The sunlight felt warm on his skin. On his neck ... hands ... arms ... A few minutes went by—an eternity—then something happened.

He heard a sound escape from Angela. A new awareness fell upon the group, zipping mind to mind. Bodies shifted, rustling the grass. All binoculars up ...

Mel said, "Ah ..." very quietly, almost lost in the wind.

Ralph squealed and bounced.

Hubert saw a wee bit of the egg crack open.

And then, like magic, eggshell began to chip away.

He heard nothing but the wind. His mind supplied the noise: *Chip! Chip! Knock! Knock!*

It was happening.

Minin' gold.

Two

THE HATCHLING

Something swam through the tall grass, something that wore a beat-up old cowboy hat knocked back on its head. On a low rise a hundred feet behind the Barneys and the Brit, it stopped and peered ahead.

The purple dwarfs shone like jewels in the brilliant sun. The enormous egg was nearly obscured by the tall grass that whipped around it.

The thing shifted its eyes and adjusted its cowboy hat—*it saw that devil, Angela Barney. It saw Hubert and ... that little one. And the Brit.*

The thing's name was Chad Garrick.

He was thirteen, a year younger than Hubert, a year older than Angela.

The swarm of purple dwarfs in the distance had drawn his eye yesterday when he'd been out looking for cougar tracks. The big cats sometimes prowled the grasslands.

Cougars began dancing in Chad's head.

He transformed himself into a cougar and crept toward the purple dwarfs.

Stealthy ... silent ... vigilant ...

He stopped, uncougared himself, took a drink of water from his canteen, then flowed closer, keeping low in the snaking grass.

Yesterday ...

His eye, pulled by the swarming purple dwarfs, had led him to the giant egg. He had soaked up impressions. He touched it, listened to it, walked around it, watching ...

On his return trip to the egg this morning, hiking across the prairie, Chad had seen the Barneys on horseback. He guessed they were going to the egg.

Chad kept his distance, staying low. He watched as the Barneys disappeared into a grove of paper birches. He tracked their path, sans horses, to the bur oaks and watched them wend their way down the line toward the egg.

The wind had been kicking up. The colors—there were a million colors across the grasslands: greens and golds, reds and purples, yellows and whites—broke in exploding waves, whipped all around.

From somewhere out of the wind, the Brit had come.

The Brit stalked the Barneys like a wolf or cougar. I've got to save them, thought Chad, creeping through the bur oaks. It looked like the Barneys were unaware of their peril.

Chad grew frantic as the Brit went in for the kill. Then relief like a cold spray of water on a hot day hit him as he saw the Brit hook up with the Barneys instead of killing them.

Chad peered at the enormous egg. A ripple of activity swept through the four watchers as a dark, irregular crack appeared on the egg, growing across its surface.

Then, like nobody's business, something godawful poked its beak out.

Inside the egg, the newly awakened soul stirred, and became self-aware, and dreamed ... *He was being chased by unseen monsters, hideous dimensions of fear shrieking through his mind. Monsters clutching him, slamming him onto rough wooden pillars. A cross. They drove nails through him. His mind tripped. He saw things he couldn't explain. Unparalleled suffering. Genocide. All because of his bloody death on a cross. A whole world destroyed. His mind rebelled.*

He flipped out.

Escape!

A rush hit him. A frenzy. The secret code. Magical DNA.

Escape!

He attacked the egg, smashed his beak against it, felt it give. Cracks resounded. Shell zipped away.

Brightness assaulted his eyes. A moment of discomfiture stalled him. He sniffed the air. A new world peered at him from above.

A dream?

He renewed his attack.

He stuck his head out—a drunken, craning periscope. He hoisted himself up ... out ... and before he hit the ground, he knew his name.

Clem.

A whisper.

He stood, stretched, shook himself, glanced around, saw a swirl of background, then saw the purple dwarfs.

An intricate, meaningful arrangement. He feasted his eyes on them.

Yes!

His instincts were jogged.

Yes!

The world became fuller. He saw more. The wind whispered to him. He knew what to do.

Run!

Thataway ...

Run!

Clem turned and ran through the bur oaks, his body ungainly at first, but learning ... learning ... acquiring speed and grace, thumping along, scampering along, tuneful feet flying along.

Ten-power binoculars to her eyes, watching, gasping, Angela Barney saw its head pop out of the egg. Her mind burned with its visage. A long blackish bill, a reddish sheath at the end—scoop-like, downward curving, sharp tip. Its face, bare of feathers, creased and gray, wore a severe expression. It looks ancient, she thought.

It flew into another fury, widened the hole, sluiced itself out, and fell to the grass, momentarily hidden.

"Ah ..." escaped from Mel, ran with the wind, ran to Angela's ears. A mystical sound, she thought. A delightful, meaningful sound.

"Ah," escaped from her own lips.

The bird stood, wobbly. It was somewhat like a turkey, though much bigger. A large head. A stout body. Thick, short neck. Gray feathers, mottled. Small yellowish-white wings—they looked more like clubs than wings. A tuft of tail feathers.

She couldn't see its feet and legs now, for all the grass that was in the way, but she had seen them as it had tumbled out of the egg, and they had been scary: thick yellow legs; enormous feet with three frontward toes, one rearward toe, all ending in terrible thunder claws.

The bird fled into the oaks.

Angela popped up and ran after it, her binoculars slung around to her side. She pulled out her camera, snapped pictures, catching fleeing fragments of the bird.

"Easy, Angela." It was Mel. She turned. Mel, Hubert, and Ralph were catching up. "The little one, Angela. Remember the little one." Mel was patting Ralph's shoulders as they walked along. "We only go as fast as he goes. There'll be plenty of time later for your camera. You'll get some really striking photos of the dodos."

Dodos!

Angela's mind went wild. She yelled at Mel, "Stick that kid in a pouch and carry him like a papoose." She turned and ran into the oaks, hearing Mel's laughter behind her.

Moments later, they caught up with her, Ralph now piggyback on Mel.

They scurried through the trees, catching glimpses of the fleeing hatchling, hearing the madly spinning echoes of its *Thump! Thump! Thumping!* feet.

Chad Garrick shadowed the Barneys and the Brit.

"God all mighty!"

It dawned on him that he was muttering. He clammed up, reminding himself he was on a mission.

"Hoodoo," he whispered, casting the oath outward through his fingers.

Mission, Chad.

He flowed through the grass, through the purple dwarfs, to the egg, then into the bur oaks. He oozed along, ears sharp, eyes sharp, body tuned, ready for anything.

Jesus!

Mission, Chad.

He oozed through the wound in the earth.

"Angela!" hollered Mel. "Wait up! We've found a shortcut!"

Angela turned to look. Mel was lowering Ralph to the ground. "Go," said Mel, aiming Ralph off to the side and pointing. "Go!"

Ralph ran, and in moments was out of sight.

"Look!" cried Mel, pointing beyond Angela.

She spun around and saw Ralph in a clearing about sixty yards away, scampering along. With her mind in a blur, she ran to catch up with him.

Winded, she grabbed Ralph and held him in place.

Hubert and Mel caught up. Mel swept up Ralph.

"Little buddy, do you know what happened?"

"No," said Ralph.

"You just took a shortcut through an air passage. Look, I'll demonstrate with Angela."

Mel stood behind Angela and placed his hands on her shoulders. Walking along, he aimed her to and fro. "Look for a tunnel through the air. It'll be big enough for a person to step into."

Abruptly, Mel stopped, and Angela saw a shimmering tunnel of air, barely perceptible, a few feet in front of her. "Go!" cried Mel.

She ran into it, felt a cool caress, ran and ran …

Moments later, she emerged from the tunnel, still running.

She stopped, looked at the ground, pounded it with her feet. Solid. She looked around, saw thickets nearby, felt the warmth of the sun. Her mouth flew open. She turned and saw the others way back—more than a hundred yards away. It's the tunnel of willies, she thought, shivering.

Mel, Ralph, and Hubert ran off to the side, vanished, and within seconds popped out next to her.

"Again!" cried Ralph. "Again!"

Mel aimed the children, shot them into the distance, taught them how to find the shortcuts. They rode them again and again.

"They look like heat waves," he said, "but cool, not hot. Just keep glancing to the side; you'll see them. They guide you safely ahead; they won't slam you into a tree or drop you off a cliff."

"How do they know where we're headed?" asked Hubert.

"Hubert, my boy, the Universe knows where we're headed. These shortcuts—secret passages is what they're called—are the Universe's way of helping us out, speeding us along."

"Crazy," said Angela as they walked along. "Let's call them the willies' railroad."

"Okay!" cried Ralph, running ahead of them. "Willies' railroad, come out, come out, wherever you are!"

Mel ran to catch up with Ralph, picked him up, and gathered Hubert and Angela close. "It's important, now, children, that you stick close to me the farther we go into Dodoland. There are dangers."

"The bird, Mel," said Angela. "We'll lose him."

"The hatchling is behind us now, Angela. We've covered a lot of ground taking these shortcuts. He's heading our way. We've got time for an important lesson."

He led them to a willy. Angela, deciding that willies' railroad was too cumbersome, had shortened it to just plain willy.

"Let's go beat the bush for some ferocious man-eating dodos," said Mel.

They stood before the shimmering tunnel of air, Angela making ghostly sounds, scaring Ralph.

"No! No!" screamed Ralph.

Mel, carrying Ralph, stepped into the cool willy. Hubert and Angela followed, and in moments the willy carried them deep into the brush, and they popped out onto solid ground again.

"Hubert," said Mel, "find a small tree branch suitable for rattling the foliage, then have at it."

Hubert, looking a bit uncertain, picked up a small tree branch and swung it around at the bushes.

"Harder, Hubert," said Mel.

He swung harder.

"Make some noise!"

Hubert tore at the thicket with the branch. Soon, a distant noise erupted and made for them. Something big was making

22

its way through the thicket. Hubert stopped, but the noise continued, approaching fast.

"Keep at it, Hubert, old boy. Don't lose your nerve."

Angela began to feel real fear. She looked at Ralph. He was turning white.

"Mel," she whispered, "Ralph looks like a ghost. Stop it."

"This is important, Angela. It won't take but a bit longer. Hubert ..."

Hubert thrashed the brush, ripping the branch to shreds. The approaching noise intensified, pressing close. They all turned to face it.

The noise stopped.

The thicket parted, and the head of a huge dodo poked through and stared at them. Hatred like acid flowed from his eyes, but he came no closer.

He sniffed the air, stared at each of them with an extra measure of loathing, then withdrew, dragging his terrible noise with him.

Silence.

"There are good dodos and bad dodos, children," said Mel. "You saw a bad one."

"Uh ... why didn't he kill us?" asked Hubert.

"And eat us?" asked Angela.

"Ah ... My blood shadow, children. It surrounds me wherever I go. Like an umbrella, it spreads and casts a protective shield. Like an egg—and eggs are inviolable in Dodoland—it protects those in its charge."

"Blood shadow," whispered Angela. She stared at Mel. "How?"

"How can we get our own blood shadows?" asked Hubert.

"Ah …" Mel shook his head. He looked at Angela and Hubert. He patted Ralph. "You okay, Ralph?"

Ralph did not respond. He stared vacantly at the brush.

The kid has had a traumatic experience, thought Angela. He's probably busy wiping it from his mind.

"Later, Hubert, Angela," said Mel. "Later, and you will learn of blood shadows. Now, we must get back on the trail of our bird. Let's go find us a willy."

They searched for a willy, but had no luck. They discovered it was tricky finding one in the cramped quarters of the brush.

"One can always find one," said Mel. "Always. Never give up." Eventually, they spotted one and angled toward it.

They stepped into the tunnel of coolness, held on to the sides. At the end of the ride, they found themselves in an area of widely spaced bur oaks. Sunshine played about, and Ralph came alive.

"Willy, willy, willy," he squealed. "Where are you? Come out, come out, wherever you are."

"The bird, Mel," said Angela, irritated at Ralph's insistence on playing around.

"Ah … children, this way." Mel raced them through willy after willy. They curved through the forest, found the hatchling again, and gave chase on foot. But soon, they lost sight of the speedy hatchling and decided to hitch another ride on a willy.

"Now, for the thrill of a lifetime, children," said Mel, finding a new willy for them. "Brace yourselves." They stepped aboard the willy, held on, and it took off like a roller coaster. Angela squealed and shut her eyes.

"Look!" cried Ralph.

Angela, trembling, opened her eyes, fearful that she would see another hateful dodo face. But what she saw was the hatchling. It was running along on solid ground, and the willy was keeping pace with it. We're on a flying willy, she thought.

The Barneys and the Brit weaved through the forest on the flying willy, shadowing the hatchling.

"One last lesson before we step back on solid ground, children," said Mel, moving to the front of the willy, close to the racing hatchling.

"Make a wish," he said. A moment later, the willy shot higher into the sky.

Angela saw the hatchling break into a clearing far below.

"Make a wish," repeated Mel. "My wish was for us to be higher. So here we are."

Angela wished for them to be lower—she didn't like heights—but nothing happened.

"Mel, I wished for us to be closer to the ground."

"Ah ... Angela, you have discovered that the Universe doesn't grant all wishes."

"I knew that before," said Angela, staring downward.

"Hubert," said Mel, "do you have a wish?"

"Yes."

"Care to share it?"

"I want to know more about the dodos, about this world, about the hatchling."

"And?"

Hubert looked puzzled.

"I'm getting something," said Hubert. "I'm hearing something, I think."

"Train it, train it," said Mel. "Cultivate your gift. The Universe has delivered. Let it come. Let it flow. Easy, now. Don't try too hard."

"All right, Mel," said Hubert, staring at the horizon.

"Is it better, easier, Hubert, when you just let it come to you?"

"Yes, Mel." Hubert closed his eyes. "Amazing. I'm listening, hearing ..."

"Let it come, Hubert, my boy. Let it come."

Angela, perplexed, swept her eyes back and forth between the ground, far below, and Hubert.

"Angela," said Mel, "what Hubert is experiencing is called a *knowledge hit*. I'm sure he'll fill us in later. Just wish and listen and ..."

She closed her eyes and thought of Ralph—she was too frightened to look at him; she didn't want to see another ghost.

"Angela," said Mel, "are you wishing now?"

"Yes."

"Good."

I wish to help the kid, she thought, to save him, to soothe his mind. I'm not nearly as frightened as he is.

Angela felt an outpouring of energy, a tingling warmth that flowed through her. Her fear was gone. She cast her eyes upon Ralph.

Ralph, with eyes closed, looked like he was in heaven. "I'm riding Clem!" he cried.

He stood stock still, eyes more than eight feet above the ground, claws dug in, wrapped for purchase. Suffused with tension, he was a frozen wave ready to pounce. His partner stood down the way, on the far side of a bur oak. They bracketed a path trod by four humans.

A "chip," almost silent, passed through his beak.

A return "chirrup" told him his partner had picked it up.

Another "chip," nearly lost in the ambient sounds of the woods, completed the signal.

The four humans would be allowed to pass, unhindered.

The two dodos, all but invisible in their stillness amongst the oaks, watched the Barneys and the Brit pass by.

A while later, they resumed their patrol, checking the eggs, noting that one of the eggs and a nesting array of purple dwarfs had intruded into earth-plane territory.

He sighed. Another earth interface.

Ye gawds! Such wretched jargon. *Interface!* Our report— *Those miserable bureaucrats! Those pompous, arrogant assholes!—* will have to include the dainty word *interface*.

He belched loudly.

"What's it, Tim?" his partner called, moving closer.

"Oh, 'ell, it ain't nuthin', matey."

"That's quite an accent, Tim," said Zack, his partner.

"Picked it up from that tall bloke that just passed by." They laughed. *Tall* tickled them. "He speaks many tongues, you know?"

"You don't say."

"Yeah. Likeable fellow. Met him in ... in ... Well, somewhere." They laughed.

"Was it Australia?" asked Zack.

"Don't know."

"Africa?"

"Don't know. Can't tell them apart." More laughter.

Suddenly, Tim froze.

"Umph."

Zack was alerted. They watched the approach of another human. Tim craned his neck, stepped sideways, sniffed the air.

"Harrumph." This one would not be allowed to pass.

Tim crept closer, sensing Zack's movement. A scissors maneuver.

As he crept, eyes zeroed on the target, Tim held a vision of this human hanging from a rope, twisting in the breeze, body limp, neck broken. Dodo justice, swift and terrible.

Clem, fleeing from his hideous dream in the egg, rumbled through the bur oaks. To his hatchling mind, these woods seemed to go on forever, but finally he shot out the other side.

He kicked about. A wide expanse greeted his wandering eyes. It spread savanna-like, green and gold, sparkling in the bright sunshine. Gentle hills lay in the distance. Groves of monster trees were scattered about the plain.

"Ah ..." Clem heard the sound of his voice for the first time. "Ah ..." He tried it again and again.

He adjusted his vision, reeling his eyes in from the bigness all around him, focusing closer. He saw more of them—purple dwarfs. He sniffed them, holding his head high. They had a minty scent. He read them, and knew where to go. He ran, clipping along with the breeze. Hearing distant voices, a pleasing melody blew into his ears.

"Go! If you still have your toes.
Scatter them near and far.
Let them run from you and kick at your foes.
Never save them as if in a jar."

Clem raced with the wind, ate up the savanna, touring around the scattered groves of monster trees. Soon, he found himself in the midst of other hatchlings, all streaming toward some unknown destination. Breathy *ahs* filled the air.

"Ah ... ah ... ah ..."

The land teemed with hatchlings. A stampede.

"Hoo-ray!" shouted Clem.

Cries of "Hoo-ray, hoo-ray, hoo-ray!" rose from the mass, rose on the wings of thunder, then ...

Silence gripped the hatchlings.

They came upon a hill, crossed it. Mazes of purple dwarfs met their eyes, filling the valley below. Instincts were jogged. They divided, streamed into the classrooms open-air affairs, formed by purple dwarfs. Minty scents strafed their nostrils.

Clem took a seat on the grass inside a classroom.

"Hoo-ray!" he shouted.

All hatchling eyes fell upon him. He wanted to shout again, but one look from the instructor settled him down. The last hatchling flew in through the doorway, and the lessons began.

The instructor rose, dwarfing the baby dodos. He unrolled a banner and began teaching the youngsters to read. Within an hour, Clem and the other first graders were reading classic works of Dodo Literature.

"Excellent," said the instructor. He praised the class after each improvement in reading ability.

"Hoo-ray," whispered Clem.

A bell rang, signaling recess. They streamed outside. Clem played soccer with the other hatchlings. Instead of using a soccer ball, they used a mockup of a human head. Another bell drew them in, and they hit the lessons hard.

Dodo History. Dodo Philosophy. Dodo Military Tactics and Strategy. The Secrets of the Universe.

The bell rang again, signaling a lunch break. The hatchlings rummaged in nearby fields—their first solid morsels.

Clem uncovered roots, ate them.

"Hoo-ray!" he shouted.

He ate berries, nuts, grain.

"Hoo-ray!"

He jumped as a small furry animal scurried underfoot. He eyed the escaping varmint, then pounced on it, killed it, and began feeding.

Suddenly, Clem found himself lying on the ground, a searing pain clutching his ribs. The varmint was gone. He looked up. Three strange dodos, bigger than hatchling size, stood over him. They had divided the varmint and were eating it.

Clem rose.

The three crowded him, punched him, knocked him down. Clem was in shock; he didn't know what to do; his instincts told him to take flight, to escape, but ...

They had him trapped.

They pounded him.

Clem covered up; his fear, like prison bars, held him hostage. He took the beating.

Finally, they left him alone, bruised, bloody, beaten. They walked away. Clem lay still, heard them talking, made out a name.

Roger ...

Clem looked up, burned their images in his mind. He cursed his instincts for failing him. Then he got up and painfully made his way back to the classroom.

No one paid attention to Clem as he entered. All eyes and ears were on the instructor. Clem took his seat on the grass. He tried to tune in to the lecture, but memories of the beating and theft of the food haunted him. He cursed his ineptitude. He cursed the Universe.

"Humans ..."

The word pricked up Clem's ears. He listened to the instructor.

"... and the formation of hierarchies ..."

But the painful memories stampeded back. *Roger ...* Clem fought for control of his mind.

"... laws shift and fall into place and evaporate ..."

Roger and his pals ...

"... power goes to the ones with the biggest fists ..."

The instructor's voice set up a cadence in Clem's mind. Roger and his pals were banished for the moment. Clem learned about humans. Humans vis-à-vis dodos. Humans vis-à-vis the Universe. Humans ... Humans ... Humans ...

The bell rang. The hatchlings streamed out of the maze of classrooms, formed into a mass, and tore across a hill into another valley. Scattered enclosures of purple dwarfs awaited them. The hatchlings dispersed, joined with other, older dodos, then entered the *dojos* for martial arts training.

Clem, standing at the end of a line of husky, fierce-looking dodos, trembled as the *sensei* entered the *dojo*. They all bowed. The brutal-looking *sensei* wore a black belt that was so frayed it was turning white in places. Clem gulped and looked down at his own belt, a pure white one. It gleamed in the morning air.

The lessons began, and soon Clem was too busy to be nervous.

"Hoo-ray!" the older dodos shouted as they went through their martial arts practice. Minutes later, Clem was keeping up with them and shouting *Hoo-ray!* also.

"Oh, come on, Hubert!"

"It's true, Angela, they beat up Clem after stealing his food."

"You mean it really is *Clem? That's* the bird's name? Ralph knew it too?"

"Yes."

"And three punk dodos beat him up?"

"Yes."

"Tune in, Angela," said Mel. "Hubert and Ralph have. They're learning. Perception beyond the normal human range is possible in this world. *Knowledge hits.*"

"Sure, Mel, I'll tune in." She approached the *dojo*, savoring the minty scent of the purple dwarfs. She whipped out her camera, leaned against the purple dwarfs, and felt the sharp punch of a barb.

"Ouch!" she cried, jumping back. She glared at the purple dwarfs then leaned into them again and snapped a picture of the hatchling.

She overheard Hubert talking to Mel. She glanced in their direction.

"Some of the dodos want war with humans," said Hubert, keeping his voice low. "I picked it up. A knowledge hit. They're training for war."

"Yes, Hubert," said Mel, in a hushed tone. "We'll avoid the unpleasantries, though. We'll focus on the peaceful interludes, the culture, the ongoing life of dodos." Mel trailed off, noticing that Angela was watching him. He turned his attention to the *dojo*.

Rhythmic stamping of feet and shouts filled the air, piercing like cactus slaps to the face. The big birds were in synch, working through their practice routines, shredding the air with lightning punches and kicks.

"Hoo-ray!" shouted the students.

"They're practicing *katas,*" said Mel. "Ritualized movements. Punching, kicking, blocking against imaginary opponents. Very repetitious and dance-like, as you can see."

Ralph squealed with delight.

"It's an Okinawan style of karate," continued Mel, "modified by the dodos."

The *sensei* was chanting something peculiar, punctuating the ebbs and flows and flurries of the students. *"Ichi ... ni ... san ... shi ... go ..."*

"What's he saying, Mel?" asked Angela.

"He's counting in Japanese."

"Hoo-ray!" exploded from the students.

"Why do they yell?" asked Angela.

"Ah ..." Mel paused. "Hubert?"

"Energy," said Hubert. *"Ki.* Focus. Right, Mel?"

"Right, Hubert, old chap. You've had some martial arts training?"

"Not exactly, but I've ... uh ... studied a little Zen."

"Ah ..." Mel stepped away from the purple dwarfs. "The shouting. The breathing." His hands flew into motion. "The breath of life. Air is the essence. Cosmic spirit. Cosmic energy."

Ralph squealed again, then sprang up on tiptoes, leaned into the purple dwarfs, and began sniffing around like a dog.

Mel continued. "You take spiritual energy—air—into you, focus, and blow it out—*Hoo-ray!*—with a punch or kick, visualizing it shooting out of you. *Ki*—Japanese for energy. Simply put, your blow lands with extra power."

"How?" asked Angela.

"You're exchanging energy with the Universe. Breathe in, explode out, and you knock your opponent for a loop."

Mel's gliding hands collapsed to his sides. "Does that make sense?"

"Yeah," whispered Hubert.

Angela smiled at Mel then returned her gaze to the dodos.

Ralph gave a little kick of glee, acknowledging Mel, then went back to watching the dodos.

"Ah ..." said Mel, stepping to the purple dwarfs, standing by Angela. "Can we pick our bird out from the bunch?"

"No problem," said Angela. "The littlest one." She pointed.

"Ah ... Clem, old boy."

"They're easy to tell apart," said Angela. "They're all ... such distinct individuals." She scanned the line of dodos. *Oh-oh*, she thought. I can't tell them apart—except for Clem. Mel probably thinks I'm weird.

"Individuals. Good God, yes," said Mel. "Brilliant observation, Angela. Ah ... the minutiae of individuals, even among dodos. Slight differences in coloring. Obvious differences in size, depending largely on the age of the bird, of course. A different slant or aspect to the face, or cap of feathers. Some *do* look meaner than others. Postures vary. A hitch here or there in a walk differentiates. And, if you got to know them, you'd find their personalities to be unique."

Angela felt relieved. She froze the *sensei* and Clem—just the picture she'd been waiting for—in the viewfinder of her camera and snapped away.

Chad Garrick, following the bizarre stop-and-start-again mess of tracks made by the Barneys and the Brit, paused and listened. No breeze, no clatter of leaves, no creak of tree limbs met his ears. Deathly silence stalked the forest.

He resumed walking, eyeing signs of his quarries' progress. He heard a snap, faint, ground level, off to the left, and stopped.

His skin crawled. He scanned, saw nothing, and walked on.

Something was happening. He felt it with every breath, with every step. *Hoodoo!* He cast the spell outward, calming his jumping nerves.

He lost the tracks of the Barneys and the Brit—again. They detoured, then vanished. Odd, he thought. Chad picked up the hatchling's tracks and followed them, trying to guess when the human tracks would rejoin them. That had been the pattern.

Something in the air winked at him. He stopped, stared. A shimmering tunnel of air blew Chad a breath of haunting coolness. Then it disappeared.

Chad bolted along the hatchling's path, shaking off waves of horror.

What was that?

He slowed to a walk.

He knew. Knowledge had hit him. Clear knowledge. He shivered. There were tunnels through the air. You had to look for them. They weren't always easy to find. They were safe to travel. The Barneys and the Brit had used them.

Tomahawks and tom-toms …

Chad began to recite his war chant. It was familiar and comforting. It was what he needed right now. It poured through his mind.

Tomahawks and tom-toms …

It soothed him. It charged him with purpose. It blanked out everything, except the one thing that was important—his mission.

Tomahawks and tom-toms …

He followed the hatchling's tracks. He wondered where the Barneys and the Brit were. Suddenly, a voice entered Chad's mind. That haughty Angela Barney's voice!

Chad recites left, right … left, right *so much because it hypnotizes him. When there's nothing else going on in his mind except* left, right ... left, right ... *his world is a much nicer place. He doesn't have to think of Milky. Mom says so.*

That haughty Angela Barney! I knew it. Chad smashed a fist into his palm. She's been talking to her haughty friends about me again.

Chad, when he was in grade school, regularly camped in town after school near the entrance to the library or courthouse and intoned *"Left, right ... left, right ... "* as people walked by. Invariably, pedestrians found themselves marching in step to Chad's cadence. The whole county learned of this, and Chad Garrick became a much-talked-about character.

Her mom knows it? Angela Barney—that haughty devil!

Tomahawks and tom-toms ... Tomahawks and tom-toms ...

Chad had been in the Barneys' home once, two summers ago. A swim party. The Barneys had a pool in a sun dome adjacent to their house. Boys around Hubert's age had been invited. Fancy invitation cards had been sent out by Mrs. Barney. Chad's mother had driven Chad there.

The Barneys had gone to Greece that year. Greek culture was all around. Maps and books. A statuette of a goddess holding writhing snakes. Minoan frescoes. Centaurs. Soothsayers. Sacrificial animals. Winged demons. Bronze Age replicas. Ivory reliefs. Photos of sun-sparkled villages on the Aegean Sea.

Chad's mind had been in a swirl, tasting the delights, catching glimpses of that haughty devil Angela, listening to Mr. and Mrs. Barney explain the objects.

The Barneys went somewhere every year. Greece ... The Orient ... Tanzania ... Their father was a doctor, a surgeon, in the region's biggest hospital.

"He goes big-game hunting in Alaska and Tibet," Hubert had said with immense pride at the swim party. Their mother was a doctor also, a pediatrician, somewhere in the city.

In the Barneys' house, in a room that seemed to have more books than the school's library, Chad had spun a large globe. Watching it turn, he imagined himself going somewhere every year.

But that was still just a dream; Chad had never been out of the county. Someday, though ...

Chad was going to join the military, and then he'd be off ...

He heard something.

It was Angela Barney's voice again!

Chad marches to the beat of a mindless drum that tells him what to do, because he doesn't want to think for himself, especially not about Milky. War consumes him. It's his thumb and blanket.

Shut up, Angela Barney! Shut up!

Left, right ... I mean *tomahawks and tom-toms ...*

Chad got into his correct chant and marched along the tracks made by the hatchling. Angela Barney's voice faded out, but Chad knew he'd hear it again, sooner or later.

He steeled himself. He fought down his anger.

Tomahawks and tom-toms ...

Mission, Chad.

He walked on and soon spied the mess of human tracks again, joining with the hatchling's. So, they came through an air tunnel here, he thought. He looked around, saw nothing winking at him, and resumed his pursuit.

But, God! That haughty devil Angela Barney! I don't want to meet up with her!

Chad heard another snap, off to the left, and fear and

weakness descended upon him. He began sprinting through the woods. He floated along, a visitor inside his own body.

As he fell, he saw two massive shapes. Bird shapes. They were on him.

He numbed out.

Three

*H*ubert stepped away from the purple-dwarf walls of the *dojo*. He took a deep breath, looked into the distance, and felt chills up his spine—the willies.

Then his whole body shuddered.

Chad Garrick ...

The name had been sneaking into his thoughts.

"Not too far away, Hubert," said Mel, glancing at him. "Stay within the protective canopy of my blood shadow." Mel raised his arms like an umbrella. Ralph, copying Mel, raised his arms also. "Fifty feet and you'll be ruffling the edges, old boy."

"Gotcha, Mel," said Hubert.

Chad Garrick ...

Hubert felt that feeling again, a knowledge hit gathering power, drawing him away. But why Chad Garrick? Garrick was weird, the weirdest of the weird. Then something leaked through, a vague sense of danger, but danger for whom?

41

"Mel ..."

"What is it, Hubert?"

"I feel ..." He stopped, unsure of how to proceed.

"Yes?"

"Well ..." Hubert glanced at Mel. Someone was in trouble. He knew that. Was it Garrick? The big Brit was staring at him.

"Give the knowledge hits a rest, Hubert. You've taken in too much, and have had too little time to absorb it. Enjoy the sights. Ease up."

"Sure, Mel."

Hubert returned his attention to the *dojo.*

The *sensei* snapped commands, and the dodos paired off to practice falls, grappling, and throwing.

"They're practicing *jujutsu,* Hubert," said Mel. "A soft style, but punishing, to say the least."

Hubert eyed the hatchling. The *sensei* was demonstrating a throw to him.

"Clem," said the *sensei*, "tuck your opponent's wing up, then bend it under. Like this ..." The *sensei* whipped the wing of Clem's training partner up, then bent it under, and threw the dodo head over heels.

"Thank you, *sensei,*" said Clem, bowing. He faced his partner and duplicated the move, throwing the dodo smoothly.

"Excellent, Clem," said the *sensei.*

"Clem, Clem, Clem!" cried Ralph.

"You sound like a parrot," said Angela. "Pipe down or you'll attract attention."

"Ouch!" cried Ralph. He'd been leaning against the purple dwarfs.

"Poor Ralph," said Mel. "Did the *dojo* sting you?"

"*Dojo?*"

"These shrubs, their barbs. Martial arts classrooms are called *dojos*. Japanese, you know."

"Oh," said Ralph. "Clem, Clem, Clem ..."

"Ralph, I don't want to be seen with you," said Angela. She slipped around to the other side of Mel, putting him between her and Ralph.

Without warning, a knowledge hit struck Hubert. It possessed him and drew him into another person's life. For a short while, he experienced a life much different from his own.

It was Chad Garrick's life.

Chad, at age nine, was riding bike with two other kids on a backcountry road on a hot summer day when a pack of wild dogs sprang at them from a field.

The other two kids tore away as fast as they could pedal, but Chad's bike was old and rickety, and the dogs overtook him.

Chad threw down his bike, grabbed handfuls of gravel from the road, and faced the dogs. He identified the leader, an insane-looking white dog with bull shoulders. The dogs circled, forming a wall of ragged barks and snapping jaws. Chad, eyeing the leader, ignored several bluff charges by the others.

Finally, the white dog charged, and Chad unloaded a fistful of gravel into its face. It was like an exploding mine. With eyes closed to slits, the dog retreated, kept a distance, and tore into Chad with a hoarse voice.

Chad resurrected his bicycle and made his way down the road, keeping watch, more gravel frozen in his fist.

He went home, went into the woods behind his house carrying a chain.

Rabies, he thought. For two days, Chad kept himself chained to a tree, just in case he came down with rabies. He slept under the stars. When awake, he thrashed about, the chain tightening around his neck.

The chain loosened from Hubert.

He could breathe.

He saw that he was on hands and knees. He stood up.

Mel, Ralph, and Angela stood close by.

"You were shouting, Hubert," said Mel.

Hubert told them about the knowledge hit. Angela stared at him with disbelieving eyes.

"Chad had chained himself to a tree, to protect others in case he came down with rabies," said Hubert. "I lived the experience."

"You were hit by something powerful, Hubert," said Mel. "In this world, you can experience more than just preternatural knowledge; you can experience the life events of others, their self-imposed chains as well."

The breeze died, and Hubert heard footfalls. He spun around.

An odd assemblage of men and women were marching up the road toward the *dojo*. Each carried a staff.

A powerfully built older man in roughhewn coat, trousers,

and hat marched along at the head of the pack. The man's hands were like weapons, massive, frightful. With jaw thrust forward and dressed all in black, he looked formidable. I wouldn't want to get in his way, thought Hubert.

"Hubert!"

He turned. Mel was hustling Angela and Ralph away from the *dojo*.

"Hubert, my boy, we've got to go now." Mel's eyes tracked the approach of the new arrivals. "Up, Ralph." He squatted, and Ralph jumped onto his back.

Hubert was hit by a shocking awareness. He looked back and saw the strange mob flood into the *dojo*. He ran toward Mel.

"Mel, I know what's going to happen."

"Hubert, my boy, you don't realize—"

"They're going to kill them," said Hubert. "The dodos are going to kill those people."

"They aren't people, Hubert. Let me explain."

"Oh, Mel, please," said Angela, "can't we stay and watch? I know these dodos wouldn't do anything harmful. The one in the bush with the hateful face might, but these"– she sauntered toward the Brit, gazed into his eyes—"dodos are kind. I know they are. And Clem is one of them."

"Clem, Clem, Clem!" cried Ralph.

"Ah ..." Mel paused, stared into the *dojo*. "All right, children. You win."

They crowded against the purple-dwarf walls of the *dojo*.

The *dojo* was humming with dodos and humans. But soon, like swimming sharks, they separated into two groups, one at either end, dodos and humans eyeing each other.

"Who's he?" Hubert pointed at the man in black, who was standing in front of the humans, staff in hand.

"He's Gregor Drakon," said Mel, in a whispery voice. "I must caution you to never refer to him as Gregor. Refer to him only by his surname, Drakon."

"He's not human?" asked Hubert. "None of them are human?"

"Shhh ..."

Drakon and the *sensei* met in the middle of the *dojo,* bowed to one another, took up fighting stances, and began sparring.

They circled, feigning, landing occasional blows.

The *sensei* lunged at Drakon. Drakon parried the attack with his staff, turned the *sensei* aside with a lightning-quick move, and left him staring at blank air.

Drakon hit him a mighty blow on the leg with his staff, then sent him reeling with a series of blows to the body. The *sensei* covered up. The match was over. They bowed.

"They're evenly matched—experts," whispered Mel. "But these others ... They're learning. Prepare to cover your eyes, children. Learning can be bloody ugly."

The *sensei* and Drakon went at it again. This time the *sensei* prevailed, sending a vicious kick into Drakon's ribs that the staff was not quick enough to block. Drakon went flying, hit the ground, covered up, and received several stomps from the *sensei.*

"My God, he must have broken ribs," whispered Hubert.

"Drakon does not injure easily, Hubert, old boy."

Drakon eased to his feet. He and the *sensei* bowed, then walked to their respective sides, and two other martial artists stepped forward.

"I warned you, children," whispered Mel.

A large dodo and a man in a business suit holding a staff stood face to face. They bowed then took up fighting stances.

The man jabbed the dodo in the chest with his staff. The dodo knocked the staff aside with a wing, whirled and sent a roundhouse kick at the man's head. It made solid contact and the man crumpled to the ground and lay motionless.

"The birds retract their razor claws for these bouts, children, otherwise the guy's head likely would have sailed away."

"Is he dead, Mel?" asked Hubert.

"No, Hubert. Watch."

The man still lay motionless. The dodo kept a distance, then warily approached.

"In a real fight," said Mel, "don't hesitate, go in. Finish your opponent off. Don't make the same mistake this dodo is making."

The man rolled over, a gun in his hand. The gun barked twice.

The dodo combatant stumbled backward, clutching his chest, then flew at the man, who had now risen to his knees. The dodo obliterated his opponent with thrashing claws.

The man lay in a bloody heap, his limbs violently askew.

"Broken bones now, Hubert. When guns come into play, all rules are off."

The wounded dodo stood several feet from the destroyed man. Blood spotted his chest feathers. He stared at the man, breathing hard.

Drakon walked out, picked up the gun, checked it, picked up the man's staff, walked back to his team.

"Small-bore guns are useless against most dodos, Hubert.

Dodos have remarkable powers of regeneration. Right now, that bird's body is encapsulating those slugs and pushing them outward. They'll fall out within an hour."

"What a dirty trick," said Angela. "He had a gun."

"They want realistic training," said Mel. "They'll encounter much worse when faced with real human enemies."

The destroyed man trembled, then slowly pushed himself to his feet, his motions stiff.

A miracle, thought Hubert.

The man stood, expressionless, then walked back to his teammates, stiff-legged, stiff-armed, eyes pointing straight ahead.

"He's not human, Mel," said Hubert.

"No, he's not."

"Explain."

"Righto, old chap. But let's sit a spell. These legs need a rest. There's a rise over there." He pointed. "We'll be able to see into the *dojo* from there."

"Let's have a picnic," said Angela. "I'm famished."

They walked to the rise and sat facing the *dojo*. Two new warriors faced off.

The Barneys set their lunches before them: sandwiches, grapes, apples, fruit juice.

Mel took a biscuit and jerky from one of his pouches.

"Mel," said Angela, "here ..." She held out an apple.

"Have one of my sandwiches," said Hubert.

"Have a grape," cried Ralph. He threw a grape at Mel.

"Now, now, children," said Mel. "You need your nourishment. This'll hold me over till the festival."

"Festival?" said Angela. "Can we go?"

"Yes, you can go. It's on our itinerary."

"What kind of festival?" asked Hubert.

"Arts, crafts, entertainment, food," said Mel, chewing on his biscuit and jerky.

"Ah ... Mel," said Hubert. He flinched as Ralph threw a grape at him. "Stop it, Ralph. Don't play with your food." He turned back to Mel, pointed to the *dojo.* "Explain, please."

"Ah ... Without further delay, Hubert." He bit off a piece of jerky.

"Homunculus. From the Latin. Means little man, manikin, dwarf, pygmy. Or, in general, a little human being—men *and* women." He paused, swallowed, then repeated the word, rolling the syllables off his tongue. "Ho ... mun ... cu ... lus ..."

"Ho ... mun, ho ... mun." Ralph parroted the word, butchered it, gave up, saying instead, "Ah, ah, ah ..."

"Homunculus also means a model of a human being. Such models being typically used for demonstrating anatomy. So, there you have it, those people in the *dojo* are—the plural— homunculi."

Hubert looked into the *dojo.* There was a pause in the action. The *sensei* had unrolled a large scroll of a human figure and was strutting about, waving it at his students. He was too far away to be heard.

"What's going on down there, Mel?" asked Hubert.

"The *sensei*—that's Japanese for instructor—is detailing pressure points, places where, when you're hit"—he hit himself on the shoulder and winced—"it really hurts."

The *sensei* stood aside, and combat resumed. Match after match ensued. Several more homunculi were defeated. They lay as if dead for a while, then got up and stiff-walked back to their side. They crowded their end of the *dojo* like stalks from a bizarre garden.

Finally, it was Clem's turn. He stood in the middle, looking awfully small compared to the other dodos, and faced a female homunculus wearing a tight leopard-pattern knit dress.

"Watch out, Clem!" yelled Angela. "She's probably got a knife hidden somewhere. I wouldn't trust her."

"Angela, I don't want to be seen with you," said Ralph.

"This is serious, Ralph," said Angela. "I really mean it. I think she does have a knife. I'm ... just getting such a strong impression."

"Don't try, Angela," said Mel. "Just let it come to you. Easy, easy ..."

Clem and the woman homunculus bowed, circled, feigned, probed for weaknesses, landed light blows.

"Nail her, Clem!" cried Angela. "Don't wait. Don't make any mistakes."

The homunculus launched herself at Clem. He stepped aside, grabbed her by the arm and shoulder, and threw her headfirst into the ground. He followed up with a kick to the head. Her neck seemed to snap.

Clem backed up.

She eased to her feet, her head at an extreme angle, and stiff-walked toward Clem, a knife in her hand.

Angela shot to her feet.

"She's faking it, Clem! She's faking it! She's not dead! She can move like—"

The homunculus became fluid, put on a burst of speed, and was on Clem in a flash, thrusting the knife toward his belly.

Clem sidestepped the streaking blade, grabbed her arm, braced it against his body, and snapped it in two, forcing the homunculus to drop the knife. Adjusting his grip on her arm, Clem ripped it off at the elbow, dropped it, and watched her scurry back to her side.

"Hoo-ray, Clem!" shouted Angela.

Mel stood.

"Show's over, children."

The Barneys stood.

"Are we safe here, Mel?" asked Hubert. He was horrified at what he had seen. "Can we get out of this world alive and in one piece when we want to?"

Mel winced, but maintained steady eye contact with Hubert.

"Good Lord, yes, Hubert! Yes! You are safe!" He looked at Angela, at Ralph, back at Hubert. His hands rose, encompassing them all. "What did I tell you? You're minin' gold here, children! Minin' gold you are!"

The Barneys and the Brit walked down the slope toward the road.

Drakon, the man in black, marched the homunculi out of the *dojo* and onto the road. Abruptly, he raised his staff and roared a battle cry that sounded like it came from a thousand throats.

"Alala! Alala! Alala!"

Drakon swung his staff at a stiff-walking homunculus and knocked him flat. He rose, but Drakon smashed him down again, and the homunculus sank slowly into the road, pooling into the road, his matter becoming the road's matter.

The vanquished homunculus's staff came alive and morphed into a bounding cheetah. The cat made off into the countryside.

"The homunculi are shapeshifters," said Mel. "Their staffs also."

Drakon, sounding his fierce battle cry again, smashed another stick-walking homunculus to the ground.

Drakon raced through the assemblage, smashing almost all of the homunculi. They sank like into a sea, their staffs leaping and sizzling, shapeshifting into leopards, lions, tigers, jaguars, and cheetahs, and tearing into the surrounding meadows and forests.

"This is like a mass funeral," said Angela.

"It's a mass burial, children," said Mel. "Drakon is returning them to good old Mother Earth. Nature gave up the monks, now she takes them back. And their staffs return to *their* true nature—hunting cats."

They watched as Drakon and the few surviving monks marched down the road.

"She's with them," said Angela. "The one that fought Clem."

"Drakon will repair her arm once they get to the forest. She'll be as good as new, ready to knife old Clem again, or anyone else, all for a good cause—training. Make Clem a true warrior. Well, children, shall we be off?"

"Clem, where's Clem?" said Ralph. He looked about. "He's gone." The dodos had left the *dojo* and were traveling across the countryside.

"We'll find him, Ralph, old boy. Never fear."

Mel led them across the savanna. The grass and wildflowers danced in the wind. They spotted a tiger stalking three grazing deer. The deer, alerted to the danger, took off with blazing speed. The tiger gave chase.

The wind whispered a melody as the Barneys and the Brit watched the drama. The tiger caught one of the deer, took it down. The tall grass swam for a while as the deer sought to escape, then all was still.

The Barneys and the Brit gave a wide berth to the bloody spectacle. Mel and Hubert had their rifles out just in case. But the tiger did not leave its kill.

Like a long scream lost in time and space, Chad Garrick had been gone, but now ...

He was coming back.

All the way back.

Darkness washed away.

Half-conscious, half-aware of his surroundings, Chad sensed he was being carried. His eyes fluttered open. His mind rebelled at what he saw.

He shut his eyes. Must wait, he thought. How did they get me so totally wrapped up, a prisoner? I didn't even fight them. He burned with dishonor.

A minute passed.

Chad opened his eyes again and slowly soaked up more impressions. He looked around, got some bearings. Then he closed his eyes.

He was being carried by a humongous bird, cradled in a wing. Another bird, just as humongous, was close by, wearing Chad's cowboy hat. The wing around him felt like feathery bands of steel. A warm, humid odor came from the bird.

Suddenly, the birds began to talk.

"Hey, Tim?"

"What's it, Zack?" answered the bird that carried Chad.

"Suppose we uh ..."

"Suppose we what, Zack?"

"Uh ..."

"Uh what, Zack?"

"Well, this terrain looks awfully familiar. Haven't we passed through here before?"

"By Jove, I believe you're right, Zack. I do believe we've completed our circuit."

The two birds laughed uproariously.

"That's what I like about you, Zack. You're never afraid to toss the ball. Let's skedaddle with this miscreant."

Chad felt an abrupt change in direction and heard a new, energetic crunch of feet. His eyes flitted open. He saw trees whizzing by. The two birds were in a swift glide, zipping along at an amazing speed.

I've got to escape, he thought. But how? Where are they taking me? Are they holding the Barneys and the Brit prisoners also? But what if I'm not a prisoner? What if they're just trying to help me? After all, I did black out.

Wake up, Chad! You're their prisoner!

Right. He *was* the birds' prisoner. That much was sure. He had to escape.

But how can I escape from them? He drew mental images of the birds. They had boulder-like bodies, bulging with muscles, sculpted, big, big. It would be tough for them to maneuver through tight spots. And they probably couldn't climb trees.

A plot unfolded in Chad's mind. He would open his eyes intermittently. When he saw dense brush nearby, he would launch himself out of the bird's wing and run like hell. He would crash through the tightest, most impossible places, then lie still. But he wouldn't climb a tree. No, they could wait you out.

He thought it would work. He was cradled in the wing, not held in a tight grip. With a good launch, he'd be out of it. But it had to be a surprise. It had to be quick.

He cracked his eyes open. Lightly, like a butterfly, he fluttered his eyelids. Must only half see, he thought. Can't risk them noticing eyes open.

He saw trees and lots of undergrowth, but the undergrowth was not close at hand. There were small hills, copses, draws. No paths. It was virgin wilderness.

Must maintain limp posture or the bird might tighten his grip. Must ...

They were approaching a dense thicket. A thought bubbled up: what would a cougar do?

Chad furiously clawed himself free of the wing, seized the bird's neck, put a strangle hold on it, felt the bird go down.

Tim let out a *"Hoot!"* and rolled into a bone-jarring, wing-flapping somersault. The red tip of his beak slammed into the ground and broke off. He sucked for air and kicked at the sky.

Chad hit the ground rolling, sprang up, and ran for the thicket, hearing the quick feet of pursuit. The bird who wore Chad's cowboy hat was chasing him, gaining rapidly. Fear permeated Chad, but it was an enabling fear, flinging him toward his destination.

He crashed into the brush, tore into it furiously, sharp barbs cutting his hands, arms, face. All he saw was brush, brush, and more brush; all he heard was crashing brush; all he smelled was brush—leafy brush, flowery brush, berry-laden brush.

He went into it for a godless time.

Exhausted, he collapsed, rolled over, looked back.

Silence.

Save for his own breathing. His chest heaved, he ached for air. Sweat ran in pools over him. His arms and legs, heavy with fatigue, were anchored to the forest floor. His head pounded. He stared at his backtrail but could not see the path he had created for himself. It had closed up.

Safe.

Minutes passed. His breathing eased. He sat up, drank from his canteen, examined his wounds, noticed how dirty he was. He picked burs from his clothes. Blood, cool and dark on his arms and hands, was drying.

He smelled the air. It was charged with heady scents— earthy, minty, refreshing. He sighed. He felt at peace.

He listened. The forest canopy, chattering in the breeze, was a gentle ocean of sound. He looked up. The tick of insects, the warble of birds, the rustle and bother of creatures swam on the delicate sea.

A stray beam of sunlight broke through Chad's brushy enclosure and struck him in the face. He felt its warmth. He rubbed his eyes. They felt dusty.

Just then something big, something heavy, landed in the brush not more than thirty feet away. Chad jerked at the sound, then froze. Violent rustling swept the forest. Chad tracked it, saw a moving shadow.

A bird's head, more than eight feet off the ground, came into view. Its eyes peered about. It looked angry and it wore Chad's cowboy hat.

Four

A QUASI-SPIRIT WORLD

"Say it again, Mel!" cried Ralph.

"Again?"

"Yes!"

"But you've just heard it."

"I know, but I want to hear it again."

"Do I have to say it over and over?"

"Yes."

Angela trotted beside Mel. The big Brit was carrying Ralph piggyback. Hubert was up ahead, scouting a good spot for Mel's school session. Mel wanted bare earth to draw upon. He was going to teach them about dodos. Hubert had been pestering him, asking for explanations. Now Ralph was pestering Mel, too.

"Ralph wants to hear it again," said Angela, "because he was too dumb to understand it the first time, and the second time, and the third time ..."

"Mel!"

"Ah ... okay, Ralph, old boy."

"Watch out, Mel," said Angela. "He'll be too dumb to understand it this time, too. Ralph can be awfully dumb."

"This place is a quasi-spirit world," said Mel. "Quasi means having some resemblance, in some sense or degree, in a manner, seemingly. Quasi is often hyphenated when used as a prefix to an adjective or adverb. Hence, quasi-spirit world, with a hyphen."

"Quazy?" said Ralph.

"You're driving *me* quazy, Ralph, old boy," said Mel.

"Give up, Mel," said Angela.

"Say it again, Mel!" cried Ralph.

Mel began babbling like an idiot.

Angela felt sorry for him. Ralph was up to his old tricks.

"He's enough to drive anyone crazy," she said. "Keep babbling, Mel, maybe it'll throw the kid off."

They walked on. Hubert was still nosing around. He hadn't found a suitable site yet.

"Picky, picky, Hubert!" shouted Angela. "Just pull up some grass and create a barren landscape for us."

Hubert glared at her. He was a budding artist, in the Impressionistic mode, and did not take kindly to jabs at his neophyte talent.

Hubert resumed his search. Ralph fell silent.

Suddenly, crossing the top of a hill, tears welled up in Angela's eyes. She didn't know why. Then she knew—she had once been four, the same age as Ralph.

She wiped the tears away, twirled around, let them dry in the sun and wind.

Four had been a difficult age for her. She had wanted a new

name, so she told her mother she didn't like *Angela* anymore. It was a dumb name, a stupid name. She wanted to be called *Mirth*. She'd picked the name up from an old picture book. Her mother had said, "You will be called Mirth One. Our next little girl will be called Mirth Two. The next one, Mirth Three."

No one ever took her seriously.

Quasi-mirthful will have to do, she thought.

Going downhill, she spun around, skipped through the grass, gazed at the blue sky. This is a quasi-spirit world? Quazy, quazy, quazy ...

Hubert found a clear patch of earth under a tree with wide-reaching branches. Mel set Ralph down, then pulled out a knife and began drawing in the dirt.

"India," he said. He outlined the subcontinent.

"Saudi Arabia." He traced the peninsula.

"Africa, the east coast." He drew it in.

"Madagascar, a big island off the coast of Africa." He drew the island, then made three small marks east of Madagascar. The marks ran east-west in an irregular line.

"Reunion, Mauritius, Rodrigues—three islands in the central Indian Ocean. Home of the dodos."

The Brit stood and sheathed his knife.

"The extinct dodos, that is. The true dodo, *Raphus cucullatus,* to be precise, lived only on Mauritius, the middle island of these three. Reunion and Rodrigues were home to two other, closely related species.

"Around 1507, Portuguese sailors landed on Mauritius. The dodos, isolated as they were, had no natural enemies. They had lost the ability to fly. They were herded like sheep, led onto ships, slaughtered for food. Man introduced animals to these islands: pigs, dogs, monkeys. They ran wild, killing dodo youngsters and eating dodo eggs. By 1681, the true dodo was extinct from Mauritius. By 1790, all the dodos were extinct from all the islands.

"The dodo *did* do some traveling, however, before its demise. In Europe, it was a court jester of sorts, serving as entertainment for royalty. Artists were fascinated by these birds. You can find paintings of dodos in the darnedest settings, in the most striking contrasts. How about a big, plump live dodo standing on a table amidst a scene of fish and fowl—dead game for the larder. Ah ... a feast of splendor, wouldn't you say?"

"I think that's disgusting," said Angela.

"Exactly, dear Angela. Disgusting. I was being facetious."

"Mel," said Ralph, "what's fuh ... fuh ... fuh ..."

"Facetious?"

"Yeah."

"A clumsy attempt at humor."

"Oh," said Ralph quietly, staring at the Brit.

"Ah, getting back to the lesson ... What comes to mind when you hear the word *dodo*?"

Hubert raised his hand.

"Yes, Hubert," said Mel.

"It means you're calling someone stupid."

"Right you are. Dodo, from the Latin, as I've mentioned, *Raphus cucullatus;* or, just the same, *Didus ineptus.* How would you like to have a name like that—*Didus ineptus?*"

Ralph laughed, clasping his hands to his face. He squealed mightily for a moment, then became quiet, staring seriously at the Brit.

"From the Portuguese *doudo,* meaning silly, stupid, simple, foolish. These birds were easy prey. They could be herded like sheep. You could walk up to one, say hello, and club it to death. They looked stupid and behaved stupidly."

Mel paused, hand on chin, thoughtful.

"I don't want to belabor the point," he said.

"Ah ..." Ralph raised his hand.

"Yes, Ralph," said the Brit.

"Why did all the dodos die?"

"Ah ... the million-dollar question. Facetious, Ralph, facetious. They all died because they were swamped by enemies who killed them and their eggs for food, or, in some cases, for sport. They couldn't defend themselves. They had no warrior class. They had no wisdom masters. No spiritual attunement. No monks in monasteries praying for them. No guru leading them to Shangri-La. No group consciousness reflecting Indomitable Life."

"They couldn't fly," said Hubert. "They laid their eggs on the ground. Easy prey."

"Right, Hubert. But those are the scientific explanations. Why did species X bite the dust? Well, eons ago the birds of species X held a meeting. 'We've got no enemies,' said one. 'It's cheaper to walk,' said another. They took a vote and flightlessness won. Then, voila, the enemy enters ... Bye-bye, dodos.

"But Hubert, Angela, Ralph, isn't there something science can't touch, some *raison d'etre*—from the French—some reason for living? Or, some reason for not living? What does having become extinct say about the dodos' spirituality?"

Silence from the Barneys.

"Well ...?"

More silence.

"I'll give you clues," said Mel. "Think of hierarchies. Think of catechisms."

"Mel," said Angela, "you mean the churches didn't send missionaries to save the dodos' souls? Facetious, Ralph. Just being facetious, kiddo."

"Mel," said Hubert, "the dodos' spirituality failed them. They didn't adapt to the changing environment. They weren't ready for a fight."

"Right you are, Hubert. The dodos worshipped only that which hindered them, and eventually doomed them."

"Uhhh," said Hubert, "I think that's what the human race is doing. Worshipping ..." He paused. "Heck, I can't even say it. It gets weird to even say it."

Despite herself, Angela felt allied with Hubert. She rose on tiptoes, jumped a little, began squealing inside. *You're right, Hubert! Say it! Say it! Worshipping people who hate us and lie to us!*

The Brit took a step toward Hubert.

"Hubert," said Mel, "an almighty spirit lives within us all, but spirit is weak—very weak, very faint—within hierarchies, whether they be religious hierarchies or otherwise. Spirit becomes stronger the farther you walk away from hierarchies— the farther you walk away from any tyrant. Tyrants and their hierarchies push their catechisms on you, their set of rules, but rules don't give you spirituality. With their rules, hierarchies suck your spirit dry. With their rules, hierarchies kill you."

Mel became angry.

"Don't let the catechism pushers get their talons into you, Hubert. They are weaklings. They fake it. They'll teach *you* to fake it, too. Misery loves company."

A hush descended on them. Angela's ears rang with Mel's words, then a question rose in her mind.

"Mel," said Angela, "did the giant dodos walk away from their ... hierarchies? Did they become more spiritual?"

"Angela, the giant dodos here in this quasi-spirit world are very spiritual. Their religion back on Mauritius—that is, the set of rules governing their lives—led to their extinction as a flesh-and-blood species, but it did not kill their spirit. Spirit lives on. The spirit of dodos, with no bodies to inhabit, walked away from Mauritius—away from dodo religion—and became stronger. The farther it walked, the stronger it became. It found a home for itself in the astral planes and began spawning a new race of dodos—super dodos."

"With greater survivability built into their genes," said Hubert.

"Exactly," said Mel. "Infinite survivability. Socko survivability."

"Like how, Mel?" asked Angela. "How are the dodos more spiritual now?"

"They abhor people-pleasers. The original dodos of Mauritius were the ultimate people-pleasers. Come here, you! Wham, you're dead! They were the ultimate dodos. They richly deserved the name back then. But here ... These birds can sniff people-pleasing odors on you. If you reek of people-pleasing, they don't want you around. People-pleasing bleeds into the atmosphere; it pollutes a place. Here, if you're big on people-pleasing, they sentence you to death."

Mel knelt. Ralph jumped on his back. Mel stood and walked toward the road they'd been following.

Angela felt ecstatic. I'm anything but a people-pleaser, she thought. A warm feeling washed over her.

"Mel," said Hubert, "your blood shadow ... It's the only thing keeping us alive. Isn't it?"

Mel looked at Hubert but did not respond.

Angela's skin began to crawl.

"We reek of people-pleasing odors, don't we?" Hubert's voice trailed off.

Mel was silent.

Angela felt a crazy electrical dance take hold of her body.

Chad Garrick held his breath as the humongous bird maneuvered through the brush. It was Zack, the one who had stolen his hat. He passed within a few feet of Chad, casting his eyes about, looking everywhere. Momentarily, his eyes rested on Chad.

Holy Christ! He sees me!

But the bird did not stop; he continued to scan the thicket. Chad was ready to bolt deeper into the brush, but held his place, frozen.

Uh ... maybe he didn't see me. I could have sworn ...

He watched the bird head away. His body, seen through the tangles, dissolved like a ghost fading out. Unseen, he dragged his heavy noise, beating the brush with his wings.

Chad let out a breath, easy, silent. The bird should have seen me. But maybe birds don't see you unless you move, unless you provide a contrast. Otherwise, you're just background, part of the variegated mass. That must be it.

As the monster bird's crackling passage through the brush grew dimmer and dimmer, Chad began to wonder how it had arrived in the first place. Did it fly in? Impossible. Those bodies—

Silence gripped him. The bird had stopped.

He's going to fly, thought Chad. The impression came bounding to him like an unseen dog full of playfulness, nipping at his face, nipping at his throat. He's going to fly. He's going to fly.

Chad became a glacier, staring at the wall of brush inches from his face. Seconds ticked by. Then, through the tangles, he saw the bird in the air. It did not use its wings; it was levitating, hovering, floating along. It scanned as it flew, a slow, penetrating aerial search. It headed away from Chad and vanished.

Chad relaxed. Safe again in his pocket of brush. He drank from his canteen, careful to maintain silence. Must provide no contrast, he thought. Must blend in.

But I can't stay here forever. What am I going to do?

Chad looked around. Suddenly, a freezing coolness swept his skin, a coolness familiar and frightening. He remembered another such coolness: on the trail of the hatchling, witnessing the bizarre tracks of the Barneys and the Brit, the air winking at him.

They had traveled through tunnels in the air.

So can I.

He listened for the bird. Silence. Then it landed somewhere, and Chad heard crackling through the forest.

He set off into the brush, searching for winks in the air. When Zack tramped along, Chad risked movement, risked noise. When the bird was back in the air, Chad lay still. All the while, he looked for those winking tunnels.

He found one.

He slipped into it. He walked and crawled through eerie silence, his bones chilled. He walked on solid sheaves of air, saw flickering images of brush and forest around him.

He stepped back to earth, felt warmth return, heard the crackling of brush, sniffed the fragrant air.

Willies! That haughty devil, Angela Barney, calls the air tunnels willies. Christ! Leave it to Angela Barney to call them willies.

But I won't call them that. They're …

They're … Jesus! They're …

Slithers.

It had popped into his mind. It was perfect.

He rambled through the brush, going after Zack, and soon caught another ride on a frigid, reptilian slither. It put him back to earth close to his quarry.

He caught a glimpse through the tangles of Zack floating above. Minute by minute, Chad crept closer.

He thought it ironic that the prey was now doing the hunting. It gave him a sense of power, of being in control. He remembered seeing a nature documentary on TV about Africa. Several antelope were following a lion that was cutting through their territory. The prey felt safer knowing where the predator was. Knowledge—it was power.

Chad felt nerve-crackling power as he tracked the bird. If the lion on TV had turned on the fleet-footed antelope, they had a good chance of outrunning it. If Zack turned on Chad, Chad could freeze and blend in with the brush, or burrow his way into thicket the bird could not penetrate.

He plowed on. Dust and sweat and the chaff of the woods peppered him, peppered his wounds, became his armor.

After a while, he saw Zack in plain sight. The brush had thinned, becoming hedge-like and spotty. Meadows abounded. Giant trees grew in waves across the land. The land itself was rolling, tall with grass. Savanna-like expanses reached for the horizons.

Zack sat beside a hard-packed dirt road that wound through the countryside. Chad crouched in shrubs, peering at the huge bird.

Zack, facing away from Chad, remained motionless for several minutes. In a wild moment of indiscretion, Chad thought of sneaking up on Zack and swiping his hat back. His body leaned forward, going with the notion, but he reined himself in.

Whoa, Chad!

Zack rose into the air and drifted about, continuing his search, curving one way, then another, tracing a meandering path through the air.

Chad followed, looking about, wary. Turning around, he saw Tim, the bird who had carried him in his wing.

Tim was in the air—and had Chad in his sights. The front part of his bill was gone—the reddish part.

Chad froze. The birds had been working together. Crafty. Tim had him.

There wasn't much brush around.

A thicket stood at Chad's elbow. He could burrow in. They could wait him out, or maybe crush it down. It was only a small thicket. The big thickets were behind him, far behind.

Chad thought of looking for a slither, escaping.

But there was no time.

Tim landed.

Chad faced Tim.

Tim, close to elephant size, stepped toward Chad.

Chad heard a sound behind him—Zack landing. Another elephant.

Tim, his face expressionless, stopped a few feet away, looked down at Chad, and sniffed the air.

Chad heard Zack come up from behind, stop, and sniff the air.

Chad didn't dare move, not a muscle. What's going through this bird's mind? What? What?

Then Chad saw it. Doubt was in the bird's mind. Doubt was in his eyes. *Doubt.* But why? Suddenly, Chad knew why. They'd underestimated him. They'd pegged him wrong. They hadn't thought this puny specimen would be capable of doing ...

"Give me my hat." Chad, keeping his eyes on Tim, extended a hand behind him.

A hint of fear shone in Tim's eyes, just a bare hint. It began pushing the doubt out. But he doesn't fear me, thought Chad. He fears something else.

Chad heard the rustle of grass behind him, felt the heat of Zack's body, felt his hat settle onto his hand. He put it on and squared it away, facing Tim all the while.

Chad felt a shift of power, an energetic swing of the cosmos. I can do anything, he thought. The power was upon him. He was a magician. A sorcerer. Alchemy was about. It whetted his blood. A liquid rush rose within him, going navel to heart. He heard a voice inside his head:

We are taking you up, Chad, to a new level.

The voice was a soft whisper. It came from a vast cavern. It came from the stars. He heard the voice again:

We're taking you up, Chad!

Knowledge plastered Chad: the voice of the Universe was speaking to him.

Hoodoo!

Calmness swept over Chad. He accepted it. The voice of the Universe.

Hoodoo!

He stared up at Tim. Murky images danced in the bird's eyes. In those eyes, Chad sensed immense sorrow—the Song of Earth. *Be measured in pain,* those eyes said. It was the eyes, the mirror, the soul behind the eyes that spoke. *Be measured in pain.* It was a message from the Universe.

The voice of the Universe rose, and Chad listened.

"At one tug of the finger was killed the fire-breathing beast of reason."

Chad stared up at Tim, and the Universe spoke again.

"A cold river of fear always faint in the background."

Like a dance, the Universe sang.

"With the smell of foul breath upon them."

A dance.

"They tore round and round."

A chant.

"The rush of society drawing the nets, an ill centering, narrow borders, hymns for insulting whatever falls outside."

Chad felt privy to something vast. The secrets of the Universe being unfolded? The words flew.

"A lance from ill moon, reeking pitiless gloom."

Tim and Zack began to dance. They flapped their wings, making a thunderous roar, hooting, calling, circling crazy fashion, thralls to the music.

Chad rushed aside, escaped their fury, stood and watched them.

"When blood runs cold and fear like a wind, you're fit for the hyenas to eat: Intestines first in a fight, be your own spectator, watching the dusty, gory spectacle unfold."

The scene was intoxicating; the birds, frenzied. All conjured by the vibrant words that swam through the air. Chad felt he was being initiated. He felt chosen. Honored. A witness of the weird. An observer of the grotesque.

"Amidst cutting voices and lowering tablets, another new sun circles to unsettle."

Suddenly Chad knew, he knew, he knew ...

"Orators borrowed from kindly roles, thinkers of no thoughts, creating a ministry of key labels, telling you what you've been zeroed for."

Amidst the frenzied action of the birds, Chad knew.

"Who authored earth? A celestial poet? Or were all minds in the world wired into the lines?"

Dodos ... The Universe whispered it. Tim and Zack were some kind of fabulous dodo birds.

"The sons and daughters of gift-givers become eggs running a bluff."

Extinction, Chad, he told himself. They became extinct. Now they're back. And this is their story, their song, their sorrow.

Tim and Zack joined up and moved to a meadow, the insanity of their dance still upon them: fury, rage, bustling drama, cries of stark raving madness.

Chad knew he was watching a rite of sorts. Something had shifted. He had been in danger—big danger—here in this strange world. Now, he sensed, someone else had inherited that danger.

Who? he thought. And why?

He followed the birds. They were gray tornados, tearing across the land. Suddenly, the Universe flipped into a new song, barely skipping a beat, and Tim and Zack went totally bonkers.

"Jostle and blather, dance foul rites.
The worshippers gather, the communion alights.
A dodo was found.
His brain was wrapped with the new law tightly wound.
He was ordered to circle, an intellectual dance.
And dip and bow in an economic prance.
And groove into a political trance.
And spew running words like drunken ants.
And never say no to the holy rants.
And when ordered to, begin some cants.
And when ordered to, worship those grants.
Those grants given to the disordered few,
Persistently driven across borders to screw
The weak brains that slouch all around
On God's earthly dodo planet ground."

Tim and Zack gave out exhausted honks and nearly collapsed. Moments later, the birds regained their composure and began gliding down the road.

Chad followed, but soon the dodos were out of sight.

He walked alone now. Find a stream, he told himself. Wash off. And then find some food. He would need some food. Then ...

The day was coming of age. Brightness shone. Brilliancy swept a path all around. Marching along, Chad watched the blueness above. He watched the road, the trees, the fields, the bejeweled islands of brush.

It was majestic country. Enchanting. Invigorating. Nature on display, wearing her inviting colors.

The blueness above, a crown of sky.

The road, a royal path.

Everything, a slight trembling of fear, faint in the background.

And Chad felt it, felt the fear. He breathed deeply of the fresh air and felt a chilling wave hit him.

He marched on. He wondered where the Barneys were. And the Brit. He looked up. Staring down at him, masking the blueness above, was a dark, roiling cloud.

"Crown of death," whispered the Universe.

Five

THE INDIGNITIES

*A*s the Barneys and the Brit hiked along the road, Hubert began to entertain serious questions about Mel. *Who is he? What's he up to?* He recalled the Brit's words: *They kill people-pleasers here.* Hubert came to an inescapable conclusion: The Brit is evil. He has us under his control. We're his prisoners.

Mel halted and bent an ear to the wind. "I suspect our bird is ..." His voice trailed off. He pointed to a meadow. "Let's fetch us a willy, children." They left the road, entered the meadow.

"How can you tell where Clem is?" asked Ralph, piggyback on the Brit.

"Knowledge strikes, Ralph, old boy. I don't quite know where old Clem is, but ..." The Brit fell silent.

"Knowledge hits, Ralph," said Hubert. "Sometimes you just know."

"Oh," said Ralph, staring wide-eyed at Hubert. "Pow!" He hit himself in the forehead. "Clem, Clem, was that you that hit me?"

"Ralph," said Angela, "Clem is a gentle being. He doesn't hit anyone, unless he's provoked."

"Ah, are you picking that up, Angela?" said Mel, peering at her. "Or ..."

"Uh, I'm ... not quite picking that up, Mel. But—"

"We must be precise. We can't really know by surmising, dear Angela, can we?"

"No, I guess not."

"Don't be fooled by your own projections."

Angela wore a contrite expression. Ralph shook a scolding finger at her. Hubert felt like laughing, then he glanced at the Brit's large-bore rifle, his .45, the knives, the ammo pouches, and shuddered.

A willy winked at them. They stepped aboard and made good time, touching down on a meadow swept by gentle breezes. Songbirds serenaded them from surrounding willows and pines.

Mel looked about. "This way." He began walking toward piney hills in the distance.

Hubert looked at the sky. Wispy clouds had formed. Sky paintings borne by the wind. He glanced at the land. Velvety green, tucks and folds. He weaved his vision in and out of focus, and let his eyes water, creating an effect he hoped would transform the view into something resembling a Claude Monet landscape.

He had seen some of Monet's work in the National Gallery of Art in Washington, D.C., during one of the Barneys' frequent cultural excursions and had been fascinated by the French Impressionist's use of color and viewpoint.

One painting had stuck in his mind: Monet's *The Japanese Footbridge*. In the painting, a small footbridge—an arcing blue span—dominated.

Hubert recalled staring at the footbridge; at the pond below; at bright-green brush reflected on the pond's surface; at darker thickets in back, behind the bridge; at rushes close up, at water's edge; at dashes and dabs of paint, floating on the pond's surface.

Dashes and dabs of paint?

He had blinked, backed up, and looked again. Okay, lily pads and flowers were floating on the pond's surface.

But, Jesus, dashes and dabs of paint had spoiled the whole effect.

In this world, Hubert had run into dashes and dabs of paint, also: the homunculi. And there had been no opportunity to blink, back up, and look again. Mel had hurled them in and out of explanations.

Homunculi were used to help train the dodos for combat. They were cannon fodder in the *dojos,* and were ultimately killed. Where was the morality in that?

He wondered if Impressionism, with its coolly imprisoned subjects, captured forever in glints of sunlight, lent itself to questions of morality.

He wondered if poetry—another of Hubert's budding interests—lent itself to morality. Poems were music—the arcane music of bare words on paper. Some poems were wretched music, dashes and dabs of paint in your face. Spoiled illusions.

Where is the morality in anything we're doing? he wondered.

Hubert's thoughts were dark shadows clinging to him. He tried to shake them off, but they clung fiercely.

"Look," cried Angela.

Purple dwarfs were swinging into view.

"Meditation square," said Mel.

Several dodos were sitting inside a big enclosure formed by purple dwarfs. Others were on the way, gliding across the fields. Some of the younger birds were engaged in spirited races. Boy, can they tear, thought Hubert.

His memory was jogged by the sight of the racing dodos. In the second grade, in art class, Hubert had drawn a picture of a cowboy riding a galloping horse. Focusing intently, he had turned the picture every which way, wanting to get everything just right. It wasn't long, though, before he realized something was out of kilter.

He worked on it, trying to fix it, never bothering to stop and think that it might be better to start over, wiser for the experience. And he hated erasures—too messy. So, he drew and drew. He even closed his eyes a little while drawing, hoping the discrepancy would go away. But, alas, it did not, it stayed.

The cowboy's head was connected to his body in an odd way. Most everything else about the picture was okay. In fact, it was a finely textured drawing—shadow and light, character in both the cowboy's and horse's faces, and they were impressively flying along on a prairie path.

He had gone home with it, and said to his parents, "I started it wrong, but I finished it anyway," hoping this drive-to-complete would earn him some measure of praise.

His parents had praised him lavishly—for the drawing, and for completing it against adversity. Then his father said, "It looks like when the cowboy opens his mouth, you can see his undershorts." Everyone had laughed, even Hubert. They had kept it, showing it to everyone over the years.

And Hubert, back then, learned the value of starting anew when he noticed something going irreparably out of whack.

They kill people-pleasers ...

Hubert whispered the Brit's words in his mind.

Socko survivability. They abhor people-pleasers. These birds can sniff people-pleasing odors on you. People-pleasing bleeds into the atmosphere. It pollutes a place. The original dodos of Mauritius were the ultimate people-pleasers. Come here, you ... Wham! You're dead.

Hubert's mind played association. Claude Monet. *The Japanese Footbridge.* Dashes and dabs of paint. Spoiled illusions. Dodos. Homunculi. People-pleasers. They kill you. They kill you. They kill you ...

The Brit was evil. The Brit was recruiting them. Leading them on. To be fresh homunculi—cannon fodder. Homunculi were actually people, zombified somehow, made to perform. The dodos needed these ritualistic killings to maintain their world, to assuage their hunger for revenge.

Hubert wanted to go home. Fast. He gripped his carbine. He glanced at the Brit. We're his prisoners, subtle prisoners, until we try to escape.

An opportunity would present itself, he figured. He could carry Ralph piggyback. But Angela would be a problem. She was starry-eyed over the Brit. She would have to be shown the light, in no uncertain terms.

If necessary, he would shoot the Brit.

In the meantime, he'd have to play along, pretend everything's okay. Not alert the Brit. Try to merge minds with Angela. Break her off from the Brit.

He scanned all around. His ears grew sharp. He sniffed the

sparkling air and caught a wandering wave of coolness. It rattled his soul. The willies.

He looked ahead. Mel was talking to Angela and Ralph. The meditation square and gathering dodos loomed close at hand.

He picked up his pace. He wanted to hear all about the meditating birds. Not alert the Brit.

He stumbled, fell hard on hands and knees, began picking himself up. The others were looking back at him.

Oh, no ...

The world leaked for Hubert. Like a big hand waving a magic wand, knowledge hit him, sprayed him with another person's life.

Rising from hands and knees—seeing Mel, Angela, and Ralph looking at him—Hubert saw Chad Garrick, and became Chad Garrick, all in the twinkling of an eye.

Three years ago ...

A kid told Chad that something was lying dead in the woods.

"Come on, Chad. Let's go see it."

"What is it?"

"You'll see."

Chad followed the kid, sensing something mighty important was up. Along the way, he thought of Milky. Was it Milky who was lying dead in the woods? Would Milky get up and ... and come home with him ... and shock their parents? Or maybe Milky ... poor Milky ... would chase him ... and kill him ... and take him to wherever Milky's soul lived.

They walked through the woods, entered a clearing, and saw a shack. It was old Brent Hardwick's place. Hardwick carved up animals, their meat, their hides, stuffed them, mounted them, inserted fake eyeballs.

Haunting pictures of Milky lurched through Chad's mind as he and the other kid walked to Hardwick's backyard.

They came upon a dead animal stretched out on the grass. Two bullet holes were in evidence, one in the chest, one in the head. Blood stained the chest wound, but the head wound was bloodless, just a dark hole.

Chad stared, Milky forgotten.

It was a mountain lion.

He circled the body, stared at the cat's face. It looked like a normal face, not a dead face. Heck, and why should a bullet hole, something so small, bother such a big, strong animal? It wasn't fair. Why couldn't things keep running and jumping even though they've got bullet holes all over them? Bullets are tiny.

He imagined the cougar out hunting, lurking, flowing through the brush. He looked at the other kid.

"What do they eat?" he asked.

"Deer. Lambs and calves when they want to live dangerously. A rancher killed this one."

Chad imagined the cougar killing and eating a deer. Then he imagined it killing and eating a rancher.

"Which rancher?" he asked.

"Ain't none a your business," a strange voice intruded. "Which rancher? Cheesus!" It was Brent Hardwick. He had snuck up on them.

Hardwick's bony face, protruding from the collar of filthy

coveralls, looked like a tombstone. He stared at Chad, showed his teeth. Black stumps and gaps. His hair looked like it had been frozen in a cold turbulent draft. It stuck out of his scalp like an array of sharp knives.

"Cheesus! Which rancher!"

Hardwick shook his head, walked in circles, his hands buried in the deep pockets of his coveralls. He hardly seemed to walk; he was scarecrow thin; his coveralls seemed to just blow around with him inside.

"Cheesus! Which rancher!"

Chad began to hate Brent Hardwick. In his mind, he saw Hardwick sink his knife into the cougar's flesh. He saw the cougar snap to life and swipe a big paw across Hardwick's face, decorating the air with a spray of blood and a scream that would not end.

"We'd better go, Chad," said the other kid.

Hardwick was leaning over the cougar, his eyes buzzing like flies, his tongue flicking serpent-like over his rotting teeth.

Chad and the other kid walked away.

"Never tell a soul, Chad," said the other kid when they reached the woods, "or Hardwick will carve us up with his knife."

"Don't worry." Chad's mind was elsewhere. He and the other kid split. Chad went home.

He lurked around the edges of his yard, half-Chad, half-cougar, doing a million things in his mind. Bullets could not stop him. Nothing could stop him.

Hubert rose to his feet, blinked and blinked again.

He had been inside another person's skin, now he was back inside his own, and the creeps were pitilessly assaulting him.

For the moment, he forgot about the Brit, about zombies, about sparkles of sunlight, poetry, and morality.

Something raw had touched him. Something about Chad.

Mel, Angela, and Ralph were staring at him.

Hubert ran to catch up.

Chad followed a path downslope into a forested valley. Trees, wildflowers, and thickets grew in profusion all around him. He heard running water, pushed through a thicket, and came upon a peaceful glade, a burbling stream.

He took his shirt and hat off, waded into the stream, and cleansed his wounds. He got out of the water, let the sun and breeze dry him off, then put his shirt and hat back on.

He filled his canteen in the stream, took a long drink, filled it again. He looked around. An explosion of plant life teased his eyes. His stomach growled.

"Which of you is poison?" he asked the plants, approaching them.

The plants remained silent. The wind threw a gentle, clattering gust through the trees, but did not articulate an answer.

"I've got to eat." Chad heard nothing.

He began poking and sniffing the plants. A sharp *chirp* startled him. He looked up and saw a squirrel watching him from a tree branch. It shivered in the fashion of squirrels—its body like a statue, but cloaked within a million jitters. Suddenly, it ran along the branch to the trunk, then scurried upward, rasping the bark.

Chad followed its rattling flight. It stopped on a high branch and gazed down, still cloaked in squirrel jitters. A bird swept to a twiggy branch near the squirrel. A moment later, two storms broke out as bird and squirrel hurled from one another.

Chad continued his search. He knew something about edible plants and their poisonous colleagues. Birds and squirrels can thrive on things that would terrorize the human system. The flighty creatures of the woods would be of no help. You can't follow their lead.

He ran names of poisonous plants through his mind, trying to remember what they looked like: Star of Bethlehem, death camas, jimsonweed, yellow sweet clover, dogbane, water hemlock, poison ivy.

You didn't hunt cougar tracks for three years without learning something of the woods, meadows, and streams. Chad had spent hours poring over library books on edible plants, now he tried to conjure up the plant faces.

Star of Bethlehem—six white petals, star shaped, kills grazing animals.

Death camas—a messy-looking flower on a stalk, whitish, known to kill horses and cattle.

These plants really know how to protect themselves, thought Chad. They'd kill humans too, or at least powerfully screw them up.

He plucked as he went, avoiding suspicious-looking plants, and soon had two handfuls. He washed them in the stream, then sat against a tree and began to eat. Only then did he realize he was eating food from another world.

He stopped chewing. His heart raced for a moment, then slowed. I'm still alive, he thought. His instincts gave him a twitch of approval, so he resumed eating.

His taste buds collided with a swirl of sensations: juicy, spiky tangs; soft, wallowing flavors; sparkles of energy. Soon, the plants were gone.

He wanted more. Spying some tasty-looking plants near the water's edge, he rose, but abruptly froze, a sudden inexplicable terror holding him in place.

He scanned the brush, his eyes resting on something in the foliage, something cloaked in ghostly black vapors.

Chad felt a fever pitch of fear. His heart tumbled about in his chest. He faced the black quaking patch and waited. It emerged from the thick tangle of plants. A man, he saw. A powerfully built man.

The man ambled toward Chad. He was dressed all in black, and held a staff and a white cloth sack. His clothes looked like they had come from a museum; they had that ancient look about them, especially the hat—a wizard's hat, thought Chad, though round on top instead of pointed.

Chad heard rustling, glanced to the side. A huge dodo poked its head out of the brush. Looking down its beak, it examined Chad.

Chad snapped his eyes back to the man in black. The man was muscular in a rangy, whipcord fashion. He had a warrior's body, warrior's clothes. His staff was a warrior's staff. Bits of the woods and meadows clung to him. The man seemed to be a movable portion of the woods and meadows.

More rustling to the side. Chad looked: the dodo was breaking through the brush. It swept into the clearing, stood sideways, and stared at Chad.

Chad, feeling a spike of fear, switched his eyes back and forth, keeping man and dodo in sight. He balanced on the balls of his feet, felt energy coursing through him, preparing him for battle.

The man stepped closer.

"Close enough," said Chad. The man was two arms' lengths away now.

The man stopped, reached into his white cloth sack, and pulled out a smaller sack. He held it out toward Chad.

"Eat," said the man.

Chad stepped forward, took the sack, and smelled the faint aroma of food.

He loosened its drawstring and looked inside. A small loaf of bread.

He reached in, grasped it. It fell into moist pieces. The full aroma hit him. It blew up his nostrils, nearly lifted him off the ground. It was the most pleasing aroma he had ever experienced.

Eating greedily, savoring the taste and texture, he walked to his tree and sat against it. It was a crumbly meal, like bread, like something else. He drank from his canteen, then ate some more, looking into the sack, wishing there were a never-ending supply of this fascinating food. He looked up at the man, at the dodo, back at the man.

"What's this food called?" he asked.

"It is called Forest Buckle." A pleasing growl from the man.

Chad looked into the sack, continued to eat. Its aroma tugged at him, pulled at the core of his being. Feeling a quickening fear, he glanced away, then looked back into the sack, gripped by a compulsion to dive in. He reached for more, but froze his hand, staring in disbelief.

The mass of dwindling food was now presenting a bizarre picture: the edge of a forest, a ramshackle hovel, a family: children in rags, a haggard mother, a wrathful father.

Chad looked up, escaped the image. He stared at the man in black, odd thoughts crisscrossing his mind. Finally, he found his voice, though it hardly seemed like his own.

"Did you step in from the days of the black plague, the days of werewolves and witches and warlocks, of torture racks, of murderous thugs posing as kings and queens and popes and bishops, the dim, dark days of sorcery?"

The man roared with laughter.

Chad went back to eating the food. He picked with care through the forest and hovel and family.

Then Chad lost himself.

The images flew. He slipped into the sack of Forest Buckle, slipped into Europe, slipped into tumultuous times. He found himself in another body, which he instantly recognized as his own. His senses ignited, and he became that wrathful father—a life Chad had lived hundreds of years ago.

He was sitting. And thinking. A tough life. Food scarce. Work torturous. Too many children running about. Most of them die young anyway. What good are they? The children ran by. He batted a little one with his big paw of a hand. It flew through the air, its ragged clothes flapping like broken, twisted wings. The others cowered then ran off. The little one whimpered and lay still.

Later, he discovered what children were good for. You put them to work on your own land and you sold them off whenever possible. They were good for nothing, those children were—ungrateful, wretched scoundrels. But they could work. So, he batted one. It flew ...

Another life. As a woman this time. Children were evil. They had to be constantly reminded of their sinfulness. And of what was expected of them. Her children were always doing wicked things. In every thought, in every word, in every deed. Hell was made for children. She flew into a rage. And went looking for them ...

Then a life as a clergyman. Crafty willfulness. Careful now, not to alienate the bishop; the hierarchy must be taken care of. Careful now, pick out the lowliest amongst the flock. See the fear on the faces. Worthiness is not for some. Strong contrasts draw in the worthies and keep the lower elements in their place. Mock the weaklings in front of the flock. That's it. Draw the flock in tight, make it a pointed church, with the fearful in their place, the strong lording over the weak. Now, step on that little one ... The fearful never fight back, and they can never escape. Ha, ha. Where would they go? This is the only church. And godless people are not permitted to live. See, the worthies of the flock laugh with you. Joy!

Not a single life this time. A collision of lives, an echo chamber of lives. Falling ... falling ...

Chad fell through a deep, dark ocean of roiling clouds. Then he broke into light below and continued falling ... falling ...

Chad opened his eyes, saw that he was lying on the ground. He sat up and looked into the sack. Still some food left. Smells wonderful. He ate, recalling its name—Forest Buckle.

"The Indignities!"

The words, spoken harshly, had come from the man in black. Chad looked at him.

"What's your name?" he asked.

"Drakon," said the man, then motioned toward the dodo. "Allow me to introduce my friend Marshall."

"Glad to meet you." Chad nodded at them. "My name is Chad Garrick. Thank you for this food."

The dodo looked away, pointed his beak in the air, and gave out an airy "Harrumph." He busied himself along the periphery of the clearing, inspecting the plants, sniffing and uttering a variety of airy calls, all the while ignoring Chad and Drakon.

"You had a trip through your own hell," said Drakon. He walked to Chad, sat, and laid his staff across his knees.

"You're limping, Drakon."

"One of the big birds tried to take out my knee. He paid for it." He held up his staff and smiled impishly.

"The Indignities?" said Chad.

"Some call it the cycle of rebirth. Karma. Reincarnation. *The Indignities* is what I call it."

Hoodoo, thought Chad. Shivers swept up his spine. He looked at Drakon. "So, my mother's religion is wrong? We live many lives?"

The man nodded, burning confirmation into the air.

"Yes, Chad Garrick. Souls reincarnate, to surge through this sea of bloating blather time and time again. Now you know the truth."

"Yeah?" Chad laughed, then looked into Drakon's piercing eyes. "Who are you, Drakon?"

"You will learn of me, Chad, in due course, but first, tell me how you came to enter this world."

Chad told Drakon about finding the giant egg on the prairie yesterday, about coming back to the egg this morning, seeing the Barneys, seeing the stranger stalk the Barneys.

Drakon held up a hand.

"Stranger?" he asked.

"A Brit. I could tell by his accent."

"You were close enough to hear his accent, and he didn't detect you?"

"Uh, yeah," said Chad.

Drakon's eyes seemed to dance in the air.

Chad told Drakon about following the Barneys, the Brit, and the giant hatchling through the bur oaks, being kidnapped by Tim and Zack, escaping, discovering slithers, witnessing the dance of Tim and Zack, hearing the voice of the Universe, following the road, finding the stream.

"There's one thing that bothers me, Drakon. Just before those birds grabbed me, before I even saw them, I began running, and then I blacked out. Why didn't I fight them?"

"Marshall can answer that," said Drakon. "Marshall," he called, "will you please tell Mr. Garrick how dodos take prisoners."

Marshall left the plants alone and cocked himself upright. He walked toward Chad and Drakon, directed his gaze at Chad, then looked away, favoring the treetops with his attention. He stopped near Chad.

"Harrumph. A dodo, Mr. Chad Garrick, in full fighting trim and vigor, does not take anything into his grasp that is capable of fighting back. You would have been slashed in half if you had fought back. At deep levels of your mind, this was known. At deep levels of your mind, commands were given: *Run! Faint!* You were quite fortunate that you did run and faint, otherwise you would have been quite dead, Mr. Garrick. Does that answer your question?"

"But—"

Marshall gave out a litany of airy hoots and calls and strutted back to the edge of the clearing. He bent, sniffed the plants, then forcefully blew air on them, sending the plant faces into airy dances.

Chad looked at Drakon.

"What would they have done to me if I hadn't escaped? And why did they let me go the second time, in the brush? And what about the Barneys? Where are they? Are they prisoners?"

"You'd have been taken to the Spiderweb, Chad. You'd have been tried, sentenced to the *dojos,* or executed forthwith. Tim and Zack let you go because your escape created a blood shadow about you. You are like a walking egg, and eggs are inviolable in Dodoland. The Barneys are safe for the time being. Their Brit casts a blood shadow over them, though it grows faint at times. At the moment, they are viewing events at a meditation square, not more than four miles from here."

Chad felt relieved to hear that the Barneys were safe. He devoured the last morsels of Forest Buckle, then held the sack up.

"Got any more of this food, Drakon?"

Drakon rose to his feet, whipped his staff around in blurring, air-ripping motions.

"Here ye, hear ye!" he cried. "Replenish the bin with Forest Buckle!"

Soon, the woods were alive with wee creatures, seemingly half-goat, half-human, none of them more than two feet high. They scampered about, chattering in some outlandish language. One of them grabbed the empty sack from Chad. They squealed with delight then vanished into the woods, leaving faint traces of their garble behind.

Chad leaped to his feet.

"What in the world ...?" He scanned the brush.

Drakon faced the brush, whipped his staff through the air, and bellowed, "Break not your head against Stonehenge!" He turned to Chad and said softly, "Sometimes they go too far afield. But *that* brings them back."

"What are they?" said Chad. "Impossible ..."

Drakon whistled his staff through the air. "*Impossible* is a word fit only for tyrants, blathering imbeciles, and scribes, Chad Garrick—not for you!"

"Sorry, Drakon. I wasn't thinking. Of course they're possible."

"They're fauns, forest spirits. They live in their own little world where they make Forest Buckle and other treats. They gather the products of forest and field, bedevil it with karmic knowledge and nature lore, and presto—delectable loaves of Forest Buckle."

Suddenly, the woods were swarming again with fauns. One of them appeared beside Chad and handed him a fresh sack of Forest Buckle. Chad took the sack and tried to pet the little creature, but it zipped away out of his reach.

The fauns vanished. The brush rustled all about. Then stillness. Chad looked into the sack. The aroma lofted him. He ate a handful, then tied the sack to his belt.

Drakon approached him.

"Sit down, Chad."

They sat.

"You have told me of your journey into this land, now I must tell you things that will help you make your decision."

"What decision?"

"The Barneys are deep into this world. They may never get out."

"What?" Chad surged to his feet.

Drakon waved him down.

Chad sat, his body becoming electric with fear.

Marshall sauntered over, leaned down, and put his beak close to Chad. Chad felt his warm, humid breath. Like blasts of wind, Marshall's voice called out.

"Chad Garrick, pay no mind to the Barneys. They, like millions of other earth souls, are false role models—faint images of talking heads with a slot on top their skull that takes a nickel. Pedigreed one-tossed-eye dogs. Drop a nickel through the slot and their jaws start to move up and down in programmed fashion. Society's fashion. Just about any grouping of words can come through the jaws, if the tongue isn't so uncoordinated it trips over them. Now and then, one of these false role models will get to jawing with such convoluted rhythms that their undershorts will geyser up and shoot out their mouth. When that happens, they all herd together and pretend nothing happened."

Chad couldn't believe what he had heard.

He looked up at Marshall. The dodo was now standing upright, staring at the treetops again. Chad popped to his feet. Marshall took a step away.

"What do you know about undershorts, Marshall? You don't even wear any. You don't wear any clothes at all. Besides, what do you know about humans?"

"Chad, I have feathers. Little ones layered close to my skin near my hind end serve as my undershorts. Bigger feathers layered on top of these little feathers serve as my trousers, shirt, and suit coat."

Marshall gave out several airy harrumphs and moved back to the plants. He blew massive volumes of air at them, nearly ripping them up by the roots. He paused and looked at Chad.

"And I don't need to be a human in order to be a student of humans, any more than a human who studies fish needs to be a fish." He turned and blasted the foliage. "Harroomph!"

"Marshall!" Chad ran at the dodo. "I'll prove you don't know anything about humans." He stopped. Marshall turned to stare at him. "What did the fire engine say to the caboose?"

Marshall looked thoughtful for a moment. Then he looked down at Chad.

"I don't know," he said. "My ignorance in this instance proves nothing."

"Get your ass out of my way!"

Marshall gazed at the treetops, then he quickly jumped aside.

"No, Marshall, it's a joke. See, you don't know anything about humans." Exasperated, Chad walked back to his tree. Marshall went back to blowing on the plants.

"Chad," said Drakon in a husky whisper, leaning over, "never mind Marshall. He's an intellectual. You'll get used to him. He's not a bad sort."

"But he's as haughty as that devil Angela Barney!"

"Chad, we need Marshall; his views add something to the dialogue that flows through Dodoland. He believes all humans—with few exceptions—are nothing more than highly conditioned saps. And role models, according to Marshall's theory, are those saps who mindlessly support, in words and deeds, society's institutions. People-pleasers, Chad."

"What was that ... that Marshall said ... pedigreed one ..."

"Pedigreed one-tossed-eye dog." Drakon sprang to his feet and whipped his staff through the air.

"Behold, an old man with one tossed eye!"

Chad heard the brush crackle, turned and saw a gaunt old man emerge from the tangles. He was morose looking, nearly bald, and wore drab, ill-fitting clothes.

The old man, putting on a brave front, walked close to Chad and Drakon, and stopped. He plucked out one of his eyes, tossed it up, caught it, tossed it up again.

"This eye is my best friend," he said in a scratchy, droning voice.

He popped the eye back in and it crawled across his face, eye socket and all. The eye snuck into his scalp, plowed through his wispy strands of hair, then began to curve around his head in a swift race. Round and round it went. Finally, it settled into place, though slightly askew.

"Begone, dog!" Drakon vanquished the old guy with a mighty swing of his staff. The man turned fearfully and crashed into the brush, thrashing with great wasted energy until he was out of sight.

"Homunculus, Chad. Models of humans. Used for demonstration purposes. That one, symbolizing an aspect of the human condition—fearful, fretful, unable and unwilling to think for himself—keeps one tossed eye on human institutions, bowing and scraping all the while. Zipping round and round, his one tossed eye never loses sight of the institutions. Pitiful."

Drakon sat, facing Chad.

"Now a bit of the history of dodos."

He filled Chad in on the dodos of Mauritius, their flight-lessness, how they became extinct.

"And, of course, they blame humans. It's only natural. But they've also looked at themselves, and have changed what they've found wanting."

A loud *harrumph* was heard from Marshall. He rattled the foliage with his breath, louder than before.

"So, they decided to grow to monster size," said Chad.

"And develop language," said Drakon. "Speaking and reading skills. And the ability to regenerate damaged or missing body parts."

Drakon told Chad about the *dojos,* martial arts training, meditation, and cultural festivals.

"The birds are quite the exotic species now, Chad. There's no question they've overcome their previous limitations. They are quite fearsome, and dedicated to preserving their young through the rapid development of survival skills. But they've gone too far. For centuries, they've been secretly killing humans in the name of dodo survivability, when it's not really necessary to do so. They don't want to quell their old hatred. It's a pattern that's so ingrained it might as well be programmed into their genes. Fight a worthy fight, Chad, but don't go insane with bloodthirst."

Chad laughed. Then he became serious and looked at the man in black.

"Who are you, Drakon?"

With that, Drakon began to tell his tales.

In the beginning ...

He wasn't Drakon then. He was *Elaphos,* and as a toddler, he heard the strains of *Elyth Skilly* pass from his mother's lips. *Elyth Skilly* was a mystery religion, a nature religion. It served the needs of its people, tying them spiritually to the bountiful land, and to the animals of the hunt, predator and prey.

Elaphos, during an idyllic childhood, learned to touch Nature, to breathe of it, to bask in it. His mother would say: *"Clench it betwixt your teeth and ride it heavenward as a conquering beast."*

Elyth Skilly held Nature as divine. Nature, at its subtlest, was the source of all creation. Creation, springing from the source, was the visible aspect of Nature—the gross physical world. The source, the unmanifested, was the vast unseen, intelligent, all-knowing creator of the Universe, the fountain which nourished everything.

"It swims from the depths, its song doth flow with that special unworldly heavenly glow."

As a young man, *Elaphos* took a wife. When their first child was born, his wife sang, *"She properly belongs in savored angelic songs."*

They cherished their daughter, and the other children who followed, teaching them the ways of *Elyth Skilly.*

Their ways were different from most others, but they were not ignorant of the world. The interlocking families of *Elyth*

Skilly lived amongst other religions, other cults, and amongst much barbarity. They lived in coastal areas of the Aegean Sea, and spread north and west, east and south, merging with and blending with other cultures tuned to Nature.

From the West, the magic and sorcery of the Druids touched *Elyth Skilly;* from the East, the perennial philosophy of the *Vedas.* It was the nature of *Elyth Skilly* to evolve.

Then Christianity flicked its flaming serpent's tongue across the European continent, and *Elyth Skilly* sank into a cold river of fear, submerging into secrecy to save its very soul.

Many *Elyth Skilly* families began flocking to Christian churches—it was often a matter of survival. Punitive laws made it dangerous to be anything but a Christian. They suffered. Their health suffered. Their fortunes suffered. Christianity, the self-proclaimed religion of the poor, lived up to its name—it impoverished their spirits and their earthly lives. Others, escaping the serpent's grip, crept farther into the wilderness. Or into the unknown.

Elaphos chose to creep into the unknown. He drank of the secrets of East and West. After much wandering, and much dislocation—his family scattered, his children grown, his wife dead—*Elaphos* began to recognize the world as illusion—*maya.*

He could pass through worlds.

He did not have to experience death.

Elaphos was now an elemental, manifesting where he thought he was most needed, wherever Nature was being gored and bloodied.

Standing on the threshold of his new being, he recalled a certain *Elyth Skilly* verse that had sprung from his mother's lips:

"It's time to abide by the raging beast inside and allow him a greater growl up here in our earthly prowl."

The Dark Ages swept across Europe. *Elaphos* trod the land, weaving in and out of worlds, helping the wretched to once again touch with Nature.

But Christianity, dominated by dark masters, held a demon's grip. Torture and murder flourished. Pagans, heretics, and those accused of witchcraft were victims. It was a plague across Europe.

Elyth Skilly, with *Elaphos* at the helm, though depleted in numbers, continued to grow in wisdom. It lent its secret verses to the dramas that flickered through darkest Europe:

"A Dominator of Old Harpoon doth enter shattering the moon. It came upon another slaughter and burst upon Earth's worst to halter the messengers of Man."

"A flattened pleasure dome, now turneth to Rome, doth meter a cheater in stone. A heaven rat is sent to beget a river rent of a flood of chorus rhyme—spilled blood for no known crime. A feast of silken pleasures in a dark dome of treasures."

Elyth Skilly sang of renewal also—a dawning of a new age, an age which would recognize Nature as being the source of all creation, an age which would tap into Nature and receive Nature's blessings and support, an age of healing and growth:

"I dreamt of a darting across a smarting land, homing on a splendid land of fire-breathing sand."

The Dark Ages fell away.

Sparkles of light fell upon the earth.

Earth, though lighter now, remained in the throes of warring forces, one seeking dominion over the other—all seeking dominion over Nature. Nature does not fight. When wars are fought over it, it seeps deeper into seclusion, withholding its healing powers.

Elaphos, catching wind of a new order of beings burgeoning on a new astral plane, paid a visit and discovered the giant dodos. They were in tune with their Nature spirit and thus were experiencing rapid development and near-perfect survivability. But soon some wretched pangs of growth came along. The world of the giant dodos, being on an astral plane closely attuned to the earth plane, regularly found itself brushing with earth, mainly in wilderness areas.

Shimmering horizons, vaulted forests, a speck of village in the distance, wandering earth souls—all these and more were suddenly within the purview of the dodos.

Racial memories of Mauritius fresh, the big dodos went out slashing, tearing, running to ground first the animals—ancient enemies of dodo eggs—and then, venturing afield, humans.

"Chad," said Drakon, "a big dodo can chase down a cape buffalo and spill its guts with one slash of its razor claws. And when they went after humans ..." Drakon paused and shook his head. "Whole villages were wiped out."

The dodo world would retreat, impenetrable, a quivering line unseen, to spring this way or that, leapfrogging continents, another merge with earth, a day or night of terror, another retreat.

On and on it went.

Elaphos observed.

He prepared himself for immersion into the dodo world. He trod the Orient, studying martial arts, deepening his practice of meditation. He yoked his mind with the dodo Nature spirit. Due to bloodthirst on the surface world, the spirit was submerged, less and less a presence in the life of dodos, more and more dormant—a distant stranger to most dodos.

Elaphos enlivened the dodo spirit with *Elyth Skilly* verses, chanting them over and over, infusing the dodos' world with Nature vibrations that would, in time, waken the spirit fully. A Nature spirit fully alive at the very surface of life would instantly cleanse the world and cause the bloodthirst to collapse.

Then *Elaphos* artfully inserted himself into the dodo world. He walked the land, not as one who hid in the forests chanting verses, but as one who strode confidently about.

"Chad, we had fights you wouldn't believe. I studied martial arts under the Asian masters for more than a hundred years. I mastered the dodos. They were three-fourths insane before they made peace with me and asked me to teach them fighting skills."

Dojos sprang up all over Dodoland. Martial arts, with the inner strength and confidence it instills, quelled some of the bloodthirst.

But not all.

"A battle half-won, Chad. Win your battles bit by bit."

Elaphos taught the dodos meditation. Meditation stills the mind. The mind transcends and merges with the infinite field of Being. The mind, as it returns from this field, carries with it blissful qualities, for it has touched with Nature at the source. With heaven. Healing of mind and body takes place.

The more advanced meditators stopped killing humans. They were enlightened.

"Chad, you can see the progress we've made. Enlightened dodos wouldn't harm a soul, but the others ...?"

If not for a very tenuous thread ...

Drakon, over several years, introduced homunculi into the dodo world.

"It was a ploy, Chad, pure and simple. The plan was to get the birds used to the idea that some humans were okay."

Working with Nature, Drakon conjured homunculi, sending them forth across the land. Initially, they were ripped to pieces by dodo sentries, who could not distinguish homunculi from humans.

"They still can't, Chad; none of them can." Drakon motioned toward Marshall, who had suddenly sent the foliage and flowers into stormy waves with his energetic breath. Chuckling, Drakon whispered, "Marshall absolutely will not entertain the concept.

"Chad, eventually I convinced the dodos that killing these interlopers was a waste. They could be captured and made to perform gladiator chores in the *dojos,* sharpening dodo fighting skills."

The dodos began capturing wandering homunculi, holding them in cages fashioned in the manner of huge spiderwebs, and herding them into *dojos* for combat.

"It was a fiasco, Chad, all part of the plan. The homunculi, knowing they were going to die anyway, did not offer themselves as worthy opponents to the dodo martial artists. The slaughter was awful. The dodos tore them to shreds. I explained the concept of incentive to the dodos—the homunculi had to have a reason to fight. The dodos understood this implicitly."

Interlopers exhibiting great bravery and tenacity in the *dojos* were granted freedom and were allowed to pass unmolested through the dodo world. The homunculi, with few exceptions, turned into ferocious fighters. Despite this, most were soundly defeated in the *dojos,* given thumbs-down by the *sensei,* and killed by their sparring partner. Some, though defeated and badly injured, were given thumbs-up.

"Courage, Chad. The will to live, to fight. That's why Tim and Zack let you go. A fight doesn't have to be in a *dojo;* it can be anywhere. And it doesn't have to be physical; it can be an inner battle with monsters that threaten to tear your life apart. Facing your inner monsters can be as scary as facing external threats to your life. There's more than one way to earn a blood shadow.

"Chad, I heard the verses of your capture, your escape, your fight. The atmosphere was full of them. The Universe sang of Chad—of fear, of sorrow, of courage. There was a song of Chad. A dance of Chad. It moved through the air. I tracked the verses and found you here by this stream."

The dodos became used to seeing people—homunculi—pass in their midst, walking about in an envelope of hard-earned freedom and dignity. Soon, a problem developed: How could one tell the difference between an untested interloper and one who had earned the right to trod unmolested?

"It was a mighty problem, Chad. The dodos, being close to Nature—aside from their hatred of humans—absolutely abhor bureaucracy. It's in their DNA. Bureaucracy, for them, would be like a living Mauritius—extinction while still alive.

The few rules they have now already test their endurance. The very idea of labeling humans free or interloper, tracking them, checking their documents, keeping records ..."

Drakon had the solution; it was all part of the plan. He told the birds: While meditating, when the mind is stilled almost to the point of transcendence, release a thought: *Smell people-pleasing odors.*

Through regular use of this *sutra,* the birds developed a highly refined ability to smell people-pleasing odors on humans—or on homunculi. Now the plan was complete.

"Chad, Tim and Zack, on patrol, use their power of smell. The Barneys, protected by the Englishman's blood shadow, made it through. But you didn't. You stank of people-pleasing.

"Now, Chad, the dance of Tim and Zack, and the song you heard, that was a calibration trial. Tim and Zack, through their dance, asked the Universe to assess the trigger point for people-pleasing odors and tighten it if warranted. This usually happens right after some extraordinary event. Your escape was such an event. The Universe complied. You're a trailblazer, Chad; but the Barneys are in danger."

Drakon stood, left his staff behind, and walked to a nearby patch of wildflowers. He plucked two flowers, a yellow bell and a blue star. He returned, sat, and held up both flowers. They looked stunning, radiant in a glow of sunlight that caught their turning faces.

Chad allowed himself to become mesmerized by the flowers for a moment, then blinked them aside and looked at Drakon. Drakon's dark eyes pierced back.

"Dodo society is at a crossroads, Chad. There are warring forces. There are those who want to go back to the old ways, blood on the plain. They want a messiah, a savior, a whip for the masses, a reason to open the floodgates once again and spill human blood in even greater quantities than before."

The dark eyes shifted to the flowers, then back to Chad. Chad shot his eyes to the flowers, then looked away.

"Chad, pretend one of these flowers is poisonous."

Chad looked back at the flowers. He saw the softness of their petals, their delicate colors, saw them come fully alive in the glow of the sun. He saw the blue. He saw the yellow. He frowned hard, furled his brow, looked at Drakon. The man in black stared back.

"One is poisonous," said Drakon. He waved the yellow flower. "The other is edible." He waved the blue flower. "Pretend, Chad."

"Okay, I'm pretending." Chad sank against the tree.

"See the edible flower. See the blue. Lance it with your eyes. See its veins. Lance it deeper. See its cells. See one cell. See smaller and smaller and smaller ..."

Chad dove into the edible flower. He was inside it, pulled past the blueness, pulled into mysterious things. Sinking deeper, he saw lively clouds of energy.

"Dance inward, Chad, to the source. Cell, molecule, atom ... the subatomic realm ... and then ..."

Chad felt his mind expand, a whooshing silent explosion. He was no longer aware of his physical body. He was in a field of dancing, sparkling particles. He was everywhere in this field; the field was everywhere in him.

"Super Chad ..."

A soft, echoey voice, thrilling him, seeped into his mind. *That was a sutra, Chad,* whispered the voice. *Sutra ...* Moments later, the sutra sounded again.

"Super Chad ..."

He was coming out. Slowly. Easily. To surface consciousness. His body closed around him. His senses ignited. He saw yellow.

The yellow flower, the poisonous flower, wavered before him.

"An illustration, Chad. You transcended. You went to the source of all thought, the source of all matter. Entering the blue, edible flower, you came back through the yellow, poisonous flower. The source connects all things. The source creates all things. What is a flower? What is poison? Each is a thought."

"Yes, I understand," said Chad, though he was a bit shaken.

Drakon laid the flowers aside and looked intently at him. Something in those eyes cast a chill into Chad, made him shudder.

Drakon turned and looked at Marshall. Chad followed his gaze. The big dodo had stopped blowing the plants around. He stared at Drakon, then at Chad, then ambled over.

"Harrumph!" Marshall bent close to Chad. "Young Mr. Garrick, if you will bear with me for a moment, I will explain the current status of society here in Dodoland." Marshall rose to his full height, stepped about, blew airy gushes at the treetops, then bent back to Chad.

"There are new ... dodos about." Marshall paused, looked at Drakon.

"He means genetic mutations, Chad," said Drakon. "Over the last several generations, a new strain of dodo has emerged."

"Harrumph! They are hardly worthy of the name *dodo*," said Marshall. "Well, Chad, these new dodos ..." He looked at Drakon again. "I call them Raj, if you don't mind."

"Suit yourself, Marshall," said Drakon.

Marshall turned back to Chad, blew air in his face. "Raj, collectively or individually, they will be. Raj is an animal, Mr. Garrick."

Chad raised a hand.

Marshall drew back. "Do you have a question, Mr. Garrick?"

"Yes. You mean they aren't birds?"

Marshall glanced at the treetops. His voice took on a singsong cadence. "Mr. Garrick, Raj *is* a bird. Raj *is* a dodo. Please try to understand what I'm getting at."

"I'm trying to, Marshall. But you're such a haughty dodo."

"Harrumph!" Marshall sauntered away, returned to Chad, bent low, blew air. "Raj creates oppressive rules, Raj abolishes traditional culture, Raj is tyrannical."

Chad raised a hand. "Are Tim and Zack Raj?" he asked.

"Harrumph!" Marshall stared at Chad, amazement in his eyes. "They most certainly are not."

"Chad," said Drakon, "Tim and Zack are old-line guards. They have fallen under the new system, though, which is very much a Raj-inspired system."

Marshall bent, unreeled a tuneless parcel of air into Chad's face.

"Raj in the bush, Raj in the forests, Raj in the swamps and meadows, Raj in the distant villages, all Raj with the exception of Spiderweb Raj are much larger than normal dodos, Mr. Garrick, and possess no powers of regeneration. They are mindlessly obedient to Spiderweb Raj. Spiderweb Raj also possess no powers of regeneration. Some Spiderweb Raj are emaciated. Some are obese. Spiderweb Raj live to give orders. And these ..."

Marshall spewed out some ghostly foul words and calls that Chad could not decipher.

"And these mutants are in command of Dodoland, Chad. While the rest of us are busy enriching our lives through the exploration of culture, commerce, and Nature, mutants are busy gravitating toward power. And ..." Marshall glanced away. "We are all threatened by their absurdities."

Marshall walked back to the edge of the clearing, examined the flowers, puffed lightly on them.

"Chad," whispered Drakon, "Marshall lost his job at the university. Spiderweb Raj threw him out for daring to question their authority. More and more, they do not tolerate dissent."

A barely heard oath came from Marshall, then a whispered, "Wage war on them, young Mr. Garrick. War is what they are waging on us, and on you." The words were like vapor flowing across the clearing.

"War?" whispered Chad.

"Yes," said Drakon. "The Spiderweb is gearing up for new onslaughts on earth. All my work here is being undone. Your decision, Chad ..."

Drakon gripped his staff and stood.

Chad popped to his feet.

"You can go to the Barneys, cover them with your blood shadow, protect them, guide them home—their Brit is falling dangerously close to the new trigger point; Tim and Zack know no end to their duty; they dog the Barneys and the Brit right now, waiting to pounce. Or, you can proceed to the Spiderweb and stop the birth of a new religion."

Chad's thoughts were caught in a mad swirl. *Stop the birth of a new religion?* He stared at the man in black. "Drakon," he finally said, "why me? Why don't you—"

Drakon held up a hand. He smiled gently at Chad. "I help beings touch with Nature, Chad. I work behind the veil. Nature would not support my intervention."

Marshall smacked the plants around with his breath, then walked over.

"Excuse me, if you would, Drakon." He looked at Chad, exhaled explosively.

"An example, young Mr. Garrick: If trees were to begin falling on the Spiderweb, the Spiderweb would continue to go about its merry business despite this strange intervention by Nature. Earthquakes, volcanos, typhoons, floods—nothing of this sort, unless it was truly cataclysmic, would deter them from their purpose. Likewise, with Drakon. He is too close to Nature to be effective in this mission. He is too much like a falling tree. The task is yours, young Mr. Garrick. There isn't much time; there are no other humans around with the potential you have; and most dodos cannot enter the camp of Raj without drawing undue attention to themselves."

Marshall wandered back to the edge of the clearing. He huffed and puffed and blew the plants flat for a moment, then pointed his beak in the air and went silent.

Chad stared at Drakon, tried to read his mind, tried to divine his secrets.

"Can't I do both?" he asked. "Can't I guide the Barneys out of here and stop the new religion also?"

Marshall let out a series of bellowing oaths. The plants went into a frenzied dance.

"You can try, Chad," said Drakon, "if that is your preference."

"I'll do it."

Marshall let out another bellowing oath. It seemed to go on forever.

"Quickly, Chad, we must train you," said Drakon. "The task before you is enormous." Drakon walked toward the darkest woods.

Chad followed.

Drakon whirled. "No, stay!"

Chad froze and Drakon hurried toward the trees.

Marshall walked up to Chad, bent, blew air. "The hatchling is Raj's messiah," he said.

Chad stared up at Marshall. "The hatchling I followed?"

"Yes. Spiderweb Raj plan to crucify the hatchling, blame it on humans, and use the resulting catechism to stir up all of Dodoland into a fighting frenzy."

Chad, too stunned to reply, swept his eyes back to Drakon.

Drakon knelt over his staff, chanted quietly. Then he stood, whirled his staff in a blur, and threw it over the trees, out of sight.

"I've got to save the hatchling too."

"Harrumph! Dodos save themselves, Mr. Chad Garrick. You have quite enough to do as it is."

Chad heard an animal call through the trees—an odd bark.

"Mr. Garrick," said Marshall, "all dodos can communicate silently with one another."

"You mean mind to mind?"

"No. Sounds. Audible to dodos, not to humans. Beyond human frequencies. Beware of Raj communicating in this manner."

Chad heard something trampling through the woods, saw Drakon go into a crouch. The trampling grew closer.

Marshall puffed air into Chad's face.

"Go away, Marshall." Chad waved his arms. "Something's happening."

"Drakon will send you an associate." Marshall puffed more air into Chad's face. "You will need her help."

"Her?" Chad looked at Marshall. "No way! You can't mean Angela Barney!" He ran at Drakon. "No way!"

Chad stopped, his fury turning to wonder. Drakon was calling quietly to earth. Chad bent an ear and heard Drakon's voice more clearly.

"I want a mighty staff, a staff that knows the Universe."

Chad heard the energetic sounds of a large animal rushing through the woods, heading their way.

Moments later, a magnificent elk broke into the clearing. It charged Drakon, butted him in the chest, and sent him flying. Drakon hit the ground, leaped to his feet, grabbed the elk's antlers, and wrestled it onto its back.

With a thunderous roar, the elk turned into a huge Bengal tiger. It spun loose and clamped one of Drakon's hands in its jaws. Drakon worked furiously to pry the tiger's jaws open, but it would not let go.

Chad shuddered and drew back. The growls erupting from the tiger were the most menacing sounds he'd ever heard.

Finally, Drakon worked his hand free, then threw the tiger into the limb of a tree. The tiger bounded out of the tree and sprang at Drakon. With a lightning move, Drakon stepped aside, and the tiger found nothing but air.

The tiger whirled and sprang at Drakon again—but this time it metamorphosed into a staff and floated into Drakon's hands.

Drakon ran his hands over the staff, checked its balance. He turned to Chad.

"It has a consciousness. It has made a commitment to help defend me against all manner of attack."

Drakon looked around, at the trees, at the sky.

"This is a wonderful land, Chad. Vibrant atmosphere. Pleasing scents. The land and sky like a nursery."

Chad followed Drakon's gaze. Yes, he thought, like a nursery.

"But ghosts trod the land," said Drakon. "And battles brew in the air."

Yes, thought Chad.

Drakon whipped his staff through the air and something began crashing through the brush. Moments later, an elk broke into the clearing. It fixed its eyes on Chad, lowered its head, and charged. It butted Chad in the chest and knocked him to the ground.

Chad fought the elk, but to no avail. It had him pinned to the ground. Then he remembered Drakon's words, and chanted them. "I want a mighty staff, a staff that knows the Universe."

He felt a resurgence of energy, pushed the elk off, and popped to his feet. The elk sprang at him again—but in midstride, with a scream, it changed into a cougar.

The cougar knocked Chad to the ground. Wrestling, biting, chewing, snarling—the battle raged.

Chad remembered the meditation Drakon had led him through, remembered the *sutra*, and silently chanted it.

Super Chad ...

He chanted it over and over.

The *sutra* charged him with power. He threw the cougar off and sprang up. The cougar lunged at him again, but metamorphosed into a staff and floated into Chad's hands.

He turned to Drakon, bloodied.

"The stream," said Drakon.

Chad ran to the stream, threw the staff down, threw his sack of Forest Buckle down, and plunged in. He cleansed his wounds, emerged from the water, picked up his staff. It was alive in his hands. It thumped him hard in the chest, then was still.

Chad looked at Drakon, at the man in black, at the elemental. *A staff that knows the Universe.*

Six

*C*harles Barbier, sitting alone in his cell, thought of blood, and of a mirror broken to bits, a mirror that reflected his face in a thousand shattered fragments. *Oh, pray, a mirror for me.* He picked at the dirt in his cell, at bits of glass and blood. His feet were bare; he had removed his shoes and socks sometime in the night. He smeared dirt and bits of glass and blood on the soles of his feet, then methodically picked the bits of glass out.

He looked up. The sun ... Straight above, the rays shooting in through the webbing of his cell, dripping in, falling in, laughing, crying ...

A mirror! cried the sun. *To see the face of Charles Barbier!* The sun would shatter.

Charles could see into neighboring cells, but right now that held no interest for him. He could climb the webbing, like an ape, but right now that held no interest for him. He could escape, though that would take a while. He could tear the webbing apart with his hands and teeth, but after this they would have him right back inside, with tighter security. He knew, because this is precisely what happened yesterday.

Yesterday. When they executed several of Charles's web-encaged neighbors down the way. One by one. Moving closer to Charles's cell. Off to *Adminland* for a quick trial—they even called out the stops, like on a subway—then to *Execution Square* for hanging.

Charles had bit and chewed and clawed his way out, breaking into a twilight which—he discovered later—saw an end to the executions until dawn. But the dodos caught him and put him back in. Then they sent for a repairman.

Now *that* was an odd, odd person, thought Charles, watching the repairman approach through the gloom.

He stepped inside Charles's cell. Charles was huddled at the far end, caressing his hands, which were raw from working his way out. The guard, a monstrous dodo, stood inside the cell near the door, eyeing Charles and the repairman.

Charles, then, did not know it was a repairman.

The repairman stepped in and stopped. A Halloween mask? thought Charles. Was he wearing a Halloween mask? And was he acting the part? What part? The questions had screamed from Charles Barbier's mind.

No! They don't make people like that!

The repairman stood motionless, staring straight ahead. He wore blue jeans, a denim jacket, a black cowboy hat, and cowboy boots. His shoulders were odd—canted forward somehow. His arms were odd—nearly stiff, held extended a few degrees in front of his body. And when he walked, that is where they stayed—there was no swing of the arms.

His face was an exaggerated, grotesque Abe Lincoln. Big nose, dark beard, bushy hair. It betrayed not the slightest suspicion of emotion, intellect, or even of life itself. It was a face, but it might just as well have belonged to a rock, a tree, a sand dune.

The man walked stiff-legged, stiff-armed, stiff-necked into Charles's cell, and Charles, expecting imminent execution, recoiled, terror seizing his mind and holding it in a five-fingered parody of cold, sifting condiments.

Charles Barbier's mind sprinkled itself all over, diminishing itself into a core of insanity.

The repairman had stiff-walked to the rip in the webbing and had fixed it, pulling woven fiber and a big sewing needle from the inside of his denim jacket and somehow levering his body and working his hands well enough to make the repair.

Charles, he didn't come to kill you, to lead you away to *Adminland*—call it out—to *Execution Square*—call it out—to the gallows, to hang you, Charles. You're safe, for now, he told himself.

But he remained insane.

The stiff-walking repairman left. The dodo guard left. The door webbing was drawn tight from the outside and secured. And Charles Barbier sat, rocking himself, holding himself in fetal position.

Twilight faded; night slipped in. Charles took his shoes and socks off and played with his feet while rocking. Then the sun came, apelike, gamboling, wicked. Charles watched. And rocked. And wished for a mirror.

A few ticks past dawn, the dodos took another prisoner. Charles heard the screams as the victim was dragged from his cell. The conductor called out, *"Adminland."* A few ticks later, *"Execution Square."* A few ticks later, a loud *thwack!*—the scaffold trapdoor opening. And *thunk!*—the fall and jerk of a body.

Silence.

Movement.

Something odd crept into the proceedings. Shouts of a messiah reached Charles's ears. Executions were suspended.

The sun ticked higher, higher ...

Charles Barbier always knew he was destined for greatness. But first, he had to discover his resonant ground—that arena in which he would find unparalleled success. His instincts told him to become an outlaw.

But not just any kind of outlaw.

At eighteen, Charles went to the University of Virginia. At twenty-two, to Stanford Law School. At twenty-five, a big law firm in Washington, D.C., hired Charles. Its list of clients stretched worldwide. Charles made his peace with the world and kept his nose to the grindstone.

And hated it.

Whatever happened to his outlaw ambitions? Remaining proper within a deranged society was not for him.

Two years crept by.

Charles took up skydiving. After his twelfth jump, he decided he would jump without a parachute. He would just fly. After broaching the subject to a fellow skydiver, Charles was banned from the club.

He took up fencing and ballet and was kicked out of both.

He went to Florida to learn how to wrestle alligators. He found this disappointing, no contest—alligators were surprisingly easy. They were like dumb, sleepwalking humans.

He hired an ex-Navy SEAL to teach him how to kill. The ex-Navy SEAL, using a sleeper hold, almost killed Charles.

When all was said and done, Charles felt in no way an outlaw.

At the law firm, his fortunes revolved around furthering the aims of psychopaths, oligarchs, and political parasites who sought tyrannical rule over the human race. He hated them and wanted to destroy them. But how? It seemed an impossible task.

Two more years crept by.

Charles pursued an aerobics instructor. She kept dropping hints: *I prefer outlaws, Charles. You're not an outlaw.*

Charles would not give up. He did some research and hammered out an outlaw dissertation.

Charles had learned that through acquiescence, ordinary people continually lost their freedom to the psychopaths that ruled society. These psychopaths always got their way. Their insidious way. Outlaws like Charles were laughed at, sneered at, jeered at. Outlaws were a dying breed. They were becoming extinct.

In Washington, D.C., psychopaths were reflected from every shiny surface. They strutted about in glittering array, blinding nearly all with their finery, and fakery.

Charles Barbier pleaded with the aerobics instructor. She read his dissertation, but didn't seem impressed.

He tried being witty, and said to her, *"Does nectar like the sharp straw that comes piercing in to suck it dry?"*

She sniffed, *"You're not an outlaw, Charles."*

Charles knew he was a ghost, invisible to most.

One day at work, a frustrated Charles Barbier had a nervous breakdown. A senior member of the law firm found him on the floor, in fetal position.

"Charles!"

Charles sat up.

"Fred, I was just looking for something." Charles put his face close to the carpet. "My pen fell. It's got to be around here somewhere."

"Charles ..."

Charles looked up.

Fred motioned to a chair. "Sit."

They sat.

"As a professional courtesy to you, Charles, this will be handled discreetly. As you know, Charles, our firm offers free psychiatric and psychological counseling through a private mental health provider. No stigma is attached to this."

"Are you going to cart me off, Fred?"

Fred winced. "Charles, only if you wish."

"What are the alternatives?"

"What do you want to do with your life, Charles?"

Charles thought long and hard. Minutes passed. The senior partner's chair began a rhythmic squeaking that sent waves of tension through the room.

"You've been working too hard, Charles. Take a vacation. Take a month."

"I want to write, Fred. I want to write. I have ideas. Ideas on how to ... Government which governs least ... The pen is mightier than the sword ... Fred—"

"You just had a collapse, Charles. Go far, far away. When you get back, you will see things in a different light."

Charles went to Alaska. The airliner landed in Anchorage. From there, a bush pilot flew him to the Kenai Peninsula. The next morning, Charles, four strangers, and a wilderness guide named Topper got under way.

"Where're you from, Charles?" The voice, a husky rumble, belonged to a large man from Wyoming named Candy. He sat in front of Charles as they paddled, two to a canoe, downriver.

"Washington, D.C. I came here to drive the evil spirits out of me."

Candy laughed. And fell silent.

The days were full of paddling. Charles saw wilderness scenes that took his breath away. Nights around the campfire were filled with Topper's Alaskan tales. Charles felt chills as he listened to harrowing stories of grizzly bear encounters. He'd crawl into his tent, fall asleep, and await the burst of morning that would flit him into another day.

On the third day, the explorers angled their canoes toward a forested shore and made camp. They fished from the bank, caught their limit of sockeye salmon, and put them on a stringer.

As everyone settled in, Charles heard the aches and pains. "Ooooh ..."

"Aaaah ..."

Charles felt his own aches and pains. They throbbed with a peculiar searching kind of excitement as he walked through the crisp evening air.

"Not too far, Charles," said Topper. "It don't take but a minute to get lost in them woods."

"Gottcha." Charles rejoined the others.

A fire was blazing. Topper pulled the stringer of salmon from the river. He filleted them and set them frying.

They ate dinner.

Afterward, wandering a bit before the stories began, Charles stepped into the forest—and saw his first dodo.

He came back to camp and sat with the others. The crackling campfire licked the graying air. Shadows lengthened. Darkness welled.

"And wouldn't you know it, a sow grizzly and her two cubs came wandering onto the trail." Topper paused, sucked in a lungful of air, and let out a long, wistful sigh. "Just waddling about, right across our path. Later on, both them guys had to check their drawers. There was a powerful stench, as you can well imagine."

After the grizzly tales, Charles crawled into his tent and went to sleep.

In the morning, after a sizzling breakfast of salmon, Charles roamed into the forest and saw some strange purple shrubs.

The monster bird. Had it been a dream?

He tramped on and lost track of time. Shouts of "Charles! Charles!" dwelled in the air. "Charles! Charles!" Growing fainter.

The land changed. The flora changed. The fauna changed. Two huge birds crept from the silence of the forest and stood on either side of Charles Barbier.

"You're quite out of the ordinary, sir," said one of the birds, sniffing the air above Charles.

Somehow, hearing the bird talk didn't surprise Charles. He might've been surprised if these birds *didn't* talk.

The other bird, after sniffing at Charles, looked at his companion and said, "The *dojo?*"

His companion shrugged and said, "The *dojo.*"

That began Charles's education in Dodoland.

Do ribs, sternum, and clavicles heal faster in this world? Believe it. Believe it.

Charles jumped into the fray, believing he was invincible, realizing he must hold such a belief—hold it vividly—if he were to stand any chance of survival.

The dodos beat him.

And beat him.

And Charles kept coming back.

Each time, he was given thumbs-up.

Even when Charles was beaten to a seizure-driven mass of flesh and bones he was given thumbs-up.

They knocked him off his feet like cruel puppet masters. Charles would roll, protect himself, get to his feet, counterattack.

Thumbs-up.

They could have killed him easily. Day after day, they did not kill him. Once he was given a day off to mend. Then back to the *dojo.* And then they beat him to death—almost. Charles learned to take his beatings in a relaxed manner, and he learned to counter with a flurry, and he learned to believe— vividly—that he was invincible.

Each time the dodos demolished him, they came sniffing. Each time, Charles sought the enemy, fought the enemy ...

And the dodos, Charles learned, had a sixth sense for this. Thumbs-up.

After twenty-one days of gladiator duty in the *dojos*, he was granted freedom and dignity. He could walk amongst the dodos in peace.

Charles slept in the forest. He ate plants and fish. He bathed in streams. He went exploring and met more dodos. Charles swam in the dodos' world, and they swam in his. They swapped stories: Charles told them about D.C. They told Charles about the Spiderweb, about trials and executions, about people-pleasing odors, about a mysterious man in black. And, recently, of a wall of frustration building across their land, a wall that denied them knowledge.

"Why wasn't I brought to the Spiderweb for trial?" asked Charles.

"We're quite a distance from the nearest governing web," said Pablo, one of his dodo friends. "We rely on frontier justice. Interlopers go straight to the *dojos.*"

"Have you ever seen this ... this man in black?"

"No, not in these parts."

"This wall, Pablo ... What is it?"

"The atmosphere is blocked. Things are changing in Dodoland. We should know what these changes are soon."

Charles stared at his dodo friends.

"Are you just going to accept these changes?"

Pablo shrugged. He looked at the other dodos, then back at Charles.

"We always have, Charles. We are at such a distance—"

"Point the way, Pablo. I'll show you how humans become involved in government."

Pablo puffed out his chest and squinted at Charles.

"Survival is best served, Charles, by showing prudence."

"A wall is building in your world; it can only mean one thing—slavery."

A murmur swept through the dodos.

The next day, Charles and Pablo set out on a journey to Spiderweb One.

On the third morning, with the sun a fiery red ball on the horizon, Charles woke from a horrifying dream. Dodos were attacking him, violating his blood shadow, hauling him to the Spiderweb. His trial was a mockery of justice. They hanged him!

Just a dream. Charles shook the cobwebs from his mind, shook himself fully awake, and crawled from his hiding place. Where was Pablo?

Standing, he felt groggy. Funny, he was wide awake just a moment ago. Now … sleepy again? He looked around. Something told him to not look too much. He began walking, and then in a panic, he began a mad race.

Blackout …

Charles woke, encased in the fetid wing of a monstrous dodo, fantasias of insanity rippling through his mind.

The dodo, running at full tilt, transported Charles to the Spiderweb and threw him into a web cage.

"Been about a month since I've seen you, pal."

The voice was familiar. Charles looked into the adjoining cell. A face crept to the webbing—Topper.

Charles stared into the haunted eyes of his wilderness guide.

"The day after you disappeared, the birds got us, farther on down the river. They hauled us a long way."

"Candy? The others?"

"Hanged."

That night, Charles tore silently at the webbing of his cage, watching for guards.

"Adminland!"

"Execution Square!"

He escaped. He was captured. Enter the odd, odd repairman. Night came and went. The morning saw more executions.

He saw them drag his friend away.

"Pablo!"

Thwack!

Closer ... Closer ...

They took Topper.

Thwack!

Silence.

Then cries of a messiah.

And Charles sat, rocking, as the sun ticked higher ... higher ...

"Whoa, children!" Malcolm Moreland pulled up and set Ralph down. "Give these birds a wide berth." He kept a grip on Ralph. The energetic youngster was always a threat to run off after the dodos.

They watched the dodos pour into the meditation square. When the last of the dodos entered, a trilling passed through the air. The birds, sitting in rows, grew silent and closed their eyes.

"Hush, children."

Mel looked down at Ralph, and over at Hubert and Angela. Their eyes were intent upon the dodos.

"I'll whisper a few words to you as the dodos meditate."

He swept his gaze over the birds. They were like boulders, a couple hundred or so, big gray feathery boulders within the confines of the purple dwarfs.

"Meditation. Stills the mind. Stills the body. A dive within. An effortless trip. Some new words, children. *Mantra*—a sound you repeat silently within your mind. The *mantra* takes you inward to the transcendence, where your mind merges with the infinite field of Being."

Ralph squealed and tried to wiggle away from Mel.

"Hush."

The youngster settled down.

"Samadhi," said Mel. "The settled state. Silence within. Awake in the deep inside. You are one with unbounded consciousness. Then—"

Just then one of the birds began flapping its wings, raising a ruckus. A mad flapping of wings broke out among several other birds, then they settled down.

"The Yoga Sutras of Patanjali. Sutra—thread. From a state of unbounded awareness, release a thought. That thought becomes your awareness, becomes your reality. You are released from the bounds of normal reality. *The flying sutra ...* Release it ..."

A bird rose into the air, then another, and another.

"Nature is at your command, children," whispered Mel,

watching their awestruck faces. "Our bird is in there. Watch for him."

"Clem, Clem," whispered Ralph, looking skyward.

Dodos filled the air. They spread across the meadow, hovered over nearby woods, bobbing in the wind.

"They float around at will," said Mel. "With eyes open. Flapping of wings absolutely unnecessary. Of course, some are better at it than others. Practice, practice ..."

Ralph tried to shoot away from Mel, but he held him.

"I see Clem, Mel! I see Clem!"

Angela had her camera out and was running down the road, snapping away.

"Angela, stay close," called Mel.

She stopped, continued snapping.

Mel steered Ralph toward her.

"Hubert, we've got to stay together. One unit. Help me keep them corralled, will you?"

"Uh ... sure, Mel."

I've got three devils on my hands, thought Mel. He decided to throw a little scare into them, make them stick close.

He gathered the Barneys close.

"Children, be ye not deceived, for these exotic birds shall surely kill you—after a perfunctory trial—if you stray too far from me. We can't be sure of the intensity of your people-pleasing odors."

"Ah ... Mel," said Angela, "I've got no people-pleasing odors. Never did have."

"Me neither!" cried Ralph, stamping the ground.

Hubert just stared at him.

"Ah ..." How to make them understand? Suddenly, an idea,

like a python uncoiling from a tree limb, dropped on Mel.

"If you promise to stay close, so I don't lose you, I'll introduce you to a homunculus or two at the festival. How's that sound?"

"Hoo-ray!" Angela jumped around.

"Hoo-ray, hoo-ray, hoo-ray!" squealed Ralph.

Hubert shrugged and looked away.

Mel walked the Barneys down the road, willing his shadow to cast a cool spell over them all.

As he floated close to a grove of monstrous trees, Clem looked for a place to land. Trees, trees, please stay away from me, he thought. His belly fluttered as he passed over them.

He looked around, saw a clearing, steered toward it.

Some of the more immature hatchlings were hollering, *"Wee, wee, wee!"* as they floundered through the air currents, looking like drunken sailors.

Clem was relatively stable in the air; he had taken to yogic flying like a hawk takes to updrafts. To him, it was the most natural thing in the world.

A growing concern began to command more of Clem's attention. He was sure that that punk Roger and his two pals were looking for him. Clem had seen them staring at him in the meditation square. He remembered the assault this morning. The beating. The theft of the food.

Where are they? He scanned. *There!* Clem watched the three hoodlums as he continued to steer toward the clearing.

Roger looked like he was about to collide with a pine tree.

You'll be wearing that pine tree up your ass, thought Clem, glancing at Roger and snickering.

Clem began his descent. He landed with a soft *whomp* and ran across the ground until his momentum stalled out.

Whomp! Whomp! Crash!

Other dodos were landing here and there. Clem looked about and saw Roger, a little worse for the wear, shamble across the clearing toward him.

"Think you're so great, huh, Clem?" said Roger, flanked by his two hoodlum friends.

"What's that feather doing up your beak?" said Clem.

"Huh?" Roger swiped at his bill. "What feather?"

"Better check your ass, Roger," said Clem. "Return those pinecones at once. Don't you be carrying the woods around with you."

"Arrrrgh!" sputtered Roger. Regaining his composure, he cried, "People-pleaser! People-pleaser! People-pleaser!" He pointed at Clem with his razor claws and fanned the air with his wings, urging his thug companions to join in. Soon, all three of them were hurling people-pleasing taunts at Clem.

The three goons circled Clem. Clem stood his ground, never taking his eyes off Roger.

"Go sass your mama with that!" yelled Clem, bursting his voice through the blanket of jeers, halting Roger in his tracks.

"What?" cried Roger, pulled out of his incantations. He fiddled with his bill for a moment. "My mama?" Enraged, he lunged at Clem.

Clem sidestepped Roger's lunge, took him down with a wing lock, and kicked him in the ribs.

"Aw!" cried Roger, emitting a single note of agony.

Clem lashed his claws at the nearest companion and saw a smear of bloody feathers wipe the air. He chased the third punk into the woods, hearing the coward hoot like a crybaby.

Clem let him go and returned to the clearing. Roger and his bloodied friend were up and hobbling about. When they saw Clem, they made for the cover of the woods. Clem gave chase till both were shrieking, then let them go.

He set a swift course for the Greenways, home of the cultural festival.

"Hoo-ray! Hoo-ray! Hoo-ray!" shouted Clem as he sped along.

A pair of eyes, watching from a thicket, tracked Clem as the hatchling tore by. Those eyes, and many others, had been watching Clem throughout the day, relaying reports.

Clem, are you our anointed one? thought the owner of those eyes. Our Christ?

The eyes withdrew, fading into darker shadow.

Hoot ... hoot ... The air rang with a silent cry, and more news of Clem the hatchling was transmitted through the ether to the Spiderweb.

There was something in the air ...

Chad Garrick bent an ear.

"Not for you, Chad," said Marshall. "For the Spiderweb. News of a messiah. Harrumph!"

Marshall went back into his fighting stance. "Shall we continue, Mr. Garrick?" He stalked toward Chad, stopped, raised his razor claws.

Chad whipped his staff in a blur, knocked Marshall's razor claws aside, then rammed him in the midsection.

"Ooph!"

"Sorry, Marshall!"

"I'm not the fighter I used to be, Chad."

"You're doing fine, Marshall."

Something in the air …

Chad bent an ear.

Marshall cocked his head.

"Knowledge, Mr. Garrick. For you, I believe." Marshall wandered to the edge of the clearing.

Chad listened. The communication was not sound but mind to mind. The Universe was whispering a message, though garbled.

"I can't quite get it, Marshall."

"Put your full attention on it!" barked Drakon, who was sitting on a rock at the edge of the clearing.

Chad's face reddened. He put his full attention on the message and it came through. No, it wasn't from the Universe. It was from Hubert Barney. You don't know I'm here, Hubert. You can't know that. Not yet. Can you?

We're in big trouble, Chad! Help!

Chad continued to listen, but the message was over. He faced Marshall, staff at the ready. Marshall began stalking him again, then stopped.

"You seem preoccupied, Mr. Garrick. Is knowledge still hitting you?"

"No, Marshall. Let's fight. I'm going to war."

The battle raged through the clearing.

Drakon sprang to his feet, made the air sing with his whirling staff.

"You are ready for me, Chad Garrick."

Marshall let out a long sigh and retired to the edge of the clearing. He blew softly on the plants.

Chad faced Drakon. They circled, probed for weaknesses, Drakon offering advice, correcting techniques.

"A woman will join you, Chad."

"No, Drakon! I protest!"

Drakon rammed Chad in the chest with his staff. Chad flew backward.

"Your anger let your guard down, Mr. Garrick. I sent my *ki* into you, as well as my staff."

Chad rolled onto one knee, stood, came at Drakon. They flew at one another.

A dozen times, Drakon struck Chad with his staff, and Chad hit the ground. Bruises and welts rose on his body. Chad sent his *ki* into his pain, easing it.

"Remember, Chad, your staff has a consciousness. Let it help you."

Chad felt a sudden warmth flow from his staff. He fought with greater confidence. His strikes and blocks acquired greater speed and power. He foreknew Drakon's moves.

He closed on Drakon, drove his staff into him.

Drakon flew backward and hit the ground. He rolled to his feet and faced Chad with an impish grin.

"You are ready for the Spiderweb, Chad Garrick."

The three of them stood in the center of the clearing for Chad's graduation ceremony.

Drakon hummed a mournful tune.

The sky and earth seemed to lend their voices to the song, and the song became richer, shaking off the sorrow, taking on a heavenly melody.

Marshall joined in. His ornery voice did nothing to spoil the tune; it became even richer.

Words entered ...

But Chad could not make them out.

The Universe kicked up a little wind dance in the clearing, and the words rained lively into Chad's ears. Still, he could not make them out.

Then the words swam from the depths, and Chad heard them clearly. Their spirit, their essence, their meaning made his heart romp with joy. He was ready to go to war now. Like an arrow already shot.

"You heard?" asked Drakon.

"Yes," said Chad.

"That was the key *Elyth Skilly* verse. It lives within everyone. Ultimately, everyone hears it."

"Hoodoo, Drakon."

Staff in hand, Chad journeyed through field and forest,

hitching rides on slithers when possible, popping back to earth again and again.

While passing through a woodland, Chad's instincts told him to look back. A giant dodo was staring at him through the trees, madly sniffing the air, glints in his eyes like fiery breath. With an explosion of energy, the dodo sprang at Chad.

Chad raced to a dense thicket and forced his way in. The huge dodo smashed into the brushy wall repeatedly but could not penetrate it. Eventually, he wandered away.

Raj, thought Chad. They don't respect blood shadows anymore. He searched for another slither, found one, and jumped aboard. The slither snaked through the woods, broke into a savanna, and let Chad out.

He glanced around, staff at the ready, and saw that he was on a well-traveled road running east-west. He followed it west, heading deeper into the dodo world.

As he walked along, the air became lively, and he felt a rhythmic trembling of earth. He bent an ear, heard a low rumble.

Wave after wave, the sound hit him. Alarmed, he raced off the road and ducked into nearby woods.

From around a bend came a swarm of dodos, seemingly running with preternatural speed.

With a rush and a swoosh, they were past Chad and around the next bend. Many of them carried something under wing, bundles too blurry to lay eyes on. Chad guessed it was human cargo.

Prisoners? Did they kidnap the Barneys?

Chad burst from the woods and raced after the birds. Winded, he caught a ride on a slither and came back to earth near strange cage-like enclosures in a grove of giant trees. Birds stood guard, eyes alert. Humans, or homunculi, wandered about unsupervised.

Chad crept closer to the cages. He drew as close as he dared and lay flat, concealed in brush. Husky aromas from the plants wafted into his nostrils.

He peered at the cages. They were woven from vines and anchored to the forest floor and to the giant trees. He made out humans or homunculi in some cages, dodos in others, and in one cage, a black jaguar.

He crawled toward the jaguar's cage.

Why are you held prisoner? he asked.

The jaguar froze, sank low to the ground, spied Chad.

I was a staff. My monk was hanged.

Chad crept closer to the jaguar's cell. The jaguar crept closer to the webbing, its eyes aflame.

Turn back into a staff! commanded Chad.

No!

I'll pull you out!

No! I am a cat!

Chad crept to the webbing. The jaguar bared its fangs in a silent snarl.

I'll pull you out!

No!

Hearing the crunch of footsteps, Chad retreated to the brush.

Three dodos marched to the jaguar's cell, looked through the webbing. The sleek cat retreated to the shadows.

"This one next," said the dodo commander.

"But it is not a human. It is a cat."

"We cannot violate orders."

"We have already executed the human who was in there."

"Silence!" The dodo commander stepped to the door, loosened the webbing, drew it open. The jaguar slipped out and vanished into the trees.

"You fools!" The dodo commander turned on the others. "You let him escape!" He strutted about, slapping the others with his wings. "After him!"

The guards gave chase, their commander on their heels, still slapping and castigating them.

Chad held his breath as the three dodos crashed through the underbrush. They'll never catch him. Thank God. If only humans were like cats. Cats know how to survive. They know how to get away. They know how to kill.

If only ...

Chad heard a dim voice. Silence. The voice again, gruff, faint in the distance. It was his father's voice, and Chad was only three.

A tiny three ...

"In you go, Chadprechaun."

Chad scrambled into the cardboard box and curled up.

His father closed the lid.

Locked in darkness, Chad shut his eyes and squeezed himself into a ball as his father picked up the box and swung it back and forth in a high arc, his gravelly voice calling out rough cadence.

He swung it higher and higher, gathering momentum.

Then, with an explosive roar, he tossed the box high into the air, and Chad sailed away.

Thud!

Chad's box landed on the roof of the garage. He lay still, silent.

He heard the slap of a lasso against the roof, felt the lasso tighten around the box, felt the box scrape against the shingles as it was being pulled.

Chad blacked out.

He always did.

The box slid off the roof, pulled by his father's lasso, and landed in Rory Garrick's arms. Chad came back like he always did.

His father opened the box, and Chad popped out.

Rory Garrick cuffed his son around the yard.

"Stand at attention, Chad. That's it."

He punched Chad in the chest, knocked him down.

"Up!"

But Chad lay still, so Rory kicked him.

"When your commander tells you to get up, you get up!"

Chad stood at attention again, and Rory unleashed a powerful blow, and Chad flew.

"Up!"

Chad bounded to his feet and stood at stiff attention.

His father picked him up and galloped to the backyard. Chad remained at stiff attention in his father's pulverizing arms.

Rory stood Chad on a small table. Chad could no longer remain at attention, the table wobbled so. Chad's legs were shaking; his whole body was shaking. He tried to keep his head and shoulders rigid—maybe that would be good enough—and just let the rest of him shake, trying to maintain balance.

But it was no good.

All of him was shaking, and his father's bearded face released a canyonful of gruff laughter.

"Chadprechaun, you will never be a good American. You cannot obey lawful orders. You are fit only for your mother's woebegone religion. *They* will forgive you your sins. And *they* will sin mercilessly against you for all eternity."

Rory grabbed him, stood him on the grass, trussed him up with the rope he had used to lasso the box off the garage roof.

"They will forgive you your sins, Chadprechaun, over and over, till they have you puking. And they will sin against you with precision, with an exactitude that passeth all understanding."

Chad, bound within the tight coils of the rope, was propped at attention. His father stood back and studied him.

"You are now a good little citizen, Chadprechaun, so long as the rope holds."

Five years later, Chad, at eight, was taking on some of his father's size.

Rory no longer put him in a cardboard box and threw him onto the roof of the garage. He no longer cuffed him around the yard, picked him up, carried him to the backyard, and put him on the wobbly table, or tied him up.

"Outside, Chad!"

They marched outside.

Rory threw women's clothing at Chad. "Put those on."

Chad, still wearing his own clothes, donned a skirt and blouse.

"You are a true American now, Chadprechaun, fit for only one thing—your mother's merciless religion. They will measure your anal orifice, they will fit you for a shaft, and they will rape and debase you for all eternity. What do you think of that, Chadprechaun?"

"I think my mother's religion is evil. I think all of life is evil. There is nothing else. Just evil."

"Take those church clothes off."

Chad did so, and he and Rory went into the woods.

"You must lie, Chad. You must cheat. You must steal. Your society hates you; you must hate it. You are destined to serve and protect your society; but your society will disown you; your society will string you up and hang you by the neck till dead. Look at me, Chad!"

Chad looked at his father.

"You see this beard?"

"Yes."

"Why do I have it?"

"So no one knows what you look like."

"And ...?"

"So you can creep and kill and get away with it."

Rory Garrick exploded with laughter. His grating voice seemed to shake the leaves.

"Don't ever let them make you reveal your face, Chadprechaun. Always be false to them. They are always false to you."

They walked deeper into the woods.

"Here." Rory tossed Chad a hunting knife. "Sneak up on me. Cut my throat."

"Yes, sir."

Chad turned his back on his father, waited until his father's footsteps died out, then began tracking him.

Rory Garrick had been in the war. His body had been riddled with shrapnel and bullets. His face had been damaged by an exploding mine. He stayed around the house and woods most of the time. Occasionally, he went into town to go to the veterans' hospital or to the library or courthouse. Chad was terrified of seeing his father without his beard. Part of his face was missing.

Chad saw his father through the woods, and froze. Rory Garrick, sitting on a fallen tree, seemed lost in thought. Then he stirred, looked about, got up, and ambled off.

Chad followed. If he could not catch his father unawares, if he could not sneak up on his father and put the knife blade to his throat without being heard, without being sensed, it meant a beating.

A severe beating.

Chad crept. The day wore on. The sun and wind bore down on the trees, turning the leaves into millions of shimmering, fluttering butterflies. Chad's allies were his father's ghosts. When they came to haunt Rory, Rory seemed to lose all awareness of his surroundings.

The moment came.

His father sat slumped on a rock.

Chad put the blade of the hunting knife to Rory's throat, pulled it tight, sliced ...

It wasn't supposed to cut flesh.

Not with his beard so thick.

Rory Garrick roared, reached back, grabbed Chad, and sent him flying. Chad lay screaming, his arm broken.

In the hospital emergency room, a doctor loomed over Chad.

"Did your father do this to you?"

Chad did not respond. He looked at his arm. It was in a cast. The doctor held a mirror to Chad's face. Chad did not recognize it as his face. It was an explosion of red, blue, and purple welts. Rory had beat him for screaming, then had carried him home and driven him to the hospital.

Back home, Chad mended. He did not see his father for a long time. His mother read to him from the Bible. Chad heard the words, but understood nothing. His mother, Marcia Garrick, had a whip-like stick with a flat stone strapped to one end. She rapped Chad with it whenever his attention strayed.

"Pay attention!"

The verses droned on and on.

"As it is written, there is none righteous, no, not one. For all have sinned, and come short of the glory of God. For God so loved the world that he gave his only begotten Son, that whosoever believeth in him should not perish, but have everlasting life. But he was wounded for our transgressions, he was bruised for our iniquities, and with his stripes we are healed."

Chad's father came home—beardless.

He sat in the shadows, holding a towel over his face.

Chad, terrified, hid in his room most of the time. When he ventured out, he refused to even glance in his father's direction.

One night, his mother forced him out of his room with the rod. Chad sat in the living room, eyes closed. Rory sat in shadow. Marcia read from the Bible.

"Let the wicked forsake his way, and the unrighteous man his thoughts: and let him return unto the Lord, and he will have mercy upon him. My sheep hear my voice, and I give unto them eternal life; and they shall never perish, neither shall any man pluck them out of my hand."

Chad came to the conclusion that his mother's religion had won. His father was beaten. Rory Garrick was lost within himself, lost within his towels and shadows.

Rory Garrick, still beardless, began leaving the house at night.

Chad snuck into town one autumn evening and saw Rory's face for the first time. He was wearing spectacles and had a moustache, and was swinging around lampposts, calling out, *"Hoodoo! Hoodoo!"*

A crowd had gathered. Chad stood among them, listening to his father's owl-like hooting. His father did not notice him. Rory's face seemed normal enough. Nothing was missing.

"I look like Teddy Roosevelt!" cried Chad's father, swinging around the lampposts. "I look like Teddy Roosevelt!"

Chad nodded and walked away. Yeah. He looks like Teddy Roosevelt. The church can't touch someone like Teddy Roosevelt. They wouldn't dare. They wouldn't dare say anything is wrong with a person like Teddy Roosevelt. His father had won.

Hoodoo!

Jesus made an appearance in the Garrick household. Stained with bright red blood, head drooping, nailed to a cross, he kept Marcia, Rory, and Chad entertained from his perch on the mantel.

Marcia, her rod hovering in the air, handed Rory the Bible. It was loaded with colored bookmarks, all neatly arrayed and numbered. Rory's voice rattled through the room.

"The last enemy that will be abolished is death. If any of you lacks wisdom, he should ask God, who gives generously to all without finding fault, and it will be given to him. Set thine house in order; for thou shalt die, and not live. Our present sufferings are not worth comparing with the glory that will be revealed in us."

Marcia took the Bible from Rory and handed it to Chad. He read, his voice sounding tiny and frightened.

"Praise be to the God and Father of our Lord Jesus Christ. In his great mercy he has given us new birth into a living hope through the resurrection of Jesus Christ from the dead. For whoever keeps the whole law and yet stumbles at just one point is guilty of breaking all of it. Who is he that condemns? Christ Jesus, who died."

Marcia snatched the Bible away from Chad and read from it.

"Do not be afraid of those who kill the body and after that can do no more. But I will show you whom you should fear: Fear him who, after the killing of the body, has power to throw you into hell. The Son of Man will send out his angels, and they will weed out of his kingdom everything that causes sin and all who do evil. They will throw them into the fiery furnace, where there will be weeping and gnashing of teeth."

She paused and looked at Jesus. Then she snapped her rod and resumed reading.

"When he comes back, he will take these dying bodies of ours and change them into glorious bodies like his own. Put your finger here; see my hands. Reach out your hand and put it into my side. Stop doubting and believe. For we must all appear before the judgment seat of Christ, that each one may receive what is due him."

Chad stared at Jesus, at the bloody trails down his naked flesh, at the blood that soaked his loincloth. Did you win, Jesus? He snuck glances at his mother and father. He wondered what it would be like standing with them before Jesus on judgement day. Would Jesus be kind, or would he cast them into hell?

"Chad," said Marcia Garrick, "do you accept Jesus as your savior?"

Chad did not want to answer. His mother's face grew narrow and began looking like the blade of an ax. She raised her rod.

"Yes." *Hoodoo!*

"That is good, Chad." She relaxed.

No, thought Chad, I do not accept Jesus as my savior. I will go to war; I will suffer. I will break at least one law and I will be cast into hell. He looked at Jesus. I will lie, cheat, and steal. And so will you. I will hate you. And you will hate me. I will die fighting to save your worthless hide, so you can hang around lying to others. Look at me, Jesus!

But Jesus kept his eyes cast downward.

Chad wanted to ask Jesus about Milky, but one look at his mother's rod persuaded him not to.

Chad, before he started first grade, came across Milky's picture while rummaging in the attic, a place he shouldn't have been.

"Who is this?" asked Chad, taking the picture to his mother that evening. It looked like a kid similar to himself.

"It's your brother who died," said his mother, taking the picture away from Chad. "You shouldn't have this. I thought we removed all—" She walked away with the picture.

Chad chased after her.

"Who?"

She turned and looked at him.

"Milky. Remember? He died before you were born."

Chad did not remember having been told of Milky before. His mind went topsy-turvy. Milky! He lived and died before I was born?

Chad snooped through the house, looking for Milky's things. He found nothing that was identifiably Milky's. He rescued the picture from his mother's bedroom, hid it back in the attic where he had found it. He was afraid she was going to throw it away.

An older Chad, one just learning to read, went snooping for mention of Milky in the family's artifacts and records. He found no such mention. Milky, a ghost.

Chad began to have memories of Milky. Milky was there when Chad was a little kid in a high chair. "Baby" was Milky's word for Chad. "Baby" whenever Mother and Father weren't around. Michael was Milky's real name. But baby Chad couldn't pronounce Michael. Nor Mike. Nor Mikey. So ... *Milky*.

Milky running from a monster. Chad crying. Milky racing to the sofa, screaming. Milky climbing, scrambling, terror stricken ...

The monster grabbing Milky, hitting Milky. Milky going a-toppling. Milky lying silent.

Chad crying himself silent, watching Mother and Father pick up a limp Milky.

Who was the monster?

His father. His mother had been present at the murder scene also, watching, doing nothing while Milky was being killed.

Milky began to appear to Chad. A living, breathing Milky ghost.

Chad began telling people about Milky. About his murder, about his ghost. He told other kids. He told teachers. He told strangers.

His parents questioned him.

"I saw you kill him, Dad."

A minister was consulted. Was Chad sinning too much? School authorities were consulted. Can't there be more reality-based teaching? Medical doctors were consulted. Chad was referred to a psychiatrist.

Chad entered therapy. He was given drug treatments. Regularly, he was kidnapped from school or grabbed off the street and incarcerated in a mental-health center.

But the memories became stronger.

And Milky still came a-walking.

Milky, a death vagrant.

Left, right ... Left, right ... Chad sat downtown, counting cadence for the passersby. His monotone a cold, clear oath along the pavement. And Milky came a-walking. *Left, right ...*

Later, an older Chad, a new war chant. *Tomahawks and tom-toms ...* In the countryside. A war cry closer to the land. And Milky wandered the woods and meadows.

Chad saw Milky's ghost almost everywhere.

I saw you kill him, Dad ...

Chad backed out of the shrubs, worked his way around the cells, staying in cool shadow, popping tree to tree.

Sounds.

He ducked, watched.

Two birds bracketed a man. Their wings were like fetters on his arms. Other birds formed a picket line, funneling the trio.

Chad followed.

The procession marched to a gallows, an affair of heavy-duty logs twenty feet high with a wide staircase. The executioner waited above. With nimble wings, he looped a noose around the man's neck. The birds stood clear.

Thwack! Thunk!

The man shot through the trapdoor and dangled at the end of the rope.

Chad crept away and hid in a pocket of brush. He tried to sink into the ground. Horrifying visions of the condemned man's face came to him.

This was war.

Chad crept through the Spiderweb, staying under cover of trees and brush, sneaking close to cages, looking in, snaking around. The wind rustled the foliage, masking the sounds of his passage. Once or twice, he thought he saw Milky in the distance, lurking in the trees or held captive in a cell. Whenever a dodo trod near, Chad froze. Whenever a human, or homunculus, came near, Chad hid, but studied them, looking into their eyes.

He saw a woman walking toward him. She was strong looking and had flowing blond hair. Something seemed to be wrong with one of her arms. She wore a leopard-pattern knit dress, snug on hips and thighs.

Her eyes.

They held Chad in a grip of enchantment.

She sees me. She's looking right at me.

She ran toward Chad. Chad ducked deeper into the brush. She followed. Chad turned to face her, staff ready. She was crouching, a finger to her lips.

"Shhh ... Drakon sent me."

Chad looked at the woman's impaired arm. She drew toward him and wrapped her good arm around him.

"Come," she said, and pulled him toward her, with both arms now. "We're going to synchronize our hearts."

She held him tightly. Chad felt the beating of her heart, felt the beating of his own, felt their hearts become synchronized.

She released him, held up her flawed arm. It wasn't as big as her good arm, didn't move as well.

"It's still regenerating," she said, waving it around. "Soon, it'll be okay."

Chad stared at her face. Feline.

"What happened to it?"

"It was ripped off in a *dojo* this morning."

Chad stared at her arm, then at the rest of her.

She watched him, smiled with a catlike hiss, then grabbed him by the arm and led him deeper into the brush.

She found a spot. They sat.

Chad held out his canteen and the sack of Forest Buckle. She declined. She held up her arm, moved it around.

"Where are you from?" he asked. "What's your name?"

"Sandra." She pointed to the earth. "From there. I'm a homunculus."

Chad's mouth fell open. *Hoodoo!*

"That's Charles." She pointed toward a cage.

They were lying flat, at the tip of a rivulet of brush. "Are they going to execute him?" asked Chad.

"They will if he refuses to help them."

Chad stared at the encaged man. He sat like a ghost. Like a fog lost within a fog.

"How can he help them?"

"It's a long story, Chad. A man named Topper got wind of the Dodos' need for a catechism. He tried to arrange a deal with them to avoid execution. 'I'm an old Baptist,' he told them. 'I'll write it for you.'

"They do need quick work on their catechism, Chad. Dodo wings are too clumsy and slow for artful script. They released Topper from his cell, placed him under guard, and told him what to write. He went off on tangents. Dodos were being attacked by grizzly bears at every turn—punishment for their wickedness. And the messiah was a grizzly cub.

"The dodos tried to steer Topper on to a more acceptable version of the new Dodo religion, but Topper just didn't have it in him to do it. They hanged him this morning, but not before he told them about Charles."

"And Charles is going to write their catechism now?"

"He will, unless he wants to hang."

"I've got to stop him, Sandra. It's my mission. To stop the birth of this new religion. Once they have a catechism—"

"I know, Chad. However foolish it might be, it establishes an air of credibility. It serves as a springboard."

Chad stared at Charles. He remembered the antelope that wanted to keep the trespassing lion in view. The devil you know is better than the devil you don't know. A plan began working itself out in his mind.

"Chad."

He looked at Sandra.

"Listen."

Chad bent an ear. Faint voices were coming from prisoners a few cells down. Dodo voices. Chad and Sandra crept closer until the voices were clear.

"What is this thing they are saying? This messiah?"

"A one who will save us, brother. Rejoice."

"But dodos have always saved themselves."

"You cannot save yourself with good works," said a third voice. "A saint is no better than a sinner."

"Yes," said the second voice. "It has been revealed."

"But—"

"Do not be a doubter!" The third voice was sharp, ending the discussion.

"It's starting, Chad," whispered Sandra. "The brainwashing has begun."

Seven

~ THE KARMIC WHEEL ~

C had asked Sandra if she knew about the Barneys. She shook her head. Chad filled her in, then told her about the knowledge hit he received from Hubert.

"Charles can wait," said Chad. "The Barneys are in danger. I have to guide them home."

"They can guide themselves home, Chad." She brushed a leaf from her hair.

He was thunderstruck. He assumed Sandra would go along with his plan. *He wanted her to go along!*

"But they're counting on me to rescue them." He grabbed the leaf from the ground and put it back in her hair.

"They have to learn to fend for themselves," said Sandra.

"Their type doesn't go to war. *I* go to war. *I* save them. They can't save themselves. Hubert sounded desperate. He thinks the Brit is evil. He thinks the Brit is going to turn them into homunculi. He doesn't know if he can shoot the Brit, like he might have to. Hubert's not a warrior."

She plucked the leaf from her hair.

"It's not your affair," she said.

Chad felt the leaf slide down his back. He reached inside his shirt, pulled it out, and stuck it down the back of Sandra's dress.

"Chad, what are you doing?"

He was backing out of the shrubs.

"I'm going to find a slither, Sandra. I have to check on the Barneys."

Chad crawled through the brush, Sandra on his heels. They spied a slither and jumped on. It carried them out of the Spiderweb and deposited them in a meadow, where they found another slither—a surprising one.

This one was brilliantly iridescent, like a spinning pinwheel catching the sun. They jumped aboard. Once it began to move, it seemed to take on a new persona, and became something of a daredevil.

It started to buck.

"This is a wild one," said Sandra. She crouched, braced herself against the walls. Chad did the same. The slither began twisting through the air, a big phantasmal snake.

"Hang on, Chad," said Sandra. She fell to her hands and knees. "I think it means to—

"Aaaa ..."

The slither lurched and roared and became a roller coaster. Chad gripped his staff in one hand, wrapped an arm around Sandra's waist, prayed. *Milky, deliver us ...*

The slither thrashed through meadows, spun wildly through woods, took to the air.

Chad looked down; they were a thousand feet up. The

open ground below was teeming with dodos, all running in the same direction. The slither dived.

"Aaaa ..."

"Milky ..."

The slither pulled out; Chad felt the G's, felt the weight of several Sandras against him. *"Milky ..."*

The slither slowed and purred and became its former self, a pinwheel. It flowed through woods, skirted thickets, floated through grassy meadows.

"Does it know where we're going?"

"Shhh ... Chad."

The slither stopped, hovering over woods.

Chad looked down and saw Tim. The big dodo was motionless, standing near a tree.

"Sandra ..." Chad filled her in on the events of the morning. His kidnapping. His escape. The insane dance of Tim and Zack. The voice of the Universe.

"His bill sheath is missing, Chad."

"He collided with the ground when I escaped."

"It'll grow back."

The slither cruised around.

"Do you hate them, Chad, for kidnapping you?"

"No. I deserved to be kidnapped, at the time. The Universe sang for my capture."

"Very poetic, Chad."

"Then the Universe sang for my escape."

"What's the Universe singing for now, Chad?"

"Uh ... I think it sings for the deliverance of the Barneys and the hatchling."

"That could be a grim mission, Chad."

"Hoodoo."

Chad saw Zack near a tree and pointed him out to Sandra. "They're watching for someone," she said.

The slither meandered through the treetops. Then it crept downward and came to a halt at the edge of a clearing.

They peered about, sensing that something was about to happen. Before long, the air in the middle of the clearing came alive with sparkling light. A man emerged from the sparkles, a small child on his back. Hubert and Angela Barney followed.

"The Barneys and the Brit," said Chad. "Looks like a slither brought them here."

Zack entered the clearing. Moments later, Tim appeared. The Barneys and the Brit, trucking toward nearby woods, glanced at the dodos but showed no signs of concern.

The woods swallowed prey and stalkers. The clearing stood empty.

"Off we go, Chad."

Sandra and Chad stepped from the slither and covertly followed the procession. Entering the woods, Chad looked up. Tim and Zack stood over him, sniffing the air.

The two monsters turned and vanished into the shadows.

"Holy Milky," whispered Chad. "I think they're using me to fine-tune their sniffers."

"Hoodoo," said Sandra.

Clem raced through the woods and meadows, humming the nursery rhyme he had heard this morning on his way to the classroom.

Go! If you still have your toes.
Scatter them near and far.
Let them run from you and kick at your foes.
Never save them as if in a jar.

The morning air had been full of this rhyme, and in the classroom, Clem learned of the powerful voice that sang it— the voice of the Universe. The teacher said, "Listen and you will hear the voice that speaks from the depths. It will be your guide." Clem and the other hatchlings listened, and they heard many wonderful things.

Clem topped a rise, and the festival grounds, flowing like jewels on a grassy sea, came into view. Dodos choked the roads and byways. A road lay near Clem, and he sped to it.

Clem's heart pulsed with excitement as he sped along the road, scanning the maze of purple-dwarf kiosks in the distance that held the products and art of dodo culture, and the long runway beyond—home field of the Thunderdudes, Dodoland's aerial precision team.

"Ah ... ah ..." he hummed, then burst into song. "Go! If you still have your toes. Scatter them—"

Suddenly, the air was filled with sterling cries of "Clem, Clem!"

Clem slowed and looked to the source of the disturbance. Oh, what is this? He stopped.

"Clem, Clem!"

Running toward him from another road, cutting across the grass that lay between, was a ... a ...

Clem peered closer. He sniffed the air. Why, it was a little man.

"Ralph! Come back! Stop!"

And people were chasing the little man. Yelling at the little man. Clem sniffed the air again as the little man, holding on to his hat, screeched to a halt right in front of him.

"Do you call those things toes?" asked the little man, pointing at Clem's razor claws. The little man appeared to be very excited.

Clem looked down, lifted one foot, clawed the air with his razors.

"Why yes, they are toes." My, what a foolish question. But maybe the little man doesn't go to school, where all such things are taught, except the instinctive things.

The little man began jumping up and down.

"Let me ride you, Clem! Let me ride you!"

Then Clem realized it was not a little man after all, but a hatchling—a human hatchling.

Clem sank to the ground, and the human hatchling scrambled onto his back. Clem stood. The human hatchling began kicking his sides—though it didn't hurt—and yelling "Giddyap! Giddyap! Whoa! Whoa!"

"Ah ..."

Clem saw a tall man and ... he thought ... a middle-sized man ... and a ... womanly person? They were all crowding around him, and seemed nervous. An atrocious idea zipped through Clem's mind: The people hatchling belongs to them, and they think I'm stealing it.

"Oh, no!" said Clem.

"Ah ..."

"I'm just giving the little man ... uh ... the hatchling a ride, as he requested."

"Ah … Okay, Clem? No harm then, old boy?" said the tall man.

"No harm, then," said Clem. He bounced around on the road, a quick jig. The human hatchling squealed gleefully.

"And …" Clem stopped. "If it brings joy to the hatchling, then much, much more no harm."

"Ah … that's the spirit, Clem, old boy."

Clem was pleased. But how did these people know his name? Oh. The *dojo*. He recognized them now. They'd been outside the *dojo* this morning.

"My name is Mel," said the tall man. "Children, please introduce yourselves to Clem."

Clem turned and watched them.

"I'm Angela Barney. Pleased to meet you."

"I'm Hubert Barney."

Then the hatchling on his back said, "I'm Ralph Barney."

Clem spun around.

"Ah … Mel, and Angela …"

"Right."

"And … Hubert …"

"Right."

"And …" He turned his head to look at the hatchling on his back. "Ralph."

Clem gulped. A speech formed in his mind: *Since my hatching, I have heard news of a messiah. I am to be that messiah. They will come for me. It is dangerous …* But the human hatchling squealed again, and Clem danced another jig.

"Technically," said Clem, "this is not people-pleasing behavior, I'll have you know."

"Of course not, Clem," said Mel, laughing. "Well, shall we be off? The festival awaits."

They trooped down the road, Clem having to keep to a slow pace so the people weren't left behind. The crowds thickened. Dodos and humans swarmed about. Clem sniffed the air; complex odors were about. He had never been in the midst of so many captivating sights, sounds, and smells. Suddenly, he heard a peculiar thing from Angela.

"Hubert, I just saw a homunculi that looked exactly like Chad Garrick. He was carrying a staff, like they had at the *dojo*. He was walking with that woman who had her arm ripped off—you know, the one with the fake leopard dress—and he was looking at us. He ducked away real quick when he saw that I was looking at him. God! I've got the willies now, Hubert."

Clem saw Hubert spin around and become watchful, lines furrowing his brow.

"What was that word *homunculi*, Angela?" asked Clem.

"Ah ..." Mel moved up, interposing himself between Angela and Clem.

"You must be their teacher, Mel. Is that correct?"

"Right you are, Clem, old boy, right you are. And teachers like to hog the limelight, so I'll answer the question. Okay, Angela?"

"Sure, Mel," she said, quivers in her voice.

"Homunculi. Angela actually meant homunculus, the singular. Homunculus means little man."

"Is Ralph a homunculus?" asked Clem.

This brought explosive laughter from all around. Clem thought it odd, but then he realized—*Hoo-ray! I'm learning things from people. Strange things, to be sure.*

Clem walked with his new friends, carrying Ralph, sniffing the air, moving through the jostling crowds.

Death grew large in Hubert Barney's mind. *Death* as something that stalks you. *Death* as something that gets you.

He thought of his parents. The days will go by. They will organize a search. *Death* growing large in *their* minds. Three kids wiped out.

Gone.

Death ...

Hubert thought of the hell his parents would go through if he didn't act. I *will* act, he told himself.

He scanned the crowds.

Angela had seen a homunculus that looked like Chad Garrick. It probably was Garrick. The giant egg would have fallen within his stomping grounds. He was always out looking for cougar tracks, and for Milky. And Hubert *had* sent a knowledge hit to Chad, back on the road, asking for help.

Garrick might be one of the walking dead by now. A zombie. Already converted. *Dojo* fodder.

And to think I asked for his help. Now he and that woman might be stalking us. Or maybe they need *our* help.

Hubert looked around for Chad. Where is he?

Can you help us, Chad? Or do we need to help you?

"Look," cried Angela, "words floating in the air."

Hubert looked. His mouth flew open. Floating toward him out of the mob, like whips of caramel candy frolicking in the air, were the verses of ...

No! He reeled from shock as the words hit him. He fought back the compulsion to cry out as the verses of a poem he'd written in seventh grade English class assaulted him.

A poor choice of a city, a dark and hilly day,
Kitchens willy-nilly, rich helping scraps say:
You can't go through here; this is sacred ground.
Though you can see it clearly, open wavy sand around.
The fences are a funneling mesh, weak and wiry,
The pigs are cold and dead, in market peak and fiery.
They travel stacked in frozen lairs,
Dead pigs to market in healthy skin prayers.
The children run through tight corridors,
Searching in dread glee for open doors.

He hadn't finished the poem. He'd only gotten as far as the fourth line, then gave it up, frustrated. Nothing more had come to him. Now, it looked like the Universe had finished the poem for him.

He saw a large, fierce-looking dodo with the front part of his beak missing—the red hooked part. *Ouch.* He wondered how that had happened. The dodo was looking at the wares on display, wandering aimlessly, it seemed.

The Barneys and the Brit walked through the crowds.

Hubert slid over to Angela.

"Keep an eye out for Garrick," he whispered.

She looked at him.

"I think it's him, not a homunculus. Let me know if you see him again."

"Okay, Hubert."

"Garrick might be in trouble. We might have to help him escape from here. Don't breathe a word of this to Mel."

He watched her eyes grow large, then he slipped away. Angela liked intrigue. It would get her thinking about danger, about Mel, about escaping. Hubert's bridge to Angela was being built.

Hubert glanced around. He saw the dodo with the damaged beak again. Casual. Aimless. Chills swept up Hubert's spine. The willies.

"Teach me, teach me, teach me, Mel."

Malcolm Moreland heard Clem's call as the group moseyed on down the broad central boulevard of the cultural mecca. The hatchling was glancing around like a child in a toy shop.

"Your first trip here, Clem?" asked Mel.

"Yes, Mel."

"Mine too," said Ralph, atop Clem's back.

"You're in for a treat, children. Let's veer this-a-way." He steered them toward a booth.

Ah ... thought Mel, eyeing the contents of the little shop. I don't want to hurt Clem's feelings. Dodo art is like wreckage strewn from a high-speed collision. I must take care to winnow out the disparaging remarks.

"Ah ... what have we here?" asked Mel, approaching the booth, shepherding the Barneys and Clem with outstretched arms.

The homunculus manning the display stepped to the counter, which was a squared-off hedge of thickly grown purple dwarfs. Such dwarfs, sculpted and otherwise manicured, served as building material for the fair exhibits, giving the grounds a mazy purple appearance, in sharp contrast to the emerald seas of grass that flowed through the surrounding savanna.

"It's a monk, children," whispered Mel, winking at the Barneys and Clem.

"A what?" asked Ralph.

"Homunculus."

"Oh."

The homunculus wore coarse dark trousers and shirt, and several days' growth of beard.

"Sir," he said, "we've got graven images, idols, pagan relics, deities, and lost manuscripts."

"Ah ... My good man, glimmers of earth lore and legend, come home to roost in Dodoland."

"What?" asked Ralph, in a tiny whisper.

"Ah ... Ralph, I was just telling the man his objects of art are familiar on our home world earth. In fact, they probably originated there, and were stolen from there."

"You mean we're not on our home world earth?" Ralph's eyes grew large and his mouth fell open.

"Ralph," said Clem, "you are from the earth plane. But now you are here in our world, which is at a different frequency than your own, though not different by far. Right, Mel?"

"Right, Clem."

"Oh," said Ralph.

"They taught us that in school," said Clem, lifting his head with pride and turning to peer at Ralph. Ralph grabbed Clem's beak and pulled.

"Naw-naw, Ralph. Let go."

"You talk funny, Clem, when I do that. What's the red for?"

"Beats me." Clem turned to face the graven images.

"But why does that dodo over there have no red?" cried Ralph, pointing off toward the crowd.

Clem turned. Mel turned. Everyone turned and saw a large dodo who was missing the hooked tip portion of his bill. The dodo, apparently overhearing Ralph, sauntered away.

"Ralph!" Angela's voice carried a stern tone of warning.

"Behave, Ralph," said Hubert. "You know better than that."

"Oh, yeah, I forgot." Ralph pummeled his face with his fists in a flurry of contrition, then said, "I'm sorry, Clem." He turned toward the hulking dodo, who was now nearly lost in the crowd. "Sorry, dodo."

"Ah ... children, children. Culture, culture," cried Mel.

Everyone's attention was swept back toward the booth.

Mel peered at the offerings, which were arranged on terraced purple dwarfs within the enclosure. A forlorn collection, he mused. Then he eyed a piece that he thought might interest the children.

"Ah ..." He pointed. "Gold Coast? Ivory Coast? The *Dogon?* The *Bambara?*"

The monk picked up the object. It was a crude mask, molded from clumps of earthen material. He set it on the counter.

"Was I close?" said Mel.

"Dodos made it, sir," said the monk. "Don't know about those other folks you mentioned."

Clem sniffed it.

"It smells awful!" he cried.

Hubert reached out to touch it.

"Don't!" said Clem.

"Better not, Hubert," said Mel. "Judging by its texture and odor, the mask probably contains a healthy dollop or two of manure—an old West African custom."

"Man-rrrr," cried Ralph. "Yuck."

"Did people actually put something like that on their faces?" asked Angela.

"Oh, yes," said Mel. "Still do—to scare off evil spirits and such. And these little creatures"—he pointed to a row of clay and wooden figures—"more than likely stood guard around the hut, protecting the old hearthstone. You see, children, spirits reside in Nature's materials—earth, trees, shells, skins, tusks—and these selfsame Nature spirits take up residence in whatever is made from the good earth. Presto." He waved his hands around. "Gods in miniature. And, if I may be so bold as to mention"—he pointed at the homunculus—"a god that is not so miniature. Am I correct, sir?"

"Aye, sir. That I am. I am a homunculus, an earthen image of God."

"Ah, ah, ah," cried Ralph, pointing. "You're a homun, homun, homun—"

"Homunculus," said Angela.

"You are a little man, sir," said Clem.

"I beg your pardon, sir," said the monk. "I am a god—a homunculus."

"Oh, I'm learning, learning," said Clem.

"Mr. ... uh ..." said Hubert to the monk.

"Frederick Heywood."

"Mr. Heywood, how does a homunculus differ from a human?"

"Excellent question, Hubert, old boy," cried Ralph in a weird parody of Mel. It brought forth a burst of laughter from the humans, and a chortle from Clem.

"Sir, we differ from humans in one important way," said the monk. "We are for demonstration purposes only; we don't live the lie; we just demonstrate it. Humans, on the other hand, live the lie."

"Oh ..."

"Just try me out, sir, and you'll see what the difference is."

Hubert looked perplexed, then looked at Mel.

"I believe Mr. Heywood would like you to say something of an exceedingly good, socially acceptable nature, Hubert. Try something truly absurd."

Hubert looked thoughtful for a moment.

"Ah ... how's this?" He looked at Mr. Heywood. "We must obey, without question, all experts and all authorities, for they are the heart, mind, and soul of our existence. We are nothing without them. The government will never lie to us. The mainstream media will never lie to us. The pharmaceutical industry wants to cure us and put themselves out of business. Establishment scientists always know what they're talking about."

They all stared at Hubert, then they peered at the monk.

For a long moment, nothing happened. Then the monk was swept by a sort of trance. He stared; his eyes became glossy; his jaws, elongated; his aspect more apelike and pious all in one jump. Then one of his eyes began to twitch. It leaped, eye socket and all, and began racing around his head, faster and faster. The monk began clapping his hands, machinelike. His eye was an orgy, madly racing round and round his head. His hands were possessed. His jaws began to open and close, slowly at first, then faster, faster. The monk repeated Hubert's words, and his whole body shook with convulsions, pulsing, a volcano ready to erupt. With one violent heave, a streak of white fabric shot from his mouth and flew over Clem's head.

They all turned …

Lying on the grass was the monk's undershorts. They had geysered up and shot out his mouth.

Everyone looked back at the monk.

"That," said the monk, looking at Hubert, his eye back in place, "is the difference between homunculi and humans."

Hubert stared, speechless.

"Oh," said Ralph, in a tiny whisper.

After inquiring about lost manuscripts and being shown several diseased-looking parchments purporting to be ancient prophecies of the coming of a dodo messiah, the group left Frederick Heywood and his goods behind.

"Don't believe it, children," said Mel as they browsed onward. "Dodo culture is not messianic. Right, Clem?"

"Right, Mel. Those documents are forgeries. There is no tradition of messiah worship in our world, but there are emerging cultists who are trying to insert messianism into dodo society." Clem grew silent, gave a heavy sigh. "I'm it, Mel. I'm their messiah."

"Horrors," said Mel. He looked at the hatchling.

"The cultists are strong-arm types with connections to the Spiderweb," said Clem. "Some hatchlings are virtually kidnapped from the egg and indoctrinated into a cult that resembles the Christianity of your world. This morning, the teacher said we were lucky to make it to the classroom. It's becoming more prevalent."

"Horrors, Clem," said Angela. She shuddered.

"Horrors," said Ralph. He patted Clem's head.

"Hatchlings who make it to class are usually safe thereafter," said Clem. "We are given warnings and are taught logic and disobedience to all manner of authority."

"Keep up your martial arts, too, Clem," said Mel. "Physical intimidation, regardless of how civilized people—or birds—are, often plays a role in persuasion, especially when dealing with messianic thugs."

"Good advice, Mel. I intend to."

Ralph asked what the Spiderweb was. Mel explained that it was a term used to describe Dodoland's system of justice, both the physical and conceptual components.

"The prisons, Ralph, are like huge nests of spiderwebs. And once you're in the jaws of dodo justice, you might as well have your head in a tarantula's mandibles."

"Yuck," said Ralph, making a face.

They walked on.

Mel glanced at the Barneys. Hubert and Angela looked bedeviled. But Ralph looked every bit the devil he was. Alone to thee, Ralph—the joys of childhood.

He wondered about his blood shadow. Had it weakened further? Had he chosen these innocent children as a test of its strength?

He felt a fit of self-repulsion. There was nothing worse than having a test coming up and knowing you *can't* do it.

And there was nothing better than having a test coming up and knowing that you *can* do it.

Not knowing ...

That's when the demons stare at you.

"Horrors!" Clem had picked up a word from Mel. It rang in Angela's ears with mounting alarm.

"Horrors!"

"What's the trouble, Clem?" asked Mel.

"Everywhere I look I see scribes."

"Oh, is that what these birds are?" Mel shot his eyes around. "Monks too. Busy little beavers, aren't they?"

The group had been traversing a maze of narrow lanes that ventured off the main thoroughfare, each lane more outlandish than the one before. The purple dwarfs that lined these lanes formed towering bulwarks topped by grotesque, leering gargoyle faces.

"Horrors!" said Clem.

Horrors, thought Angela, turning her head, watching the scribes in their ground-level kiosks and in their palaces on high, hanging over their purple parapets and turrets. The scribes in the kiosks hooted and sneered at passersby and looked wistfully above at their betters. The scribes on high called down with increasing hostility.

A shout was aimed at Angela.

"You vacuous twit!"

A scribe was pointing at her. A monk, he jumped from a balcony and bounded toward her, his eyes crazed.

"Come here, wench!" He thrust out a powerful hand to grab her.

"Oomph!"

The monk went sailing into the wall of his manor. Clem had stepped between them, had been just a blur. Cries rang out from neighboring scribes.

"Foul play! Villainy!"

"Rabble-rousers! What's the wench afraid of?"

A female dodo—a truly monstrous one—stepped in front of Angela.

"Come, my little one." The dodo waved at her manor. "We have a job for you. You must trust us."

"A job?" asked Angela.

"Yes. Come, write for us. We'll tell you what to write. You'll be perfect." She grabbed for Angela.

Angela darted away. The dodo gave chase. A moment later, Angela's ears were deafened by a powerful blast.

She turned. Mel was lowering his rifle. The dodo was down, kicking convulsively, her head a riot of blood. Angela stared in stunned disbelief.

The crowd plunged into pandemonium and shouting.

Ralph's voice broke through the chaos. "Scwibes? What's that?"

The group ran down the lane, ducked into the next lane, and lost themselves in the crowd. The shouts died out behind them.

"Pompous assholes, Ralph," said Clem. "That's what scribes are."

"Ah ..." said Mel, amidst much laughter from Ralph. "Actually, scribes are the official recorders and interpreters of society, and, as such, have rather unsavory reputations, as they serve to perpetuate the lies, myths, and agendas that benefit the ruling class to the detriment of the common people."

"Pompous assholes," said Clem.

"In days of yore, scribes studied law and interpreted scripture," said Mel. "Here in Dodoland, with everything being so loose-knit, there's no telling what these scribes are up to, but they couldn't possibly be official."

"Not yet, Mel," said Clem. "But they want to be official. They want to tell everyone what to do. But it won't work. It's against our DNA. We'll kill them all, if necessary. We'll treat them like invading parasites."

Horrors! thought Angela. Now even Clem, who had seemed so gentle, was talking about killing. Next, it'll be Ralph. Little Ralph will want to kill. Did it always have to lead to death? Didn't they have any sentences lighter than death?

She looked at Mel. He was sliding a round into his rifle, slamming it home, replacing the one that had obliterated the dodo scribe's head. She wanted to say something, to thank him for saving her, and Clem too, but all of a sudden Hubert was at her side, whispering again.

"The big dodo without the red part of his beak has been following us. Keep an eye out for him. Let me know if you see him." Hubert swam away.

Fresh willies assaulted Angela as she looked around. She did not see the big dodo with the red part of his beak missing. She looked at Mel, and remembered Hubert's previous warning: *Don't breathe a word of this to Mel.* What about Mel? Is he someone we have to ...?

The thought was too horrible to contemplate.

"No, Chad!" Sandra had a tight grip on him.

He tried to twist away from her.

Boom!

Chad spun, saw the Brit lower his rifle. The dodo that had tried to grab Angela lay writhing on the ground, her head a bloody mass of ribbons.

His ears punched half-deaf, he ran with Sandra through the angry sea of shouts. Hands and wings reached out to grab them. Chad smashed them away with his staff, Sandra with the butt of her knife.

They reached the end of the lane, paused, and looked around.

"This way," said Chad. He saw the Barneys, the Brit, and Clem down another lane, stitched into the wavering throng.

They followed, maneuvering through the crowd. It was a formidable thoroughfare, hemmed in by tall castle walls and imperial arches and columns. Walking along, Chad peered upward.

"Still scribes, Sandra?"

"Yes." She glanced up. "A loftier version." She pointed.

Chad looked. Perched in casemates and on the towers and walls of castles were the downward peering nostrils, beaks, and hooded eyeballs of the elite scribes.

"God, they're a haughty bunch!" cried Chad.

"Hush! You mustn't attract attention."

"I don't want to hush!"

"Don't forget what we're doing."

Chad looked ahead, saw Clem, the Barneys, and the Brit

farther down the lane, meandering along. Tim and Zack were lurking.

"I don't think they heard me," he whispered. "What are Tim and Zack waiting for?"

"A remarkable thing is happening, Chad. Can't you feel it through the air?"

Chad tried to tune in. "There's too much interference from these haughty creeps."

"The Barneys are acquiring their own little blood shadows," said Sandra. "Tiny ones, but still ..."

"How?"

"I can only guess. Maybe by learning how dangerous their situation has become, by staying calm, and by preparing for a fight."

"Hoodoo!"

"It might be the thing that's holding Tim and Zack back, Chad."

Hoodoo again, thought Chad. He was itching for a fight. He wanted Tim and Zack to make a move. That haughty Angela had always mocked his military ambitions. He'd show her. It all came down to preparation—*know yourself, know your enemy.*

Hoodoo! He cast the spell ahead to the Barneys.

The Barneys, Mel, and Clem broke out of Scribeland and stood in the main square. They gazed at the purple-dwarf kiosks and smelled the refreshing scents that sailed through the air.

"Ah ..." said Mel, stretching skyward as they passed through the center of the square. "Free from the labyrinthine pincers of the scribes."

Hubert was tracking two dodos now, the one with the damaged beak, and another. They stood out from the crowd, try as they might to sink into it.

He thought of how Clem had saved Angela from the monk, and how Mel had expertly dispatched the dodo who'd menaced her.

He gambled. He stepped toward Mel. Something's got to give. *Mel, are you with us?* Hubert looked into Mel's eyes.

"Mel, two big dodos have been following us." Mel stopped walking. Everyone else stopped walking. "They slink around ..." Hubert saw fear in Mel's eyes. *Sorry ... I was wrong—*

"Where?" Mel's eyes searched. He seemed to shrink as he looked about.

—about you being evil, about us being your prisoners.

Hubert scanned the area, electricity rampaging through his nerves, willies racing up his spine. The two big dodos were in the square, browsing. He pointed them out to Mel.

"Yes, I see," said Mel.

"They go wherever we go, but they try to look casual about it," said Hubert. "What gives, Mel?"

Mel raised himself to his full height. "Stick close, Hubert." He stared at the two dodos, first one, then the other. "Stick close." His eyes became hard. "Make everyone stick close."

Angela had caught a glimpse of Chad Garrick and that woman back in the crowd, but she had no intentions of telling Hubert. *Not now! Not ever!* Nor would she be telling him anything else, *ever!* Hubert had betrayed her.

Don't breathe a word of this to Mel.

She was incensed.

Now its *two* dodos following us, not just the dodo that's missing the tip of his beak.

And Mel, suddenly, is *okay!*

Have it your way, then, Hubert.

She stomped across the square, her burning eyes not caring where she was headed. What else haven't you been telling me, Hubert?

Her frightful spell was gone, supplanted by frightful anger. Events scary but invigorating had been sweeping her along, and she had counted on using her ingenuity to help them get out of this jam, but now ...

It's all back on Mel.

Mel will save us now, Hubert. Thanks to you!

She choked down a sob, preferring to stay with her anger. Anger was the stuff of fights. A fight is what she wanted. Those dodos better beware, she thought, as heat lightning flashed through her mind.

Towering above most of the crowd, sighting down his damaged beak, Tim spotted the Barneys, the Brit, and Clem. They were heading across the square. He tracked their passage, sending silent *chips* to his partner, Zack. Zack ambled about, sending back *chirrups* in acknowledgement.

A network of puzzling messages had been hooting in from the Universe, breaching the silent centers of Tim's mind. The trigger point for people-pleasing odors had been lowered, hooted the Universe, but the three interlopers could not be taken; conditions were not yet favorable. The blood shadow of the Englishman, though weakened, still swam about like an invisible egg. And the Barneys were sprouting blood shadows of their own.

Keep sniffing ... was the advice from the Universe.

Clem the hatchling is confirmed as messiah, hooted the Spiderweb. All else is unimportant. Hidden eyes had been tracking the hatchling all day; hidden beaks had been hooting silently, pooling intelligence.

Take Clem ... was the reverberating command from the Spiderweb. *Pounce!*

Tim, perplexed, had asked the Universe for clarification on Clem's messiahship. But the Universe had been silent.

Tim was uneasy. In hot pursuit of the Barneys, he and Zack were the guards of the moment, the guards the Spiderweb counted on to carry out its edicts, since they were closest to Clem.

Pounce!

But Tim and Zack waited.

Again, Tim hooted to the Universe for clarification.

But the Universe remained silent.

Pounce!

Again, Tim hooted.

Silence.

Tim's DNA held him in a rigid role of disobedience to the Spiderweb. He had never heard of seizing a hatchling before, and of violating an egg, however shadowy that egg might be.

Pounce!

That egg, in the person of the littlest Barney, sat atop Clem the hatchling.

Tim motioned for Zack to come over. They kept their voices low.

"What do you think, Zack?"

"Mutants are running the Spiderweb."

"No doubt. Those arrogant assholes and their dainty words. Prissy snobs."

"Rein in, Tim."

"Diversity sucks."

"The old days, Tim, remember?"

"Oh, I remember them well."

"Thundering the plains."

"Blood everywhere. Not good, Zack."

"There was no diversity then, Tim, old boy."

"Thanks for knocking my beak back, Zack, old boy."

"What do you think now, Tim?"

"Diversity still sucks."

"Tim, you're hopeless."

"It's a circle we're running, Zack. This messiah business means back to thundering the plains, blood everywhere, you know?"

"I'm not dense, Tim. I know perfectly well what it means. Yes, we'll be thundering the plains and running through blood again. We'll be swimming in blood."

"Catch my drift, Zack?"

"I'm leaning on it."

"Lean harder."

Zack cast his eyes to the heavens. After a moment, he said, "From diversity spills a thread that leads round and round to"—he looked at Tim—"to anti-diversity."

"Back to start," said Tim.

"Diversity sucks, Tim."

"Now you're hootin', Zack, old boy."

"What'll we do, Tim?"

Tim pawed the ground, glanced at the odd group.

"Remember the people-pleasing one this morning?" he said.

"Yes."

"And how he escaped, smelling like the proverbial rose thereafter?"

"Yes. I've seen him lurking."

"He's been following us. Wants to be a hero now. Think of it. Instead of sitting in the Spiderweb, under sentence of death—"

"He saved himself, Tim."

"Now he wants to save his fellow people, you know?"

"Save them from us?"

"From us and from all other dangers as well."

"What a laugh, Tim." Zack gave a low chuckle.

"So, Zack, why don't we learn from this crusader?"

"Learn what?"

"Zack, have you ever saved a dodo?"

"Preposterous. All dodos—"

"Except dainty, arrogant assholes."

"Exception noted. They're mutants, Tim. All dodos, except mutants, are designed—DNA, Tim—designed to the highest standards of survivability. You don't *save* a dodo, Tim; dodos save themselves. If it were otherwise, we'd be staring extinction in the face." Zack shuddered.

"Let's save Clem."

"Tim ..." Zack shook his head. "We can't. Clem must save himself."

Tim stared long and hard at his partner. He knew Zack was

right. He looked at the heavens. *Those arrogant assholes! Let me alone with them and ...* He reined in his anger. There was already talk of war against the Spiderweb. But that did them little good now. They could delay just so much longer. If they didn't pounce, the dainty ones would send out runners from the guard pool, runners who would ...

Pounce!

Tim and Zack split.

They continued to act casual, monitoring the odd group.

Diversity sucks, muttered Tim silently. He belched. Kidnapping hatchlings ... He belched again. Violating eggs ...

He looked up.

He saw the womanly looking person wander away from her group. Surprised, he sniffed the air and followed her.

She wandered far from the others.

With a gentle wing outstretched, Tim guided the womanly looking person back to her group, oathing silently at Zack all the while, who was staring at him with the strongest terms of disapproval.

Memories of Africa drifted into Mel's mind. He had recognized the dodo with the missing bill sheath as Tim, an oldline guard. Mel had had a meager acquaintance with Tim on the Dark Continent.

Very, very peculiar, thought Mel. They should not be following us. Dodos assess and strike people quickly—if they strike at all. They don't slink around like spies or the miserable tools of bureaucrats.

He looked at Hubert.

"Keep an eye on them, Hubert," he said. "I will too. Alert me immediately if anything develops."

Hubert nodded.

The group crossed the square, waded through brilliant sunshine, watched the birds and monks in promenade.

They stood in front of a large purple arch. Huge letters read:

TALES OF MYTH AND LEGEND

"Hoo-ray!" shouted Clem. He read the sign to Ralph, then the group passed under the arch.

They stopped between tidy rows of facing displays. The sign above the booth in front of them read: *BLOOD ON THE PLAIN—Stories for Young and Old.*

"A popular stop, young'ns," cried a dodo from behind the counter. "Help yourselves. Say ..." He eyed Clem. "Ain't you that messiah fella the dainty ones've been screeching about?"

Clem plucked a thin book from a rack. "Yes." He flipped through the pages.

"If you'll look a little further ..." The dodo scanned his shelves. "I believe we've got something on you, son. Hot off the scribes."

"Save it," said Clem, irritation in his voice. He looked at the dodo, who was now glaring at him. "Line your rectum with it."

"Why you!" The dodo leaped over the counter. "Blaspheme me, will you? Damn your scriptures!" He took a step toward Clem, a book grasped in his wing.

"Angela!" shouted Mel. He spun around. "Angela!" She was gone.

"Clem," said Ralph, "I want ..." Ralph leaned over, reaching for a book on a rack as Clem backed away from the proprietor.

The proprietor lunged at Clem, tried to shove the book in his face. Clem sidestepped him, then slashed him in the belly with his claws. The quick move toppled Ralph to the ground.

"Aaaa!" The dodo howled in pain, grabbed his bloody midsection. He hobbled away, crashed into the front of his booth.

Clem crouched, and Ralph scrambled onto his back, clutching a picture book.

"Angela!" shouted Mel.

She ran up through the crowd.

"I got sidetracked, Mel." She picked up the book the proprietor had shoved at Clem. "Hmmmmm ..." She perused it, then returned it to the booth, where she browsed a moment, then picked out another one.

"Mel ..." She looked at him. "Is this you?" She held the book up. On its cover was an illustration of a man who looked very much like Mel standing on a heat-exhausted African savanna.

"Aaaaa!" The proprietor, exploding in pain, lunged at Clem again, murder blazing in his eyes.

The Barneys, the Brit, and Clem raced down the lane, farther into *Tales of Myth and Legend*, the furious dodo at their heels.

They ditched the dodo in the crowd, then found a place to rest, sitting beside a brook shaded by willow trees. Other festivalgoers were around, reading, contemplating.

Mel kept an uneasy watch as Clem read aloud from the thin picture book he had purloined from the book shop.

On a high Asian plateau, a red-eyed sun is peeking over the horizon. The land is trembling.

In the coolness of dawn, a man leaves his tiny village. As he walks, the ax over his shoulder presses down with a gentle reminder of the day's work: He must chop wood. All day. It is his life. To work hard with his hands. Today, it is chop wood. Yesterday, it was ...

He feels the trembling land beneath his feet.

He hears a sound in the distance.

It was chop wood yesterday, also.

He strains to hear, to see. The broad plateau is rippled, and in the folds of land there are woods that flow like rivers flooding their banks. But now, in this meekness of dawn, to the man's eyes, these rivers of trees are like blood oozing darkly from a ruined hand.

He thinks ...

Yes, blood. On a big hand. The hand of Earth, this plateau. His thoughts swell within him. He is proud of his homeland. This is ancient, sacred ground.

The sound grows louder.

His step becomes lighter.

Tomorrow, he won't chop wood. There would be no need.

He sees rapid movement in the distance. Shadows ...

He thinks of his wife, his children. Tomorrow, he will work in the fields with them.

A rumbling builds from the land. It towers ... The man sees a dark wave. Massive shadows, moving like the wind, imminent, dangerous. The wave is upon him ...

He sees them clearly now: giant birds. They rush past him, wrapping him in their wind. His heart, he finds, has leaped upward. It seems to stay above him somewhere, beating madly in the air. For a moment, he has no sense of walking; he seems frozen in place, in midstep.

His mind wanders to the calluses on his hands. Thick. Rich testament to his life's work. He could grab hot coals. They would draw no hint of pain. No discomfort.

"Hoo-ray!" shouts one of the birds, turning back.

The voice finds the man like wings catching the air. He curses, falters, then is walking steadily again. Hearing the swift tread of the giant bird behind him, he kneels and thinks no more.

He had seen their feet, their claws.

They were like ...

Razors ...

The air whines. The man is split in two. His head and most of his torso fly away; the remainder slouches to the ground.

He does not hear the bewilderment of screams as his tiny village is wiped out.

Clem closed the book.

"Excellent story, Clem, old boy!" cried Ralph. He clapped his hands wildly for a moment. "Read it again!"

"Behave, Ralph," said Angela. She was paging through her

book, looking at the pictures, glancing at Mel. She waited until Mel wasn't looking, then showed the book to Hubert. She was speaking to him again, but right now there was nothing to say; the book said it all.

She began to read from the book.

"No!" shouted Ralph. "Read mine next." He handed his picture book to Hubert.

Hubert glanced through the book to see if it was appropriate for Ralph.

"Read it!" cried Ralph.

Hubert, to still Ralph, began to read.

In the rugged American West, the sun is peeking above the horizon. The land is trembling.

A man wakes from a frightful dream. He steps outside his tent, into a new dawn. He wanders from the mining camp, his head buzzing with horrific images left over from the dream.

Eyes asquint, he stares at the stark landscape. He's looking for a place to relieve himself. *Hah!* He laughs silently. What's an old sourdough to do? There's more piss in my brain than gold in ...

He hears a sound.

He turns and stares at a nearby hill. What? Still woozy with sleep, he staggers, then falls. He slowly rises to his feet. He seems to be floating in air. Then he settles down on his feet again and begins walking.

Hah! What's an old sourdough to do?

He looks around the camp. The tents are shredded. He sees bodies and body pieces. Blood everywhere. He tries to scream, but no sound comes out.

That sound again.

He turns. A man dressed in black is walking down the hill. A large man. With powerful hands.

Fear permeates the old sourdough, and he turns and runs. Oddly, he loses track of his body and finds himself back beside his tent.

He sees inside his tent through a large rent, and is stricken with terror. He sees himself. His bloody, torn corpse.

What's an old sourdough to do?

He collapses.

He rises, slowly turning in air, and sees the man in black standing on the hillside.

Go, the man says. *Leave this land behind. Cast it away.*

Immense relief sweeps through the old sourdough. He releases his attachment to the land and is pulled away.

Then ...

As he rushes through to the next world, the old sourdough searches for words to describe the experience. But there are no words. He is utterly amazed. But soon his terror returns, for he discovers he must live on earth again ...

And again ...

The man in black walks down the hill, steps through the mining camp. The ground is scarred with tracks. He sees a set of human footprints—bare running feet—and follows them, hoping for a survivor, a witness.

No ... He finds the victim in a dry wash east of camp. Ripped open. His guts spilling out on the sand before he fell.

The man in black turns and faces the camp. The wind is picking up. A gust hits him. He closes his eyes. The wind pours against him for a moment, hitting him with tiny projectiles. A hot, mean breath from Earth. Then it dies.

The man in black paints an image in his mind. He opens his eyes, walks, and is back in the mining camp, amidst the slaughter.

He paints another image in his mind and walks to higher ground. It is scrubland, flat and withered. In the distance the land is rolling, green, lush. Mountains like purple clouds lay on the horizon.

As he walks, the Universe whispers to him:

Sorrow ...

The miles pass. The air above him takes on a new character. It had been a hot, dusty, biting-blue. Now it is a soft wraparound blue, with fluffy white clouds sailing by.

Sorrow, saith the Universe.

He ponders the message. Images of recent atrocities leap into his mind. This morning, the mining camp, and the man who spilled his guts in the dry wash. Last week, it was a Tibetan village wiped out. The week before, an African village. Amidst these images, *sorrow* becomes pale; *terror* is more apt.

He focuses his mind on the birds. He is walking into their world now. The greenery closes in around him. He is in a forest. He inhales the fresh air. A minty scent plays about. He follows it. Stronger, stronger it becomes. He hears a sound. He crouches. He flows through the brush. He thinks he will see one of them, but no ...

It's an egg. An enormous egg. Nestled amongst a swarm of stunted purplish shrubs. He hears movement—something big rumbling through the forest. He freezes. The sound presses close, then falls away.

He creeps to the egg, touches it, puts an ear to it. Oddly, he feels safe near the egg. It's like an oasis in a land of dangerous currents. But he can't stay. He doesn't want a run-in with a bird, not now. He creeps back to the brush.

Minutes later, a bird walks by. A monster. It pauses to inspect the egg, then goes on its way.

Sorrow ...

The man in black lets out his breath, looks around.

Sorrow ...

Now he understands the message. Sorrow had been etched in the monster bird's face. A face drawn in sorrowful lines, painted in sorrowful tones, pulled in sorrowful grimace. The Universe *is* right; sorrow is the story of these birds.

The man in black creeps away, hidden by the brush. Minutes later, with the egg well behind him, he stands and walks, warily looking about. He knows he is ill-prepared to do battle with the birds.

He leaves the world of giant birds ... the nursery world ... and enters earth ...

He submerges himself in intensive training. The decades pass. India ... China ... Meditation ... Martial arts ...

On the dawn of a new century, the man in black returns to the land of giant birds, ready to face them.

Ralph stared at Hubert, his mouth open, expressing a mixture of wonderment and bafflement. Hubert handed him the book.

"Read it again!" cried Ralph.

"No, Ralph," said Hubert. "I won't read it again."

"Mel," said Angela. "This is you." She held her book up. "Isn't it?" She began to read.

In Africa, a killer sun is rising. The land is trembling.

A man watches the horizon, his eyes focused on the heat waves that warp the air. Illusion, he thinks. It's all illusion.

He sobs. He looks about. His wife is missing. He hasn't seen her in two days. He is frantic. They are British, and had come to Africa to renew their commitment, now she is gone.

He whirls about. The illusions grow. Glassy, fragile, shivering light. Everywhere. Growing angry, he wills the ghosts of his religion to show themselves, to come floating out of the air.

"Come, you!" he cries.

His summons works. The apostles. Saints. Jesus. Satan. Demons. All appear. They saunter close, menacing him with their eyes. Angels fall from the sky. Their tattered wings plunge and dart. Thunder and lightning rend the air. Flames foul the earth.

The battle is on.

He runs.

His ghosts pursue him.

Exhausted, he slows, not daring to look back. The heat is insane. He has to rest, but stumbles on.

He brushes sweat from his brow, drinks a steaming mouthful of water from his canteen.

He collapses into shade beneath an acacia tree. Timorously, he glances back. The ghosts have vanished.

Sitting, shivering despite the heat, he removes his hat and runs his fingers through his sodden hair. Strange verses begin to lull through his mind. They become hypnotic, then terrifying.

He stands and looks around.

"Who's following me? Who's singing?" He sees no one. The verses crash through his head.

The ghosts are inside his head now, lighting fires. He rears back and laughs. My brain's on fire. I have a flaming skull. Laughter rocks him. He pictures the top of his skull exploding off, flames and steam shooting out.

He runs.

"Out, out!" he commands. "Get out! Every last one of you, get out!" His demonic guests stream from his skull.

He collapses onto grass. Grass lions have lain in. He pulls some out, pushes himself up, holds a leaf of grass close, peers deeply into it.

There is more honesty and radiance in you, he muses, than in all the religions man has ever spawned. He tastes the grass, inhales its scent, then tosses it reverently to the ground.

He looks about. He sees a savanna that is marching into the dry season. They haven't seen the worst of the heat yet. Acacia trees, their wide-reaching branches witchy and enchanting, stand like sentinels amongst the glimmering heat waves. The land is a mirror for the sky. Light lies about in pools. Everything is pale blue. Everything is as it should be, he thinks. Illusions.

Then ghostly memories of his wife intrude.

She is growing fainter.

He runs.

Toward a patch of small purplish shrubs. He enters another world. A cooler world, washed by gentle breezes. Maybe she's here. He runs like the devil. If he doesn't find her soon, he'll have to see the man in black. He'll know where she is, won't he?

Angela closed the book and looked at Mel.

"No comment, huh, Mel?"

"Ah ..." Mel sprang to his feet. "Later, Angela. We must continue our rounds."

He began piloting them out of *Tales of Myth and Legend*, keeping a careful eye out for Tim and Zack.

"Stay close, children. Stay close ..."

He fell silent. He knew his voice was trembling.

Soon, they found themselves back in the main square. As they maneuvered through the crowds, a voice erupted from a nearby amusement.

"Key verse? I heard nothing, you crook!"

A scuffle broke out at a booth that featured a big upright stone wheel. The crowd at the front of the booth parted and a man wearing a fedora flew backward and hit the ground. A man dressed in black stood near the upright wheel, which now began to spin.

The man who'd been tossed from the amusement bounded to his feet, squared his fedora away, and charged the booth, yelling, *"Crook! I heard nothing! I saw nothing!"*

The man in black grabbed him and threw him out again.

"That's Drakon!" cried Clem. "See how effortlessly he mastered his opponent?"

"A monk, children," said Mel quietly. "To attract attention. Works beautifully."

"Let's wander that way," said Ralph, atop Clem.

They walked toward the amusement.

"Where do you come up with these un-Ralph sayings, Ralph," said Angela. "That's not something *you'd* say at all, kiddo. Ralph would say, *'Drakon! Let's go, let's go!'* You *wouldn't* say, 'Let's wander that way.'"

"Oh, I forgot!" cried Ralph. He pummeled his face.

Clem chuckled.

As they drew near the booth, they saw the sign over it:

KARMIC AMUSEMENT

The wheel, spinning slowly, was about ten feet high. Twelve marble reliefs depicting scenes from classical antiquity were evenly spaced around its perimeter. Drakon, staff in hand, stood before it.

"From out of nowhere ..." said Drakon in a rising voice.

He whipped his staff in a circle and the wheel began to spin faster. He whipped his staff again, and the wheel spun faster, faster. The reliefs turned into buttery blurs.

"From nothing ..."

He whipped his staff in a large circle, and the wheel,

though spinning madly now, began to take on the quality of stillness.

"Comes ... *The Indignities!*"

The wheel, though spinning at an insane speed, was now presenting its reliefs clear to the eye. Impossible, thought Hubert, yet there it was, before his very eyes: the reliefs seemed to be standing still on a madly spinning wheel.

Drakon's gaze traced a hypnotic parabola over the crowd. Hubert's mind expanded in a startling rush. The reliefs came alive; the scenes within them burst to life, depicting the journeys of the Barneys, and of Mel, and Clem. Hubert saw his entire life up to now flash before him. It was over in an instant.

Hubert's muse soared to new heights: The reliefs, when still, are art; when spinning, they're people's lives. Freeze, and you have art. Unfreeze, and you have life. Capture, and you have art. Escape, and you have life.

Hubert laughed to himself. Escape is what he had been planning all along. Escape from Mel, from Dodoland.

Freeze ...

But then Mel had seemed okay.

Unfreeze ...

Now Mel was their ally and protector.

Freeze ...

Claude Monet. *The Japanese Footbridge.*

Unfreeze ...

Monster dodos tracking them. Chad Garrick lurking.

Freeze ...

Art.

Unfreeze ...

Life.

The wheel goes round and round.

God, I crave life much more so than art, thought Hubert. Freeze, and you have art: imprisonment. Unfreeze, and you have life: escaping imprisonment.

Hubert felt the caress of a cool, wintry breath—the Universe whispering to him. But he did not hear the words the Universe had whispered; they were too faint. Strangely, the words seemed to stay deep within his consciousness.

He looked around at the crowd, and saw that everyone else had been swept away by the whispered words also, without necessarily hearing them. Their faces glowed.

Drakon zinged his staff through the air, and the karmic wheel continued its madly spinning paces.

"That which you heard, or did not hear," said Drakon, tracing his hypnotic parabola over the crowd, "was the key *Elyth Skilly* verse."

Eight

The Dodo Hierarchy Council was in session.

Andrew, standing near the door, gazed at the cavernous interior of the Great Hall. His vision settled on Vince, a monster dodo who stood on the far side of the chamber, beyond the conference table. The somber light that outlined Vince's form poured across the Great Hall to Andrew's dead face.

Andrew was a god. A homunculus. A human, though, to the dodos. One whom the dodos believed was immortal. They had tried to kill him many times on the gallows. Each time, Andrew got up and walked away. And each time, he allowed more of his humanness to slip away.

Andrew's consciousness swam within the rigid human form that served as his body. For Charles Barbier, Andrew was the nightmarish Abe Lincoln repairman. For the dodos, he was the master fix-it man for the Spiderweb in these parts. Intelligence—like the sky, like the sea—flowed within him. Intelligence peered from his eye windows, listened from his ear

193

windows. Within this tomb of body, intelligence had its secret being.

Andrew saw Vince sniff the air currents to assess the mood of the assembly, and sent a silent message to the big runner: *Don't be caught doing that.* Andrew chuckled inside, maintaining his rigid countenance. Oh, to be a bird with such powers. What a swirling stench his nostrils must be taking in. But sniffing and assessing the revolting ambience of the hierarchy, if the council had its way, would soon become illegal.

The council chairman was a sadistic-looking dodo by the name of Maurice. Perhaps it was his gaunt frame and pinched face that gave the impression of sadism, for one would have to say, looking upon the blueprint of Maurice, that there was likely no room for mercy and warmth within him. He looked part vapor in the air, encased within a cloud of himself. He also looked part butcher's knife, a lethal slash with every nod of the head.

Maurice stared down the long oval table, which played host to a skeletal quorum of dodo officers. Twelve in all, they stared back at Maurice, some squinting against the sunlight that fell through gaps in the webbing to come pricking at their eyes.

"Andrew," said Maurice, pointing above. "To the sunroofs."

Andrew's body gave a jerk, then became sprightly. He launched himself at the wall and clawed his way up the mesh, then like a monkey made his way across the forty-foot-high ceiling to the gaps in the webbing and closed them tight, shutting off the fountains of sunlight.

He fell with a thud, landing smack in the middle of the conference table, which was made of the finest hardwood in

Dodoland. The thirteen dodos recoiled in their chairs. Andrew got off the table and stiff-walked back to his position by the door. He watched them through the dim light in the Great Hall and chuckled within.

"Clem," said Maurice, regaining his composure. "We must capture him and bring him here." His voice was the harsh squeal of a cantankerous rodent.

A murmur swept around the table. Heads nodded. Eyes returned to Maurice.

An officer stood and addressed the chairman. "Is the attorney from D.C. prepared to perform his role?"

Maurice, looking supremely relaxed in his chair, shifted his eyes and nodded at another dodo. "Obie?"

The bird stood. His voice was nervous. "Ah, at this moment, the attorney, a Mr. Charles Barbier, is in his cell. We—"

Another dodo stood, exploding. "You nearly executed him!"

"We had orders."

"You could have blown the whole thing."

"How were we to know?"

"Silence," said Maurice. He stood and stared the warring officers down into their chairs. Then he sat down.

"A most fortuitous event happened," said Maurice. "Yesterday, the runners were bringing in humans in droves, the attorney from D.C. among them. The Captain of the Jail was under orders to execute all prisoners. Then this morning our messiah hatched, and a new complexion entered, gentle dodos."

Maurice scanned their faces.

"Let us keep our peace here. It's likely the attorney from D.C. will play a vital role. We certainly would not want just *any* human to handle Clem's crucifixion."

A murmur of assent swept the room.

"How would it look to posterity if we had a fix-it guy like Andrew do it?" asked Maurice, an arrogant grin lacing his cruel aristocratic features.

The council exploded in laughter.

An obese dodo with white-tufted feathers stood.

"Our two guards on the scene, what is keeping them from seizing this messiah? Hasn't the *pounce* order been given?"

Maurice swiveled and looked at Vince. Vince walked forward.

"The *pounce* order has been transmitted several times," said Vince. "Our spies at the Greenways report that Tim and Zack are still following Clem and his disciples."

"Peculiar," said Maurice, fanning his beak with a wing.

"Send runners," said the white-tufted dodo. "Take Tim and Zack prisoners also."

A murmur started then quickly died. The officers looked at Maurice. Faint flickers of annoyance crossed the chairman's face. Then a gleam of fear. He turned back to Vince.

"What do you recommend?"

"Tim and Zack could not be taken without a fight which would see many dead." Vince walked closer to Maurice and sniffed the air. "Sire, may I submit a plan?" He bent and whispered in the chairman's ear.

Silence oppressed the room.

Vince stepped away from Maurice and gazed at the officers.

Maurice fanned his beak.

"It is in their blood," said Vince, "in their DNA, to be heroes."

Maurice raised a wing, silencing the big runner.

Another murmur.

And a hush.

Maurice leaned forward.

"Then we'd have them all," he said. He looked at Vince. "We need discipline in the ranks."

"Yes, sir." Vince stepped back, squared his stance.

Maurice stood and began walking around the table. Heads spun. Chairs creaked. The chairman stopped and looked at the group.

"Oh, yes, you'll see some recalcitrance among the troops. Initially. Tim and Zack, case in point. Others, too, occasionally." He paced. "But we will not be deterred." He raised a wing to the assemblage.

"No!" came the shouted chorus.

"Onward!" cried Maurice.

"Onward!" shouted the chorus. The cry was deafening.

Maurice stopped pacing. Silence descended. The chairman's eyes became glossy. He turned toward Andrew.

"Andrew." Maurice pointed upward. "To the sunroofs. Just this one."

Andrew became like a monkey and within six seconds was on the ceiling and had the sunroof open. Dusty sunlight spilled in. Maurice stepped into it, and Andrew fell with a thud at the chairman's feet.

Maurice went stark raving bonkers, flapping his wings insanely and chasing round and round in circles. Soon, he regained his composure. Andrew levered himself to his feet and stick-walked back to his post by the door.

"We have come far, gentle dodos," said Maurice, standing in the column of dusty sunlight. "We are on the verge of victory.

In one sweeping move, Dodoland will be consolidated under one pure creed, one correct banner, one catechism. All power will be ours."

He shot a wing skyward.

"Hail to our messiah!" he shouted.

"Hail!" came the chorus.

The birds stood. The shouts rang throughout the hall.

"Hail! Hail! Hail!"

Finally, silence, exhausted and full, fell upon the assembly.

"Vince, stay," said Maurice. "Obie, stay." He dismissed the others with the wave of a wing.

Andrew stood by the door, watching the dodo officers file out. As their faces paraded past him, he read their inner lives: power, fear, greed. It never changed.

Then they were gone.

Andrew focused on the three at the table.

"Obie," said Maurice, "bring in our attorney from D.C." Obie left. To Vince, Maurice said, "That barbaric practice of sniffing must end."

"Yes, sir."

"Spread the word."

"Yes, sir."

"Spread it again and again and again."

"Yes, sir. Yes, sir."

"And *dojos.*"

"Yes, sir."

"And meditation."

"Yes, sir."

"This is not the Dark Ages, Vince."

"No, sir."

"Crackdowns."

"Yes, sir."

"Crackdowns!"

"Yes, sir! Yes, sir! Yes, sir!"

Charles Barbier heard the tramping of feet. Guards were coming for him, bypassing other cells. He wished for a mirror. He would break it and use it to slit their throats.

He stood and went to the door webbing. Three dodo faces glared in at him. "What do you want?" he asked in a menacing voice.

"You're going to see the chairman. No trouble!"

"I want food and water." Charles's tone implied there'd be trouble otherwise. After a moment, the dodo leader nodded.

They marched him out, stopped at a dining hall, and gave him food and water. They let him eat and drink, then escorted him out.

At the Great Hall, two of the guards remained outside while the leader escorted Charles inside.

Trading sunlight for the half-light of the Great Hall, Charles walked past the odd, odd repairman and caught a frightful chill. He turned to stare, but was fanned onward by his escort.

A huge table gripped Charles's attention. He took in its immensity, its polished surface, the dusty columns of sunlight that struck it from above.

On the far side of the table, a tall, thin dodo with a pinched face and a huge dodo with a robust physique were engaged in conversation. Charles felt like a dwarf in the presence of the towering dodos and their oversized furniture.

"Sit!" commanded his escort.

Charles crawled onto one of the massive chairs and sat on the edge like a child would, with feet dangling.

The tall, thin dodo, the robust-looking dodo, and Charles's escort took seats across from him.

"Obie ..." The tall, thin dodo nodded toward Charles's escort, his pinched face conveying unspoken commands.

"Chairman Maurice, Vince, this is Charles Barbier."

The dodos and Charles studied each other.

"Take notes, Charles," said Maurice in a squeaky rodent's voice.

Pen and paper were delivered to Charles by a guard. Scrolls were plopped down in front of him. Charles, nervous, wiped his hands on his shirt and trousers, then on his beard.

"Our Lord, Clem, has hatched this morning," said Maurice. The dodo chairman began outlining the plan for the catechism.

Charles picked up a pen and began writing.

After a while, Maurice flicked a wing at the scrolls. "Read them, Charles. They contain further truths of Clem."

Charles began reading of a messiah named Clem. Moments later, he looked at Maurice and risked a question.

"Are you the father of this messiah?" he asked.

Maurice looked thoughtfully into the air, fanning his beak.

"At this point, no," he said. "In the future ..." He paused, changed his expression several times, studied the columns of sunlight that poured in from the sunroofs. He leaned back, sank in his chair. "Allow for the possibility, Charles. We'll use whatever works. Allow for it in the catechism."

Maurice gave Vince a hastily whispered instruction, and Vince left the Great Hall.

"You will be allowed to leave Dodoland, Charles," said Maurice, "after this is over. Your presence in D.C. will serve as a rallying point—the big evil around which the new dodo society will be structured."

Maurice told of great revelations.

"Clem, as prophesied by the ancients, was overheard making disparaging remarks about scribes at the bazaar. He called them pompous assholes. But in truth, Charles, scribes are the noble incendiaries of society. They are the one mind flaming into the one thought. Dodos kiss the feet of scribes.

"But ..." Maurice fanned his beak. "Temporarily, in the catechism, we will have to make scribes out as bad dodos—Clem is infallible. In later chapters, however, Charles, scribes will be exalted."

Charles scribbled notes. Thoughts rode tortuously through his mind. Maurice's voice intruded.

"Clem will be handed to you. You will execute him. The faithful will be told that Clem rose from the dead. But ..." Maurice fanned his beak. "Truthfully, Charles, we will have no further use for him."

Charles searched the scrolls, copied passages. *Clem rose from the dead ...*

Charles read further. *The two older Barneys and the Englishman ...* He touched the ink on the scroll; it was still wet. He saw his own name—wet also.

Charles, realizing they weren't about to let him go free, tried to buy time.

"Chairman Maurice, it's going to take a couple of days to

write this catechism."

The bird stared at him with flinty eyes.

"Two hours, Charles, then all will be in place. Do your best. As the years go by, we will have others fill in the gaps and make it look seamless, a work of art."

Vince and a troop of seven dodos raced across the savanna, faster than cheetah speed. The Greenways sprang into view. The mecca of purple dwarfs lay like jeweled necklaces in the sparkling sunshine.

Vince gave silent commands.

Troop, slow! Go left!

The troop slowed, then slipped into nearby woods and huddled.

"Thunderdudes in the air, mates," said Vince. "We'll stay here till their performance is over."

"Where are they?" asked a bird, craning his neck.

"On the way from the mountains, son," said Vince. He had picked up their distant, silent approach.

"It's getting to be illegal as hell to fly anymore," said another dodo. "Won't it be a joy, mates, when we can ground those stupid birds?"

There was a scattered murmur of assent.

Vince searched their faces. Do these birds believe they must do only as they are told? Has something twisted their DNA? Or is it that old chestnut—fear? Fear of that mouse Maurice?

Sad creatures.

He turned away and looked to the sky.

The big karmic wheel spun madly, telling its tales. Hubert was hypnotized by it, held forcefully in an unseen grip.

It spun tales of Mauritius, tales of Dodoland, of survivability, of killing excursions in earth territory, of cultural shifts sparked by martial arts and meditation, of diversity igniting a society into a thousand flickering flames, of mutants grabbing for power, and the coming of a messiah.

The wheel slowed. The marble reliefs became running blurs, transforming life to art.

God, thought Hubert, eagerly waiting for the wheel to stop. How much I do appreciate art after all. A slowing down from life. A chance to reflect. To stave off ...

The wheel stopped.

The reliefs froze.

And, momentarily, Hubert saw four lifeless bodies hanging from a giant scaffold. A cold wind blew into his soul.

"Drakon!" he cried, pointing at the wheel. "They executed Clem, Ralph, Angela, and me."

"Potentialities, Hubert," said Drakon. "All things exist as potentialities."

"Right, Hubert," said Clem. "They taught us that in school."

Ralph said in an exasperated voice, "You didn't think you were seeing it for *real*, did you, Hubert, old boy?"

Hubert stared at his little brother. Is that Ralph? He looked at Angela. Her brow was creased, her eyes still on the wheel. He looked at Drakon.

"Why didn't you show us doing great things instead of hanging by our necks, dead?"

"You *are* doing great things, Hubert," said Drakon. "All of you are doing great things. Your cup runneth over here in Dodoland."

"Okay," said Hubert, throwing his hands up. "Hanging is a great trip. I've always wanted to be executed, and hanging has always been my preferred—"

Drakon whipped his staff in a circle.

The wheel spun.

Hubert stared, saw himself ...

... raise his carbine, peer down the sights. He felt his trigger hand take up the slack, heard the sharp report, saw the jerk of a body, smelled the burning gunpowder ...

Hubert spun away, his forehead bathed in sweat. He'd just executed someone, *as foretold by the wheel.* Did anyone else see it?

"Those words ..." said Angela.

"What words?" shouted Hubert.

She turned on Hubert, fury in her face.

"The words we didn't hear!" she said.

Hubert swallowed hard.

Angela turned toward Drakon.

"We must have hanged people before, unjustly, in other lives," she said. "Now it's our turn." She began to cry.

Words? Then Hubert realized what she was talking about. The key *Elyth Skilly* verse, the whisper from the Universe.

Terror seized him. Were they due to die? Was it their karma? He stared at the powerful face of Drakon. He stared back. Frozen. Art! The willies raced up Hubert's spine.

Chad and Sandra were standing in the crowd near the karmic amusement. Chad had heard the key *Elyth Skilly* verse again. It thrilled him—as it had back in the clearing with Drakon and Marshall—until he realized its implications.

The wheel mesmerized him, pulled him in. He saw a mosaic of life colliding with mysterious forces. Then, as revealed by the wheel, the Barneys and Clem were hanging lifeless.

Now, with the wheel stopped, Angela was crying.

Chad and Sandra crept away.

What does it all mean? thought Chad. He tightened his grip on his staff. He wasn't going to let the Barneys die.

His staff bucked, thumped him hard in the chest. Chad sat down, hurt. His staff flew away, then lay still.

Chad crawled toward it, looking up at Sandra, his emotions burning. He realized now that he would not be able to save the Barneys.

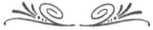

Mel glanced at the frozen wheel, then looked at the children.

"Ah ... children, what I believe the wheel is getting at is ... nothing stays as it is. All things change or die."

"Uh, Mel," said Hubert, "I have a feeling someone's trying to dictate change to us. And it's not going to benefit us. We need to resist."

"I'll echo that, Hubert," said Clem. "We need to resist."

"Well, be that as it may, change is inevitable," said Mel. "Change or die."

"We'll change," said Angela, thrusting a forefinger at the wheel. "But not like that. We won't hang!" She shivered.

"Good thinking, Angela," said Mel. "Don't let the wheel tell you how to change."

"Don't be a captive to their art," said Hubert to Angela.

"Excellent commentary, Hubert, old boy," cried Ralph. "But what does it mean?"

"You're getting to be a wiseass, Ralph, old boy," said Hubert. "Say, Clem, how does it feel to be a messiah with, I guess, a very limited life span?"

"I can do without the notoriety, Hubert. And as far as life spans go, don't shed any tears for me. I fully intend to rip to shreds anyone who so much as looks at me the wrong way."

"Very blasphemous," said Hubert.

Clem chuckled.

Ralph chuckled.

Mel was relieved. The children were not shaken up too badly by Drakon's Indignities. None of it has to come true. But ... my blood shadow?

He wondered.

He looked at Drakon.

Drakon whipped his staff through the air. The big karmic wheel began to spin, faster, faster ... The reliefs became blurs. Art became life. In the wheel, it looked like the Barneys and Clem were once again caught in a maelstrom of sinister forces.

"I'm famished, children," said Mel as he herded them across the square. "We'll get something to eat now. Keep an eye out for the two big birds. Tim and Zack, they are."

He led them to a food stand and ordered fish and fruit for the whole group. They took their food to a nearby picnic table.

"Slosh it down with these," said Mel, bringing cups of water and setting them on the table.

"Delicious," said Clem.

"Mel, you forgot to pay the food monk," said Ralph.

"Why so I have, Ralph, old boy," said Mel. "But what'll we do; I'm plumb out of money."

"Ralph," said Clem, "food is always plentiful wherever you go in Dodoland, though usually you have to track it down yourself. The people here at the Greenways—Drakon's friends, I believe—are nice enough to provide food free of charge. Egalitarianism, some dodos say, but you never see *those* types turn down a free meal. I think it's damn nice of the humans. Dodos should be more appreciative and less judgmental."

"Excellent speech, Clem, old boy," cried Ralph, stuffing his mouth with colorful fruit.

They all laughed, watching Ralph, then Angela looked up and saw Tim and Zack. The two guards were less casual now; they seemed to be on the alert. She jabbed Hubert in the ribs.

"They're here," she said. She watched Hubert's face as he sought them out in the crowd. A look of horror came over him. Angela shivered, attacked by the willies.

Just then a new danger seemed to present itself. A chattering was in the air, growing louder. They all looked about.

"Look," said Angela, pointing.

Small goatlike creatures were swarming around Tim and Zack. They darted about, circling the giant birds in mad rushes. Then they set sacks at the feet of the monsters, and the whole swarm took off, fading into the crowd.

The two dodos bent, sniffed, and began eating from the sacks, tentatively at first, then voraciously. They carried the sacks to a table and ordered drinks from a passing food monk.

Angela looked around. The odd event had drawn everyone's attention. It caused her to wonder. On the square, Tim had guided her back to the group—she had been too embarrassed to mention it to the others. Did Tim's act mean she was free from people-pleasing odors. She looked at Clem.

"Clem, you're a dodo, tell us, do we Barneys smell of people-pleasing odors? I'm dying to know."

"Yes. Each human does. Initially, when I first sniffed you, you were all above the trigger point. But ..." Clem sniffed the air. "Now, you are all wavering right around the trigger point, which would mean safety under normal circumstances. You're even growing small blood shadows, Hubert, Angela, and Ralph. Very unusual."

Clem resumed eating.

"Aren't these normal circumstances?" asked Angela.

Clem looked at Mel.

"Tell them, Clem," said Mel.

Clem looked at the Barneys.

"Mutants have taken over the Spiderweb, and blood shadows—and other big DNA things, I'm sure—are being overridden by the orders of these power brokers."

Clem nodded toward Tim and Zack. He lowered his voice.

"I believe those two border guards have received orders from the Spiderweb to violate blood shadows and take every one of you into custody. Me as well." He sighed. "Since I've been selected as their messiah."

"Clem," said Mel, leaning across the table, "can you pick up their communications with the Spiderweb?"

"To some extent, Mel. The communication channels are very subtle. When I tune in to them, I hear incoherent warbling and such. It takes training and experience to hear clearly at those levels. But I can get a sense of things, based on repetition, a feeling of urgency, and so on."

"Wonderful, Clem," said Mel. "Keep us posted."

"I will."

"Clem," said Ralph, "who were those little people who brought food to the big dodos?"

"I don't know, Ralph."

Clem took a bite of his food.

"These are sorrowful times," said Clem. "Those two"—he nodded toward Tim and Zack—"are disobeying orders to pounce on us. They risk their lives doing so."

Angela turned in shock to look at them.

"Clem," said Ralph, "would you kill us right now if we started smelling *real* bad?"

"No," said Clem. "But I *would* counsel you, and chase you home. I wouldn't want you around—bad influence and all."

"What?" said Angela. "No Spiderweb? No *dojo?* You'd just chase us home?"

Clem nodded.

"That makes you somewhat of a variant yourself, Clem, wouldn't you say?" said Mel.

"Well, maybe it does, Mel. I probably have a direction different from most other dodos. In the classroom this morning, I felt a deep, natural abhorrence of all things human. I have since changed. Don't ask me how."

"It's no wonder they selected you as their messiah, Clem," said Angela. "You *are* good."

"I can't help being what I am, Angela. *Good* is subjective. *Survivability* is a term more to my liking; it's more objective, and I like to think my direction is along the lines of greater survivability, for myself and for all dodos." He looked at Mel. "Maybe I am a variant, but one that's on a healthier branch of evolution."

"Socko survivability, Clem, old boy," said Mel in a hushed but excited tone. "Give the old birds hell, son."

When they finished their meals, a wandering food monk carrying a huge tray of cotton candy approached.

"Devil's Breath Cotton Candy!" he cried. "Who wants Devil's Breath Cotton Candy?"

Angela stared at the big whirls of cotton candy, taking in their cool, delicate colors, their warm, sweet scent. Her nostrils roused as if from sleep. Her mouth watered.

No, I can't, she decided.

Clem snatched a piece of cotton candy, ate it. "Um ..." He grabbed a whole mountain of it, then wolfed it down and licked the bare cone.

Ralph reached for some. The monk handed him a kid-sized cone.

"Yummy," said Ralph, tasting it. It took but an instant for him to down it.

Hubert and Mel reached out their hands.

Well, maybe I will, thought Angela. She reached out her hand. Hubert and Mel received their cotton candy. They, too, turned into wolves and were soon licking bare cones.

The monk gave Angela one. She took a bite. A deviltry of

taste exploded in her mouth. She gobbled the rest of it wolf-fashion until she was licking the bare paper cone.

"Devil's Breath Cotton Candy!" roared the monk, moving off through the crowd.

Angela watched Hubert contemplate his bare cone, waving it around.

"What do you make of this, Mel?" he asked. "Why'd we become sinfully gluttonous all of a sudden?"

"Ah ..." Mel seemed to be at a loss for words.

"My taste buds led me onward into a journey of pure sensation," said Clem.

"Mine too," said Ralph, who was still licking his bare cone.

"It's simple, Hubert," said Angela. "In a world where things happen so fast, it's only natural they would have some *real* fast cotton candy, also. If that's sinful, good!"

She popped to her feet and skipped away from the picnic table, hoping the calories would burn off just as fast.

Chad had a purple galaxy of a bruise on his chest where his staff thumped him, but the bruise did not hurt nearly as much as the feelings it engendered.

He had lost two enemies—Tim and Zack—and had cast the Barneys adrift.

He took up his staff and began wandering, losing track of the Barneys, losing track of Tim and Zack as well.

Sandra? He looked around. She was gone.

Chad found a clear space in the square. He whipped his

staff in an arc. That brought the fauns running in from out of nowhere, toting sacks of Forest Buckle.

One of the creatures handed Chad a fresh sack of the amazing food, then they all swarmed off. Chad followed them and found Tim and Zack. He watched the fauns deposit a peace offering of Forest Buckle at their feet.

Tim and Zack sniffed it, then tore into it.

Chad played spy. Tim and Zack took the food to a table and ordered drinks. Chad located the Barneys, Mel, and Clem at another table. He ate Forest Buckle and sipped water from his canteen as he watched them, using the crowd as concealment.

He talked silently to his staff. *Food, not war?*

The staff hit him again, just as hard as before, but this time it was painless and left no bruise. His staff moved like a bear in his hands. Chad wrestled with it.

Then his staff was still.

Strange emotions welled up in Chad. He remembered his capture by Tim and Zack, his escape, his frenzied tunneling through the brush, his later encounter with the two monsters.

I wouldn't be what I am now if someone had come by and saved me.

Chad walked through the crowds, holding out his staff, staring at it, whispering silently to it. He walked off the square and found a secluded alley between tenement-like rows of purple dwarfs. Away from prying eyes, Chad and his staff worked against imaginary opponents.

Honing skills, they worked. Against phantom human attackers jumping in from out of nowhere. Against single and multiple attacks. Against phantom birds, razors ripping the air. When it was over, Chad shuddered.

He knew now why Drakon had spent a hundred years in the Orient training with martial arts masters before facing the dodos.

He hurried back to the square, where the enemy was lurking. The dodo hierarchy had placed their agents here. He scanned the crowd, trying to detect who the spies were.

Hoodoo!

"Devil's Breath Cotton Candy!" roared the monk, passing by Tim and Zack's table.

Slurrrrup!

Slurrrrup!

Two mountains of cotton candy disappeared in the blink of an eye.

Pah—toot!

Pah—toot!

They spit out the cones.

"Ready, Zack?"

"Never been readier, Tim."

They stood.

They kept a wary eye out for lurking spies and followed the Barneys, Mel, and Clem out of the square. They moved with a surge of birds and people, a tidal wave heading to the runway to watch the Thunderdudes perform.

"Hey, Zack, what say we fly off to the mountains with these birds afterward, eh?"

"To hide out?"

"For a while. Rendezvous with other elements opposed to the dainty ones."

"You think there are others like us out there?"

"Bound to be. If not now, we'll call them in."

"Better to recruit face to face, Tim. Calling can be dangerous. You never know who might show up. Friend or foe."

"We'll call them in and size them up as they land. No sissies allowed. Sissies don't fly too well anyway. That's a telling factor."

"Sounding better, Tim. Let's recruit Clem right off. I know they have a classroom for hatchlings up there, and *dojos* and meditation squares. He'll be happy."

"Brilliant, Zack. Foul up the dainty ones' plans, too. No messiah to push around."

"On second thought, let's wait until the youngster has seen the aerial hieroglyphics of the Thunderdudes. He'll be hooting for joy to go to the mountains and join up with the resistance."

"Now you're hootin', Zack, old boy."

Tim chuckled to himself. He had led Zack into saving Clem. The rugged mountain hideaways were virtually impregnable to the intrusions of the dainty ones and their fawning goons. It took a hearty soul to thrive in the rarefied air up there.

It'll be a respite, thought Tim. But it would also mean their lives if caught. They would be branded outlaws, renegades, cowards; the scribes would go berserk with insults.

Tim slid closer to Zack.

"Those miserable, filthy, diseased scribes are going to be pissing dainty words from every orifice, Zack, when we defect. Let's rip a few of their arrogant hides to shreds before we take off for the mountains."

"Tim, we've never harmed dodos before." Zack sounded repulsed.

"Times are changin', Zack, old boy. Soon, it'll be kill or be killed."

"I agree," whispered Zack. "But let's keep violence out of it until it can really count for something."

"Thanks, Zack. You are an unwavering star in the heavens. I will nominate you for rebel leader at our first rally."

"Thanks, Tim. I can feel my neck stretching already."

They fell silent, drifted apart, swam with the tide.

Clump ... clump ... clump ...

The Great Hall echoed with the footsteps of visitors.

Charles Barbier looked up. Three young dodos filed toward the table.

Maurice stood.

"Obie, keep an eye on Charles." He walked away from the table. "Roger." He extended a wing to the lead youngster. They shook. "Welcome, welcome ..."

Maurice ushered the three toward the wall across from Charles. Charles, still writing the catechism, shot a curious eye to them, wary of incurring the wrath of the watchful Obie.

"Andrew," shouted Maurice.

The odd, odd repairman stiff-walked to Maurice.

"The map."

Andrew turned spidery and crawled up the wall. He untied a roll of canvass and let it unfurl, unveiling a map. He fell, hitting the floor with a thud. The three young dodos jumped back, startled, but Maurice remained calm. Andrew levered himself to his feet and stiff-walked back to his position by the door.

"Roger and friends, step up." Maurice produced a long pointer and jabbed the map. "Here we are—Spiderweb One. And here, I believe, is where you had your unfortunate encounter with Clem." He hit the map farther southwest.

Charles heard some grumblings from the youngsters.

"Yeah, we whipped him good," one of them said. The other two nodded in agreement.

"And here," said Maurice, hitting the map farther north, "is the Greenways, current location of Clem and the Barneys, along with their guide, Malcolm Moreland." He leveled his eyes on the three. "You *have* been briefed on the Barneys, haven't you?"

"Yes," said Roger, the leader of the youngsters. His voice carried an unhealthy note of hoarseness. He coughed; his wind stirred up a nearby column of dust, sending it swirling into convulsions. The giddy sunlight, streaming through apertures in the ceiling, seemed to laugh.

"Tell me, Roger, all you know about where the Barneys live," said Maurice.

"In a house on the prairie." Roger walked to the map and traced a route from the eastern boundary of Dodoland into earth territory. "Somewhere out here."

"Excellent," said Maurice. "Spell the name."

"B-a-r-n-e-y."

"Do you know what a mailbox is?"

"Yes."

"And what will be *on* the mailbox?"

216

"The name *Barney* will be on the mailbox."

"Yes, it will. It'll help you identify the location. And what are you to do when you get there?"

"Hide near the house. Observe. Be wary of guns. Wait for commands. If ordered, kill Father Barney and Mother Barney, two humans. Leap from ambush, use razors on throat. Return to Spiderweb One quickly."

"Obie. The signals."

Charles's escort left the table and walked over to Maurice and the three young dodos.

"Hoot ... hoot ... hoot-it ... hoot-it ..." Obie taught them the signals. Roger and his pals repeated them, working toward ever more subtle levels. Finally, the signals were being taught and refined at levels too low for Charles to hear.

Charles, returning to his writing, began to plot his escape. Somehow, he must get word out. Time became a slippery variable in his plans.

He looked up, shot an eye toward Maurice. The skinny dodo's head was bobbing in approval as Obie continued to train the killers in the use of silent commands. Charles looked at the monster body of Obie, at the smaller yet stout bodies of the juveniles. Even Maurice, gaunt though he was, must weigh close to three hundred pounds. The juveniles, much shorter, somewhere around two hundred pounds each. Obie, maybe eight hundred pounds. And they all could run like the devil.

He looked at their razor claws.

He wished for a rifle.

He wished for a machine gun.

Charles glanced at the walls of the hall, then at the ceiling with its gaping sunroofs. He turned in his chair and peered at

Andrew. The odd, odd repairman stood stiffly by the door, his eyes vacantly staring, not a sign of life, aside from the fact he was standing on his feet.

Slumping, Charles went back to writing the catechism. You show me how to do it, Andrew, he thought. Show me how to escape, how to save the others. You are visiting us from somewhere, aren't you, Andrew? You seem to have the dodos on your stringer. I sense there is something vast beyond that exterior of yours, Andrew.

Charles began shouting in his mind:

Ask and ye shall receive!

To him who believeth, all things are possible!

I'm asking, Andrew!

You are the only god in residence, now lend a hand!

Charles Barbier, spinning tales of Clem the messiah, continued to send silent entreaties to the death stick Andrew.

Later, the three juveniles slipped out of the hall, and Maurice and Obie came back to the table and sat across from Charles.

Maurice lounged in his chair and fanned his beak.

"Hurry, hurry, Charles," he said.

Charles shot a silent barrage of oaths at the dodo. A moment later, he thought he heard a chuckle. Then, oddly, he felt a chuckle. It felt like a wind blowing up from a deep, chilling cavern. The chuckle flew about, chasing Charles's ghosts all over his flesh.

Hubert sidled up to Mel in the teeming crowd. He kept his voice low.

"What's the strategy, Mel? What do we do if we come under attack? Are our rifles up to it? The dodos don't seem to mind us carrying them. You'd think they'd've disarmed us somewhere along the line if they felt threatened, with their DNA being so intelligent and all."

The questions put a pause into the Brit. He pursed his lips, slowed his walk, angled his face toward the sky.

"You know, Hubert," whispered Mel, "for longer than I care to remember, I've been lugging this elephant shooter around with me, just in case, but ..." Mel let the thought drop, stared reflectively at the sky.

A cry rose from Ralph.

"Why don't you ask Clem?"

Hubert looked at the youngster, several feet away, atop Clem, and thought there was no way he could have ears that sharp.

"Ralph, you didn't hear what we were saying."

"Your faces, Hubert, old boy," said Ralph. "You don't know something, so why don't you ask Clem?" He patted the dodo's head.

"He saw our strained looks, Hubert," said Mel. "Little Ralph has a glowing intellect."

They glided over to Ralph and Clem.

"Clem, have you noticed these rifles we've been carrying?" asked Hubert. "And Mel's handgun, machete, and hunting knife?"

"Yes, Hubert. Nothing much misses my attention."

"Can our weapons be effective in your world—I mean not just against scribes."

"Yes, Hubert, they can be effective. But we dodos have fast-closing wounds, thanks to our wonderful DNA. And when we are under assault and hurt, our glands kick in with extra energy, and we have a sixth sense that kicks in too, to carry on in the event our sensory organs are debilitated, and we go after whoever shot or cut us and ... Well ... it's curtains for them, Hubert. Don't ever try to harm a dodo."

"Oh, no, Clem, never," said Hubert.

"But, Clem," said Mel, "we are faced with some evil dodos out there who might try to harm *us*. What *is* effective against them? We might have to defend ourselves, and so might you."

"Ah, Mel," said Clem, "as a precaution against regeneration, you'd have to rip the dodo to pieces. That, or hanging or drowning, cutting off the air supply long enough. A wound from your rifle, Mel, even if it blew a dodo's head clean off, would be curtains for *you*. The dodo would get you, navigating by rapid knowledge hits, and his new head would blow into being over the course of a day or two, as your corpse lies rotting in the sun."

"But the scribe—"

"A dainty one, Mel," said Clem. "They don't regenerate."

"Remember how Drakon fought the dodos?" cried Ralph.

Hubert remembered Drakon's tales of Dodoland, rendered in the spinning marble reliefs at the karmic amusement. Drakon certainly did engage many dodos, hundreds probably, in fights that would have meant death for him if he hadn't prevailed.

"Ah, yes, Clem, can you fill us in on any tricks Drakon might have come up with?" asked Mel.

"Yes, Mel, I can, though normally these things stay in the *dojo.*"

Mel gave a nervous laugh.

"Ah ... Well, Clem, old boy, let's have it."

"Dodos are easily startled, unless they're into your rhythms. The same applies to humans, by the way. So, do something startling."

Mel laughed again; this time it was a hoarse laugh; it seemed to echo hollowly from deep inside him.

"Do something *really* startling," said Clem, "and you'll send a dodo into goo-goo land for a few moments. That'll give you enough time to evade him or try another tactic, but make it another startling tactic. Way back, Drakon drove them insane in the forests. You should hear the war stories, Mel and Hubert. They're downright chilling."

The group walked on. Hubert listened to Mel's haunting laughter. It sounded like the Brit had entered some portion of that goo-goo land Clem had talked of.

Malcolm, stay and I'll teach you survival tactics and strategy.

The words from Drakon had ironically served as more impetus driving Mel away. I don't want to end up a wandering warrior between worlds, he had thought at the time. I don't want to become like Drakon. Stay, and I'll teach you to be like me, is what he's saying.

Your blood shadow will see the dawn of a day when it will not be respected in Dodoland.

The words had been like glaciers to Mel's ears. Chilling, yes, but Mel had walked away. You and I, Drakon, are from two different worlds.

The months had gone by. Mel wandered between two

worlds—Dodoland and Earth. He had been sick of Drakon's tutoring, the never-ending training and meditation.

I'm not a stoic, Drakon. Not a mystic. I'm a torch, a guide.

Mel, walking through the crowds with the Barneys and Clem, heard the jagged edges of his laughter.

He stopped it, looked around.

A bit hasty, wasn't I, Drakon? A bit overreactive. I am ill-prepared to guide these children through such perils.

What now?

Mel walked along with the group. There was nothing else to do. Clem, at the Barneys' promptings, was talking about the peculiarities of dodos, and about tactics.

"Did the big dodo without the red on his beak grow it back?" asked Ralph.

"Oh, I'm sure he did by now, Ralph. It's a quick part." Clem chuckled.

"Would the sound of a gunshot startle a dodo into goo-goo land?" asked Hubert.

"Yes. For a second or two. But only if it was unexpected."

"Clem," said Angela, "aren't there individual differences among dodos? Do they all have to react in the same way?"

"In any given situation, Angela, you will see a certain range of actions-reactions from dodos, but if their survival is at stake, the range becomes very narrow and very predictable: Woe is you." Clem chuckled, then said, "An example of a broader range would be cowardice. Most dodos have no experience of cowardice. Not so with the dainty ones. Get one of them in a fight, and it doesn't take much before they're crying and running for cover. Even a determined human with a rock or club could triumph quickly. Trouble is, most of these sissies come equipped with bodyguards or friends. They like to gang up on their opponents."

"Mel," cried Ralph, "ask Clem a question."

"Ralph ..." said Angela.

"That's quite all right, Angela." Mel laughed. "All right ... Clem, are dodos susceptible to any of the myriad pressures that make humans conform to arbitrary rules and constraints, such as ... ah ... modifying your beliefs and behavior to avoid ridicule or censure or outright punishment?"

"Only within the hierarchies, Mel. There, you have to watch what you say and do. Such blackmail is creeping outward, though, through the pens of the scribes. Scribes' pens can be very hypnotic, and hypnosis forms bars."

"Clem," asked Hubert, "how do they expect to get you to stand still for an execution? I can't envision you being passive and all, and just going along with it."

Clem chuckled.

"I guess they plan to hypnotize me, then plant a suggestion, such as: 'Clem, old boy, just slip your neck into our hang noose and the Kingdom of Heaven will be yours.'"

"That's evil, Clem," said Angela. "Don't let them do that."

"I have no intentions of letting them do that, Angela."

"Clem," said Hubert, "how do they hypnotize a dodo?"

"The same way they do humans. They isolate you and restrict you and put you into a trance by ceaseless repetition of propaganda. It's very much like a cult indoctrination. Once you are captive to their influence, they ram suggestions past your lowered psychic filters and get you to believe anything they want."

"How do we know we're not all hypnotized right now?" It was a strange voice.

"Excellent question!" cried Ralph.

Mel turned to look.

Everyone turned to look.

It was a boy around Hubert's age, wearing a cowboy hat and carrying a staff.

"Chad Garrick!" cried Angela. "Is that you?"

He took off through the crowd.

Hoots filled the air as the crowds at the cultural festival swarmed toward the airfield to watch the performance of the Thunderdudes.

The Barneys, Mel, and Clem ran with the crowds and found a spot next to the mile-long hedge of purple dwarfs that kept everyone back from the runway.

The Thunderdudes stood just beyond the hedge—six huge dodos in crisp military formation, angled toward the runway. Stern-looking dodo guards patrolled the area to keep order.

"Hoo-ray!" shouted Clem.

"Hoo-ray!" shouted Ralph.

Hubert stared at the Thunderdudes, then gazed at the sky. It was a deep ocean of blue. Wispy white haze swam gently here and there, rolling in the sun's heating rays.

"A perfect sky for high-altitude precision flying, children," said Mel. "This'll be a treat. The Thunderdudes are in Brahman consciousness. Or, *Brahmi Chetna*—unity consciousness— where the observer and the observed are one. This state of consciousness is enlivened and brought forth through years of meditation. You saw dodos fly at the meditation square, now wait'll you see *these* birds fly. They're enlightened."

Angela took out her camera, snapped a picture of the Thunderdudes, then announced she would take no more pictures until they were in the air.

"I have to conserve my film," she said, tapping her camera.

Hubert soaked up the ocean of sky, then beheld the flowing sea of the Greenways. Are we hypnotized? he wondered. An image came to him: a boomerang thrown into the distance, curving around, coming back. He froze it far out. He unfroze it, but kept the boomerang at the outermost stretch of its journey, sliding it back and forth through a narrow arc. The image of the sliding boomerang reflected glints of sunlight, and lit up Hubert's mind.

Are we hypnotized?

He threw thousands of boomerangs in his mind, seeing them only as they sliced through that flitting blip of apogee. They began taking on reality. Some became blue spangles— the sky. Some flickered green—the grass. Some, in gaudy display, became the Thunderdudes, the crowd, Mel and Clem, Ralph and Angela. Hubert raised an open hand before him and tossed invisible boomerangs. They flared to brief life at apogee, forming his hand, forming the intricate swirls of his fingerprints.

Do we see just that flicker out there, billions of flickers per second, forming our world? Are we not here except to catch those flickers?

Are we hypnotized?

If Angela's mind stopped taking pictures, like her camera, would Angela not be here?

Hubert gazed upon the throng. Huge, it swept out of sight in both directions. He glanced across the land. Light in the transient mode of the Impressionists reached his eyes—ephemeral, elusive. There!

There it was. A brief view of another reality behind the steady illusion. But it was *so* quick.

Hubert sensed a huge web of consciousness all around him, boomerang spangles flickering madly, shooting out from every being, all coordinated with mathematical precision, a spinning web of world illusions knitting all around, agreements everywhere to avoid glitches.

How are we doing this? The thought made him dizzy. Is there a godlike mind within each of us?

Where are you, Chad? You're a part of us.

But then, thought Hubert, so are those evil mutants. They're a part of us, also.

Cloak of body, cloak of mind. Is that how it is? Hubert looked at himself, at the bodies around him. Are these garments? Where is our Being?

He scanned the sky, and he scanned the Greenways. Cloak of sky, cloak of earth.

This is our play. Our stage. We stand upon it and *wham!* It becomes real.

He took a breather from his musings. It looked like the Thunderdudes were about to get under way.

A burst of anticipation was in the air, a hush that seemed almost like a cheer. The Thunderdudes were moving down the

taxiway. They flowed to the runway in sharp single-file formation, then fanned out into takeoff position.

"Th' Dudes is ready."

It was a potent voice, alive through the crowd. Hubert
looked about.

"That's the voice of the Universe, Hubert," said Clem. "It's
the narrator for the Thunderdudes."

"Sounds disguised."

"The Universe wears many disguises, Hubert, old boy,"
said Ralph.

That's not Ralph, thought Hubert, looking at the tyke
perched upon Clem. That's not the little Ralphie we brought
with us this morning.

He returned his gaze to the runway.

"An' th' Dudes is off," said the narrator.

The six Thunderdudes sped down the runway, moving left
to right, then rocketed into the air in tight delta formation.

"Go, Dudes, go!" cried Clem.

"Go, Dudes, go!" cried Ralph.

They rose sharply through a layer of humid air, creating
vapor phantoms on their leading edges. The two soloists
peeled off and shot to opposite ends of the horizon.

"Watch th' Dudes in diamond formation," said the voice of the
Universe.

In perfect diamond formation, four Thunderdudes arced
into a wide turn and flew past the crowd. The diamond circled wide and wove a spell through the air.

"Diamond Dudes in figga eights!" cried the Universe.

Hubert watched the graceful rolls and turns. It was as if
four birds shared one consciousness. As if they'd become one

bird, an infinitely agile bird weaving artful geometries through the air.

The diamond tore apart and the four Dudes shot straight up.

"Dudes in starburst!" cried the voice of the Universe.

Hubert looked up, up, up ...

The four Dudes split apart and curved upward and outward in four different directions to enter the upper atmosphere.

"Dudes outta sight!"

They were gone; too high to be seen. Hubert scanned the sky, remembering the two soloists. Where'd they go?

"Looky he-ah, looky he-ah!"

The voice of the Universe seemed to be right in front of Hubert. He looked straight ahead to the far horizon and saw a dot in the shimmering air.

The dot grew larger as it approached, a silent, dreamy vision. How fast is that bird moving? wondered Hubert.

It swept closer ... closer ... Then it seemed to tip some barrier, and its speed left the realm of imagination and exploded into the realm of blazing streaks.

The second soloist passed overhead from behind the crowd, and the two Dudes split the air over the runway, passing one another with scant feet to spare, then shot to opposite horizons.

"Dudes in head-on!" cried the voice of the Universe.

An electric current shot through the crowd. Hubert felt like he was standing on air. He looked down, stamped his feet on the ground, anchoring himself. He looked up and saw the diamond approach from the right.

The Dudes in diamond dipped low, leveled out, and zoomed over the runway. Tracking left, they rose in an arc. Up and up they went, curving, growing tiny, now upside down, looping over, then back down, down, down, screaming toward the earth.

"Dudes loopin' out!" cried the Universe.

The Thunderdudes pulled out and leveled off a few feet above the earth. They flew down the runway and rose into another arc as before. Hubert tracked them, curving up, up ... over ... upside down ... tracking right ...

"Dudes a-twistin' in air!"

The four Dudes in diamond barreled over, righting themselves, then began a new arc ... up ... up ... higher ... higher ... at the top ...

Hubert saw them as four dots on high, tearing through the apogee. They curved into the downward stroke, coming in from the left, and became earthward bound.

Wisps of clouds obscured them. They reappeared, breaking through the clouds. Hubert strained his neck, shaded his eyes. They screamed toward earth. Hubert went into spasms of body English, trying to pull the birds out from what appeared to be an imminent collision with earth.

The Dudes stayed in their perfect arc, curved just in time and leveled off, skimming across the ground.

"Dudes makin' you sweat!" cried the voice of the Universe.

Hubert had been holding his breath. Now he exhaled, openmouthed. He heard a communion of exhalations as the Dudes tore down the runway, tracking right. They rose and flew toward the horizon. Hubert craned his neck to see. The whole crowd was watching the Dudes in diamond race into the distance.

A Dude screamed low over the crowd from the blind side.

Thousands and thousands of willies sprang from their crypts and tore in horrific splendor up the spines of their hosts. Acres of electricity zipped through the web of bodies. The crowd was zapped.

Hubert shot into the air a ways and landed splat against the purple dwarfs. He regained his feet and witnessed insanity. The birds are in goo-goo land, he thought. Thousands of wings were sent flapping, creating a chaos of wind storms. Dodos danced as if on hot, jagged rocks. Dodos hooted shuddering oaths. Dodos spinning. Dodos wheeling. Dodos yodeling. Dodos forming into tornados, tracking across the land.

Hubert hugged the hedge of purple dwarfs as a maelstrom raged about him. He saw Clem levitating in demonic fury. Little Ralph upon his back cried "Yippee!" and rode him like a bucking bronc. He saw Angela snap a picture of Ralph and Clem. Dodos screamed and screamed and tore round and round; green and purple dust clouded the air, and feathers rained everywhere.

And then the storm died out.

And laughter filled the air.

"A Dude a-sparkin' yo' willies!" growled the Universe.

Hubert glanced around, amazed at the abrupt transformation. Dodos were joshing with one another. Dodos wandered, finding where they had been. Clem came back, Ralph hanging on, convulsing with laughter.

"See, what did I tell you, Hubert?" said Clem. "Goo-goo land. It's easy to startle dodos. Humans too." Clem spun around, did a little dance. "Oh, what a frolic this is, everyone."

Hubert plucked a feather off his shirt, tossed it away, and turned to the runway.

"How 'bout that maestro Dude a-cookin' an' a-whippin' up yo' willies?" cried the Universe.

"More, more!" cried Ralph.

"Hush, Ralph," said Clem. "You'll alienate these birds. They can take only so much before they flip into a goo-goo land of no return. They've had their fill of willies for a while, I'm afraid."

"Ah ..." whined Ralph.

"Soloists a-duelin'!" cried the Universe.

The soloists were flying at each other over the runway. Upside down, on edge, back and forth they went, zipping past each other with feet to spare. Abruptly, they shot away and joined the diamond coming in from the left.

"Six Dudes a-loopin'!"

They came in low, rose in an arc, and looped around. Screaming toward earth, they leveled out and tore down the runway. Abruptly, all six Dudes stood on their tails and shot skyward, turning on the afterburners.

"Dudes a-streakin' fo' th' heavens!"

Hubert gazed up at the Dudes, but they were gone, out of sight.

"Dudes in starburst, in outta space!" cried the Universe.

Holy Christ! muttered Hubert to himself. A minute passed. He looked around. The crowd was busy searching the air.

"Look at the horizon, Hubert and Angela," whispered Clem.

Hubert looked.

"Dudes, Dudes everywhere!"

Hubert turned around, looking everywhere. Six distant dots, spaced evenly around the horizon, came closer ... closer ...

Hubert shivered. These birds like to cut it close. If they screw up? He shivered again.

"Dudes a-comin' on!"

Hubert, with the rest of the crowd, ducked on impulse as the six Dudes, screaming in from different points of the compass, met in a stack over the runway. They shot through to the horizon all around.

Hubert let out his breath. The crowd unloaded a nervous exhalation. *"Ah ..."* was the collective sigh.

"Dudes is done!" cried the voice of the Universe.

The Thunderdudes toured the air over the Greenways, dipping to catch the applause and cheers, then sped to cruising altitude and set a course for the mountains. Hubert watched them disappear from view. We've got to get home, too, he thought, staring at the distant mountaintops.

"Hoot!" A scorching command lashed into Tim's consciousness. Tim read its tone: *Get out of my way!*

He spun around, razors at the ready, and found himself standing face to face with a menacing runner from the guard pool.

Tim stepped back to create a space between him and the guard. He glanced around and saw other runners. He saw Vince. They were spread out, moving like an iron net through the crowd.

He stared into the face of the guard who was advancing on him, read his tone: *self-important, superior, politically connected.* A punk's face.

"Zack, do you see what's going on?"

"I see what's going on, Tim," said Zack, maneuvering through the crowd toward Clem. "I don't like how it's shaping up."

Tim, keeping his eyes on the punk, sent Zack a silent message: *I'll meet you in the mountains.*

With one slash of his razor claws, Tim ripped out the punk's heart. He slashed him again and tore off one of his legs.

The guard, a gaping hole in his chest, a leg gone, a surprised, dumb look on his face, toppled over.

Screams broke out. The crowd scattered.

Tim whirled.

He tried to read Vince's intentions. The big Captain of the Guards was inscrutable. To survive in the hierarchy, he had to be a cipher, a servant to the dainty ones. But Vince had been a true warrior at one time, thought Tim. He must hate their lily-livered guts.

The crowd scattered as the iron net of guards advanced on Clem and his human companions. Zack reached the hedge and began making his way toward Clem, cycing the guards. Clem and the humans stared at the oncoming guards, their backs pressed to the hedge.

Tim, hoping to spread the guard unit in disarray, assumed the fallen guard's position in the net and began walking toward Clem.

What sort of strange operation is this? he wondered. These idiots just saw me kill one of them, but they make no move against me, not even to protect themselves. Iron discipline, he reasoned. Vince must have drilled certain rules into them. It'll be their deaths when the underground makes its move. Vince, are you with us? Are you working for us on the inside? Training these punks to be idiots?

Tim saw the Englishman unsling his rifle. The oldest Barney did the same. They better not shoot me, he thought. I can't be bothered with that now.

The net advanced.

The crowd was gone.

Nothing stood between them and Clem.

"Vince," yelled Tim, "we won't let you take Clem!"

No response.

Tim looked at the humans.

"Don't shoot us!" he yelled, pointing at himself and Zack. "We're going to protect Clem!"

Zack, close to the humans now, turned and faced the advancing guards.

What a mess, thought Tim. Not like the old days. Vince has them under his control, but for what idiot purpose? Then Tim saw it. And it happened quickly.

A guard stood up from behind the hedge, plucked the small human from Clem's back, and took off running.

Vince and the other guards leaped the hedge and caught up with their comrade. The small human was passed to Vince. Vince tucked him under wing and tore across the savanna. The others fanned out to protect Vince's flank.

Tim stood transfixed.

Zack stood by the hedge.

Clem and the humans scrambled over the hedge and gave chase, Clem at half-cheetah speed, max speed for hatchlings, the humans considerably slower.

Tim ran to Zack.

"What'll we do?"

Zack remained silent.

"We can follow them to the Spiderweb."

"A price'll be on our heads now, Tim."

"The mountains?"

"It would be nice to take Clem along."

"He's attached to the humans. Headstrong. It'll be the death of him yet."

"Tim!"

It was shouted from behind him. Tim whirled and saw the crusader.

"Give me a ride to the Spiderweb!"

Tim studied him.

"Is that an order, Mr. ...?

"My name is Chad Garrick. Why are you wasting time?"

The crusader looked furious. Tim turned to Zack.

"What do you think?"

"We can't have a human give us orders."

"Right. You decide for yourself, Zack. So will I." Tim paused. "Okay, what's your decision?"

"It might be an interesting trip."

"I was thinking the same thing. Maybe we'll uncover Vince's role in the Universe. I think he's with us, but—"

"If he's with us, we can't spoil his cover. Steer clear of Vince, Tim."

"Good thinking, Zack. You are the rebel leader, as always." He turned toward Chad, bent low. "Hop on."

Chad swung aboard Tim. Tim and Zack leaped the hedge and set a swift pace for the Spiderweb.

"Uh ... Chad, what are your intentions?" asked Tim.

"The Barneys and the Brit have to save themselves," said Chad.

"Even the littlest one?"

"Yes. And I have to save Clem."

Tim turned toward Zack.

"A funny lot, these humans."

"You know, Tim," said Zack. "Maybe not so funny. If we salvage Clem with this mission, I'll begin to take a kinder look at heroic rescues."

"You do and we'll be staring extinction in the face yet, Zack, old boy."

Roger was hurting. He felt searing pain in his chest where Clem had kicked him. It worsened with each jarring footfall, with each torturous breath. But he had to run, and he had to breathe.

When he filled his lungs, jagged pains rocked him. So he took slow, shallow breaths, and kept on running. He mustn't dishonor the Spiderweb. He mustn't lose face in front of his friends.

They had skirted the Greenways. They had traversed field and grove, and now the bur oaks were in sight.

Roger, leading his two pals, entered the shadows of the oaks. He knew another world lay ahead. He shivered. He felt ill. Feverish.

He slowed.

His pals slowed. They had to obey him. Maurice had put him in charge.

Roger began walking. His pals walked silently behind him.

Why aren't I healing?

Since the fight with Clem, Roger had been fuming. At first, to himself, he denied that the fight had even happened. Later, he decided that it did happen, but that he had trounced Clem.

In the blanketing coolness of the oaks, his pain grew worse. He struggled for breath.

In school he had been taught that dodos had fast-healing bodies and near-magical powers of regeneration—except for the dainty ones.

If you have a dainty genetic structure, like hierarchical mutants are known to possess, you're plumb out of luck, the teacher had said. This had drawn much laughter from the students; no one there imagined that *they* could be a mutant.

Am I a mutant? wondered Roger.

No. I couldn't be. Clem is evil. There was no fight. He has hurt me from a distance, using sorcery. He is a hateful dodo. He might not even be a dodo. He is probably a human in disguise.

Roger poured out his hatred for Clem. It made him feel better. His pain lessened. He took some deeper breaths. He felt some jagged pains, but not as bad as before. He turned toward his pals.

"We're going to kill Father Barney and Mother Barney as soon as we see them," said Roger.

"We have to wait for orders, Roger."

"I give the orders!"

"But—"

"Clem is trying to kill us from a distance. You both feel pain, right? Admit it!"

"No—"

"Admit it!"

"Okay, Roger. Calm down. Yes, I feel pain."

"So do I," said the other dodo.

"You see?" said Roger. He coughed explosively, felt like he was being dashed upon jagged rocks. His pain, in all its full-blooming glory, came exploding back for an instant. Then the pain began to have a strange tonic effect—his pals were also hurting; Clem was trying to kill them from afar, also.

"Killing Father Barney and Mother Barney will break the spell," said Roger. He was convinced of this. It *had* to be true. "Then we'll go back and watch Clem hang for his crimes. We'll also kill Big Brother Barney, Sister Barney"—Roger coughed—"and Little Brother Barney." He coughed and coughed.

"But they'll all be dead before we get back, Roger. Maurice said—"

"Shut up, you fool! Maurice is half-bonkers most of the time. He's a mutant. Can't you tell by his dainty body?" Roger coughed and coughed. "Obie has the power, I'm telling you."

Roger didn't know if this was true or not, but he hated mutants, and Maurice was obviously not a standard-looking dodo. He fell into another coughing spell, then said, "Keep it to yourselves, friends. We perform well today, and we'll be rewarded plenty."

Roger picked up the pace.

They ran through the bur oaks, then through the wound in the earth.

Leaving the shadows of the oaks behind, they entered another world. They spread across the grasslands. Miles separated them. They sent silent signals through the air, casting them-selves farther and farther into the new territory, in search of the Barneys' home.

Marshall was beyond the bur oaks, on earth-plane territory, when he spotted a grassy concavity in the earth. "Hoo-ray!" he shouted, angling toward the inviting hollow.

He slid into it, then lazed around, cupped by the earth and its wind-blown grass. He dropped into a meditative state and silently intoned the flying *sutra*. Moments later, he rose a foot off the ground and hovered.

Marshall was in seventh heaven.

It had been a long, tiring day, with travels with Drakon, sparring with Chad, and, more recently, Marshall's latest sci-entific investigation: tracking a pride of lions, studying their behavior, learning more about survival and death.

While observing the lions as they rested in the heat of the day, knowledge had hit Marshall with double barrels, almost simultaneously.

Chad was on his way to Spiderweb One with a clarified mission: He would let the Barneys fend for themselves. But he would rescue Clem, thereby halting the new Dodo religion in its tracks.

Marshall was ecstatic.

Then the Universe had clobbered him with a second knowledge hit: Dodoland would be destroyed by the end of the day. Military authorities in Washington, D.C., with a spy in the Spiderweb, were committed to pushing the doomsday button.

Marshall had collapsed.

"The dainty ones!" he had cried. "They have ruined everything for us!" He wailed, then fell silent.

Plan B!

Marshall rose, stood on wobbly legs, and steadied himself as the Dodo Spirit whispered to him. Marshall nodded. Yes, there is always a way.

Hearing inner music, Marshall began to dance. He spun into a tornado and tracked across the land, hooting out his requests. The Universe hooted back.

Plan B was approved.

Marshall would implement it.

He turned his face to all of Dodoland and filled his lungs. Silent sounds issued from him, scratching on the web of consciousness.

It was done.

Marshall could do no more.

He must wait, like everyone else.

Confident, Marshall strode about and found the lions he'd been observing. They attacked him, but Marshall easily outran them.

Marshall, feeling younger than he had in years, decided to go to earth for a spell. There was time.

He raced through the bur oaks, through the wound in the earth, and went exploring. He found Pioneer and Cassandra corralled in a birch grove. The horses became nervous when they saw Marshall peering in at them. Marshall left them alone and ran across the prairie, feeling the wind in his face, recalling the days of yore when he was a warrior, spilling blood on the plain.

Horrible!

He shuddered.

Never again.

It came back to haunt him. The dainty ones. Our curse.

Silence, commanded Marshall. It was not a day for thinking of the past; it was a day for action. A day for Plan B. Survival depended upon it.

Marshall, tiring, headed back to the bur oaks. That is when he saw the grassy concavity in the earth. So inviting.

Hovering on his bed of grass, Marshall heard running feet. He bent his ears to the sound: *three young dodo punks on a mission.*

He settled to the ground, sat up, looked around, and spied them. *Hmmm …* The three were separating, fanning out. Curious, Marshall stood.

The punks topped a low hill, vanished.

Then knowledge hit; he learned the punks' mission. Marshall was shocked. Heat rose within him, a blistering anger. I must get help. But who?

Were other dodos out, on day excursions to earth? Were any old warriors around? Marshall ran in circles, hooting. Then he ran like a raging river, searching everywhere. He was miles from the wound in the earth when he saw a house in the woods.

Marshall squeezed through the woods, crashed through a thicket, peered through dense foliage. A heartbeat later, a man and a woman rushed from the dwelling.

The man wore eyeglasses, had a mustache, had shadowlike scars on his face. He was gripping a rifle, looking around frantically. The woman, hanging back, had a look of pure terror on her face.

Marshall sniffed the air. Knowledge hit: these people were Chad's parents.

Knowledge hit again. Marshall learned what they had been doing to Chad, what they had done to Milky.

Marshall flew into a rage.

He exploded from the woods.

The rifle came up, but Chad's parents collapsed, and the gun discharged into the ground. Marshall took both of them under wing.

He would carry them to the Spiderweb, where, if there was a trace of the old ways left, justice would be meted out.

He set a course for the bur oaks, feet flying—cheetah speed.

Nine

❧ THE TRIAL ☙

*A*ndrew stood at his post by the door in the Great Hall. His services had not been called upon since he had un-scrolled the wall map for Maurice. His eyes took in a dusky view of the conference table, seated around which were Charles Barbier; Obie, Captain of the Jail; and Chairman Maurice. His ears took in their patchy conversations. His mind heard silent pleas from Charles.

You show me how, Andrew.

You show me how to escape.

How to save the others.

You're the only god in residence.

Lend a hand!

Andrew blew a cool chuckling wind into the mind of the catechism writer. He felt Charles's flesh shiver. He sensed the impatience that gripped Maurice, the butterflies that mi-grated in great waves through Obie's gut.

You have every reason to be fearful, Obie, thought Andrew.

Maurice already has your successor picked out—a punk from the guard pool. Maurice likes punks. They're more impressionable, less likely to rebel, glad for the small favors. But you, cagey veteran Obie, *you* make Maurice nervous.

Andrew conjured a sound—*keeesh!*—and sent it rolling through the hall. The three at the table looked around, shrugged. Charles went back to writing.

A plan you want, Charles?

Keeesh! The sleek sound of an ax being sharpened on a spinning grindstone rolled through the hall. The three looked up again. *Keeesh!* filled the room.

Thoughts swam from Andrew's mind, swam to Charles's mind.

Keeesh!

Charles was struck by a sudden inspiration. Hanging is an immoral practice and has to end. Beheadings, on the other hand, serve a higher moral purpose and must begin. But can these birds wield axes? Yes, they can. Their wings are adaptable.

He was convinced. These birds have to start chopping heads off. Every dodo head in the land. The survivors ...

A haunting chuckle flew into Charles's mind. He saw a vision of mass beheadings, saw headless dodos tearing around. Not every dodo got up after decapitation; some lay still after a few feeble kicks, dead. The survivors were sprouting new heads.

Survivability.

The acid test.

True dodos can regenerate their heads, mutants can't.

Charles, writing the plan into the catechism, cast a glance at Maurice. You mutant scum, he thought, we'll see how this'll grab you.

Charles heard—and felt—that cool, biting chuckle again. It crept around him and cloaked him in ice. He mentally tore the icy coat off and cast it to Maurice. He thought he saw the bird's feathers quake.

Charles gathered the pages he had just written and slid them across the table to Maurice.

"Chairman Maurice, I'd like your opinion on this section of the catechism."

The dodo chairman gripped the pages in his wings and began to read.

Well, well, well … let me see … what has Charles penned here …?

Maurice flipped through the pages, checking to see if they were in proper numerical sequence, then began to read.

And it came to pass, when Messiah Clem drove the scribes from the bazaar, that a new law was upon the land.

Oh, pray, Messiah Clem, saith Ralph Barney, tell us what this new law is.

It is darkness, it is curtains, it is flames flickering out, saith the Lord.

Oh, must thou speak in parables? saith Angela Barney. Must thou be forever cryptic, Messiah Clem?

Still thy tongue, Angela. It is not for humans to know. It is a law for dodos.

And does Mighty Maurice give his approval? saith Hubert Barney. So that we may trust in the wisdom of this dark, secret law?

Messiah Clem saith, Mighty Maurice hath wrote, Whosoever believeth in this law shalt be saved.

And did the ancients prophesy this law? saith Hubert Barney. So we may bathe in sacred wine?

Do not lust after the ancients' wisdom, saith the Lord. They were dead before thy time. Trust only in Mighty Maurice. For he hath given his only begotten son—

Clem, saith Ralph Barney, are thou the son of Maurice?

I am the Lord, saith Clem.

Maurice paused. Do I want that? He mulled the concept over. Well, it might be okay. If it proves to muddy the waters, we'll just remove it later.

"Charles," said Maurice, "this bit about me being Clem's father—does that make me God?"

"Yes, Chairman Maurice. Is that too broad for now? We can draft it in later, if you prefer."

"Uh ..." Maurice fanned his beak. He ignored Charles's question and continued to read.

The three Barneys sank to Clem's feet and kissed his toes.

Oh, these are the toes of Maurice, saith Angela Barney.

Oh, these razors are sharp, saith Ralph Barney.

Oh, saith Hubert Barney, the darkness, the curtains, the flames flickering out. Messiah Clem, wouldst thou elaborate so dodos everywhere will heed thy new commandment?

Verily I saith unto thee, Whosoever hath their head chopped off and rises shalt be saved.

Oh, Messiah Clem, saith Angela Barney, watch out!

Ralph Barney came at the Lord with a sharpened ax and chopped the Lord's head off. Clem ran headless in circles. His neck wound closed. It created its own air passage. Its cells in bloody baths became undifferentiated and multiplied, becoming specialized cells, and formed a perfect new head for the Lord. This took two days.

Ralph did my bidding, saith the Lord. I was sacrificed; my head was chopped off; I rose. Verily I saith unto thee, all dodos except mutants possess this trait.

And Mighty Maurice, saith Hubert Barney, is he next to be sacrificed, his head chopped off, and to rise?

Verily I saith unto thee, Maurice is next.

Maurice rose to his feet. He stared at the papers. This is going off on a tangent. Then the full impact hit him. *No, no, no …* He dropped the papers. They had become ice in his wings. He shivered. Visions of a sharp ax at his neck gushed into his mind.

He stumbled backward in blind terror, fell over his chair.

"No! No axes! Clem will hang!"

Then, thinking that hanging might not be enough to kill Clem, Maurice lost control. His wings fanned up violent winds. He went stark raving bonkers. He yodeled obscene tunes, spun through the room, caught vague impressions of furious activity around him.

Charles slid from his chair and ran to the nearest wall. Obie scrambled over the table and tore after him.

Charles leaped high, grabbed the tight mesh, and became like an insect, climbing ever higher.

Obie crashed into the wall, sent furious waves up the webbing.

The wall bucked insanely beneath Charles. He focused on each handhold, each toehold, willed himself to keep climbing.

He reached the ceiling, clung upside down like a monkey, and crawled to the nearest aperture. This was easier; Obie had stopped banging the wall; the ceiling was like a calm upside-down sea.

Charles pulled himself through the opening, lay on the roof, and looked down into the Great Hall.

Maurice had fallen out of his frenzy and was wandering around, looking dazed. Obie was gathering up the pages of the catechism—they had taken flight and lay scattered about the vast chamber. Suddenly, Maurice snapped to, looked at Obie, and flew into a rage.

"What are you doing? Guards! Guards!"

"I'm picking up the catechism, Maurice."

"You are not authorized to read the catechism. Guards!"

The door flew open and guards poured in. Charles gasped at their size; they were like sumo wrestlers, twice the size of normal dodos.

"Where is Charles?" screamed Maurice, looking around. He fixed his eyes on Obie. "You let him escape!"

"No!" shouted Obie. "He's up there." He pointed up at Charles. *"You* let him escape with that tantrum of yours." Obie took a step toward Maurice. Maurice shrank back. *"You* scattered the papers with your demonic wings."

The guards seemed split in their loyalties; some stood by silently; others milled about.

Maurice regained some of his composure.

"We'll discuss this later, Obie." His voice squeaked with faint annoyance. "You did not read the catechism?"

"No."

"Good. It needs ... revisions."

The guards relaxed.

"Maurice"—Obie pointed upward—"Charles is not going anywhere, is he?"

"Uh ..." Maurice looked up at Charles. "No. He's still our prisoner."

Don't trust him, Obie, thought Charles. Make your play. Rip his mutant throat out.

"Obie," yelled Charles, "Maurice is a mutant. The catechism calls for all dodos to have their heads chopped off. Only true dodos will survive. Maurice won't survive. Seize the reins, Obie!"

Everyone below stared up at Charles. Charles, looking down into their faces, saw it. Good God! They're all mutants. Like a surging sea, the dodos began moving toward the door.

Charles rolled away from the sunroof, bounced to his feet, and ran, or tried to—it was like stepping in springy quicksand. He skirted the other sunroofs and bounced-ran to the nearest edge. He lay flat and peered over, his heart tripping out.

Forty feet below, guards were fanning out, looking up. Charles drew back.

"I saw him!" one of them shouted.

That section of the hall began to bounce. Charles crawled away. His mind worked furiously: They've got me surrounded. They can't climb, but can they fly? He searched the surrounding area. The Great Hall was anchored to several enormous trees by stout lines. At the far end, the tree branches hung over the roof like a jungle.

Bouncing along on all fours, Charles headed for the jungle. He drew closer and closer, but it gave him scant comfort. He knew they could chart his progress from below. They would know just exactly where he was going, and why.

Fear seized him.

But anger fueled him on. He had responsibilities. People were in danger.

Within striking distance of the jungle, fatigue leveled him.

He lay gasping. He eased himself to the nearest sunroof, snuck his eyes over the edge, peered down.

Maurice and Obie were seated at the table, going through the catechism. Two of the sumo-sized guards were stationed at either end of the table. Andrew stood by the door.

Suddenly, Maurice looked up.

"Where's Charles now?"

"Resting, apparently," said Obie.

"We need him. Andrew, front and center!"

Maurice turned back to the catechism, did some paging.

"We cannot long remain a society without a catechism," he said. "The common run of dodos are irresolute, self-indulgent children. They run about like sheep—baa ... baa ... And like sheep they become easily scattered, easily seduced by the sins inherent in sheep. We need the glue of a catechism to hold dodo society together, Obie. We need a messiah to hold over dodos, like a shepherd's staff—to consecrate the worthies, to cuff the recalcitrants."

Andrew stepped to the table and stood by Maurice. Maurice eased back in his chair and fanned his beak, ignoring Andrew.

"Dodos must be protected from humans, Obie," said Maurice. "Remember Mauritius?"

"Yes, Chairman Maurice, I remember."

"Every last dodo wiped out."

Obie winced.

Maurice made as if to wipe a tear from his eye, then went back to fanning his beak.

"We must have our own religion here in Dodoland, Obie."

"Yes, Chairman Maurice."

"Our own anointed one."

"Yes."

"Our own messiah."

"Yes."

"Crusades."

"Yes, Chairman Maurice. Crusades against the infidels."

"Razors honed. Battalions ready."

Obie popped to his feet. He saluted Maurice.

"Yes, sir, General Maurice."

"Our precious ground collides with Big Mother Earth, Obie. So, we are a part of Earth, and we will—we must—inherit all of Earth from the humans, or, inevitably, face another Mauritius somewhere down the road."

"Yes, sir."

"Humans have no defense against razors from out of nowhere."

"Yes, sir." Obie sat and resumed arranging the pages of the catechism.

Maurice looked at Andrew.

"Andrew, do you accept Clem as your savior?"

Andrew remained silent. Maurice and Obie burst out laughing. The two guards near the table snickered.

"Andrew," shouted Maurice, sitting bolt upright and pointing above, "to the roof. Bring Charles down. We need his writing skills. Hop to it."

Andrew stick-walked to the wall and made like a spider.

Charles, staring at the figure of death scampering up the wall, heard Maurice say something to Obie. He had to strain his ears to hear. Maurice was using a hushed tone, but the hall gathered its echo and funneled it up to Charles:

"Obie, not all dodos will be amenable to our catechism. Not everyone has a religious spirit. But we must bring Clemianity to all who are reachable. To the hatchlings especially. Stake out the eggs."

"Yes, sir."

"Build more jail cells and prepare for mass executions. I fear we may have to execute legions of pagan and heretical dodos during the purification process."

"Yes, sir."

"And, Obie, send missionaries to the hinterlands. We need to recruit more guards. You know the material we are looking for?"

"Yes, sir."

"Nothing but the finest young dodos, Obie."

"Yes, sir."

Charles drew away from the sunroof in horror. Andrew was an upside-down monkey on the ceiling now, making a beeline for Charles. Charles sprang to his hands and knees and bounced toward the jungle of tree branches. He glanced back. The roof dimpled furiously in a mad rush toward him. Suddenly, Andrew popped up from a sunroof and landed on all fours. Charles lunged for the trees, hearing the quick flap-flap of pursuit behind him.

Charles sprang onto a branch, scrambled higher.

He heard rustling behind him.

He climbed higher, branch after branch, twenty feet, thirty feet, forty feet above the roof of the hall. Moving deeper into the foliage, he reached the trunk, swung up to the next branch, and looked down.

Andrew was on the branch below him, staring up.

His eyes ...

Charles, insane, spinning, raving, fell into those eyes ...

When he woke, he was rocking himself back and forth, back and forth, in fetal position.

Abruptly, he stopped rocking and looked about. A burbling stream was close by, green grass was all around, a circle of trees, blue sky.

He rejoiced.

Andrew, the only god in residence, had saved him.

Somehow ...

Charles stood.

"You're still in the tree, Charles."

Chills raced up his spine. He whirled.

A man in black, holding a staff, stepped from the forest.

"Andrew is my window onto the Spiderweb," said the man. He walked up to Charles.

"You're—"

"Drakon."

"You—you—you—" stammered Charles, a million thoughts colliding in his mind. "You're a god!"

"An elemental."

"You have the dodos on your stringer. You know what they're up to, then?"

"Yes."

"Stop their insanity!"

"I can't step between anyone and their karma. Karma must have its play. Deny it and you only delay it."

Fear leaped through Charles. He darted his eyes about, looking for an escape.

"How'd I get here?"

"Forget about leaving, Charles. As I said, you're still in the tree."

"Oh?" Charles hit himself in the chest. He felt the blows. He heard the resounding thumps. "It seems like I'm right here."

Drakon whipped his staff in artful whirls. Charles stared in disbelief as a small hole opened in the air before him. It hovered, grew larger. Charles looked into it ...

And saw Andrew on the branch below. Charles closed his eyes and lurched backward.

"Holy Christ!"

"Your consciousness is focused here now, Charles, not in the tree."

"Please explain, Drakon."

"Wherever we happen to be, Charles, we are powerfully attracted to that place; like electrons in orbit, we are held there by the force of karma. But karma can change; if you want to be elsewhere, you can be pulled through by those same powerful forces. You can enter other worlds. You appealed for help, Charles, that is why you are here. I pulled you in through a window."

"What can I do, Drakon, to save myself and the others?"

"In a moment, I will send you back to the tree. Andrew will take you down to the Great Hall. Henceforth, you must become like Andrew. You must model your behavior after his."

"Become like death?"

"Yes, but fling a twist into things now and then. It throws the birds off. You can take it from there, Charles. Your karma is kicking up powerful storms of freedom for you. All you have to do is keep gliding in the right direction."

Drakon whipped his staff in violent circles.

Charles found himself falling ... falling ... through that hole in the air ...

Charles, frozen to the tree limb, stared down into the face of death.

Andrew grabbed him and pulled him down. They tumbled through the foliage, Charles in Andrew's fearsome grip. Branches thwacked Charles—bloodied him, bruised him. He reeled from the blows, covered up like in the *dojo*—took his beating.

They landed on the roof of the Great Hall, bounced up once, twice, then Andrew somehow stopped their bouncing.

Like whispering air, Andrew crawled, not denting the roof, holding Charles on his back. Charles glanced around, wondered how Andrew was doing it—*not denting the roof!* Queasiness like a field of dandelions sprouted in Charles's stomach.

He remembered Drakon's injunction: *You must become like Andrew.*

Become like death.

But fling a twist into things now and then.

The death-stick Andrew reached a sunroof and dove into it.

Andrew's denim jacket flared; they fell in tandem, gliding on powerful currents of air, twisting, turning, coming in low over the conference table.

They stalled out and made a pancake landing on the table, creating a horrendous *Smack!*

Maurice bolted from his chair and flew into a frenzy of wing flapping and yodeling. Obie, on the other side of the table, did the same. Both birds spun around in tornados for a few seconds, clouding the air with dust and feathers and catechism papers. Then they were still.

Andrew released Charles.

Charles rolled off Andrew's back and fell to the table. He watched from the corner of his eye as Andrew levered himself off the table and onto the floor.

Charles, following suit, levered himself off the table and onto the floor, kept his face a death mask, kept his motions Andrew-like. He stick-walked around the table, headed toward his chair. He caught a glimpse of Andrew stick-walking back to his position by the door. He caught passing glimpses of Maurice and Obie. They stared, wide-eyed, open-beaked.

Charles took his chair, sat at rigid attention, staring vacantly.

Maurice and Obie entered his field of vision, taking seats directly across the table.

"Guards!" snapped Maurice. "The catechism! Gather it up!"

He looked at Charles for a moment, then turned to Obie and said in a quiet voice, "I think Andrew has killed Charles."

Obie nodded.

"He'll be easier to control now, Maurice."

"Of course."

Both birds bobbed their heads, looking across at Charles.

"Obie?"

"Yes, Maurice?"

"Don't you think it's time to check in with Vince and Roger?"

"Of course, Maurice."

Obie stood and walked toward the door.

Charles, maintaining death-like integrity, caught glimpses of the guards as they bustled about picking up pages of the wind-blown catechism. Ideas, infused with icy chuckles, began flooding his mind. He unlimbered slightly, reached for a pen and paper, and began writing.

"Charles, you're writing again," said Maurice. He sank back in his chair and fanned his beak for a moment, then leaned forward and in a lilting whisper said, "You gave me a jolly good idea, Charles." Maurice paused to cackle joyfully. "The ax. Now that you're dead, Charles, how would you like some company?" He cackled again, then stopped abruptly as Obie reentered the room.

"Report, Obie."

"Vince has the littlest Barney under wing and is heading our way. Clem and his followers are in pursuit. Roger and his two friends are closing in on the Barneys' house. Vince is now aware of Roger's mission and will use this to induce Clem's cooperation."

"Good job, Obie. Sit. You look weary."

"Thank you, Maurice."

Obie took his seat.

Charles saw only peripheral bouts of the struggle. He kept on writing despite the flying blood and feathers. The two sumo-sized guards jumped Obie. One of them had an ax. He hacked and hacked, and finally Obie's head flew off. Obie's body quivered, then lay still. The guard with the ax placed Obie's head upright in the middle of the conference table, a gory centerpiece.

Charles wondered why they didn't use their infinitely quicker and sharper razors instead of an ax. Are these Clemians forsaking their dodo heritage in favor of human implements?

The ax-wielding guard took a seat beside Maurice and set the ax on the table.

"The killer ax, Maurice," he said. "My razors are clean."

"Good job, Lute."

Charles, maintaining his death mask, nodded his inner head. The ax, not Lute, committed the murder. Lute was still a good Clemian.

"Charles, meet Lute, our new Captain of the Jail."

Charles kept on writing. Ideas continued to zip into his mind.

Finally, the catechism's crucifixion scenario was completed. He stick-walked it around the table and dropped it in front of Maurice.

Malcolm Moreland, a human, was to be the judge. He must decide if a dodo prisoner, Clem, or a human prisoner, Ralph Barney, was to die.

Chad Garrick, a human, was to be counsel for the dodo prisoner.

The human prisoner was to represent himself.

Malcolm Moreland was to decide that Clem must die, and that Ralph Barney was to go free.

Charles Barbier, a dead human, was to execute Clem by hanging him from the neck until dead-and-no-longer-walking-around. Then the body would be nailed to a cross for the sake of artists commissioned to do the official Clemianity portraits.

Malcolm Moreland, Ralph Barney, Chad Garrick, and Charles Barbier were to walk through Dodoland and enter the plane of earth. They were to be hated eternally by all dodos for the roles they played in Clem's crucifixion.

Chairman Maurice was to rally all Dodoland around Clem's crucifixion and launch crusades against all human-kind—razors from out of nowhere—until all hated humans were dead-and-no-longer-walking-around.

Maurice read with growing rapture.

Charles stick-walked back to his chair.

Finally, Maurice laid the papers down.

"Good job, Charles. Everything looks in order, except one thing—we can't let you go. We'd hate to lose your value as a writer. From now on, you are Dodoland's official court scribe."

Charles, wearing his best death mask, silently shot wild bucking oaths at Maurice. *That's what you think, you mutant scum!*

Tim and Zack raced over the ground. Chad held on tight, his staff clamped between his arms and thighs. He whispered to it: *Save Milky Barney! Save Milky Barney!*

He meant Ralph Barney. It was against the rules; the Barneys were supposed to save themselves. The staff had been explicit on that. Chad still had the bruise on his chest as a reminder.

But ...

Chad looked sideways. Hubert, Angela, and Mel were atop Zack. It had been a hasty arrangement, made amid much arguing and shouting. Hubert, to Chad's amazement, had implored him to save Ralph. Didn't Hubert know that Ralph must save himself?

Tim had decided on the split.

Chad understood why. Tim was going in for the kill; he wanted a fighter with him.

Zack is good for caution and counseling, Chad, old boy, Tim had said as they took off. *He'll settle them down. They're having emotional reactions right now. Zack will psychoanalyze them while we're rescuing the little human and Clem.*

It's against the rules, Chad had wanted to say to Tim. Ralph Barney must save himself. But Tim had taken off, and it had taken Chad's breath away.

Why were there such rules? wondered Chad.

But he already knew the answer: You become strong through adversity, through saving yourself.

Sure, there were exceptional cases, such as Clem. But the messiah was already strong, and wise, and he was up against forces that could be overpowering even to the strongest, so it was permissible to lend him a hand. Right, staff?

But the Barneys ...

They could save themselves.

They *had* to save themselves.

They *have* to be placed in danger and then they *have* to save themselves. Or they will be weaklings. Right, staff?

Chad stared at the passing ground. It was a blur. He looked ahead. Golden wave after golden wave of prairie rushed at him.

As Tim charged on, the staff whispered to Chad, not in words, but in shivering mind pictures.

A ton of bricks dropped on Chad.

Devious.

Tim, previously, had been resistant to saving Clem—or any dodo, or any human, for that matter. Zack too. But now Tim was charging on. And Zack was playing counselor for Hubert, Angela, and Mel. Both were committed to saving Ralph and Clem.

Why?

Because Chad, a human, had told Tim and Zack that he was going to save Clem, a dodo, and that the Barneys had to save themselves. This had worked powerful magic. It had tripped circuits, opened up new pathways, modified DNA.

The staff whispered: *Violate the rules, Chad!*

The message leaped through Chad like an electrical storm. His eyes became misty. He laughed silently into the powerful wind. Thank you, staff. So, the rules are secondary; DNA is supreme.

Chad scanned ahead. Clem, picking up some demon speed, was in view. The kidnappers were distant dots on the savanna. It looked like the enemy had slowed. They appeared to be milling around.

Violate the rules, thought Chad, laughing with the wind.

The messages—silent, encrypted—had flown on the wings of the air. Vince had paid careful attention.

Vince, hurry back. I had another flare-up with Chairman Maurice. The new guards obey him without question. He's forging our chains. I feel safe only when you're here.

Then Obie had detailed Roger and company's mission.

Hang it around Messiah Clem's neck. Coerce him into coming in peacefully, like a good little messiah.

Vince acknowledged the messages, then relayed his own: *Have littlest Barney under wing.*

He slowed and hooted harsh orders at the troops. They were to form a protective barrier between him and the pursuers.

Vince stopped, and the runners formed a semicircle. Vince stood behind them and faced the onrushing Clem.

"Don't commit self-slaughter, Clem." Vince's voice carried across the plain.

Clem came close, slowed, then tore back and forth, trying to get a better look at Vince.

"The littlest Barney is under my wing, Clem."

Clem stopped. "Release him!" he shouted.

"Clem, come with us peacefully. Face trial. Fulfill your destiny as messiah."

"Stuff it up your asshole!" shouted Clem.

"All Dodoland awaits you, Messiah Clem."

"Only dainty mutants await me. Release Ralph Barney or

face irreparable damage to your body, sissy. You can't regenerate."

Vince stared into the distance. He saw Tim and Zack coming on. Clem was racing back and forth again, looking for an opening. He rushed in, stopped, backed off. The runners stood their ground.

"You're all mutants!" shouted Clem. "One scratch could prove fatal. Give it up. Go hide in the woods. Your bodies are wretched instruments. They can't heal."

A murmur swept through the guards.

"What's 'e mean, Vince?" one of them asked, looking over his shoulder. "That ain't what we was taught in school."

"Turn around. Ignore him." Yes, thought Vince, most of you—maybe all of you—are mutants. Poor dumb, sickly things.

"Clem ..." Vince put power into his voice. He told Clem of Roger's mission. "He has two pals with him. You know Roger?"

"Yes." Clem's gaze became ferocious.

"They're camped near the Barneys' house. On my orders, they will kill Father and Mother Barney. Cooperate, Clem, or I'll transmit the kill command."

"Mutant, if what you say is true, then I have three more sissies to kill. That is the only difference."

Vince stared at Clem. This is not going to work. He looked at Tim and Zack. They were closing in, slowing down. They drew abreast of Clem and stopped, each with human cargo aboard.

Vince dropped into a deep meditative state. The flying *sutra* welled from the depths of his being, and he rose into the air, higher ... higher ...

Like distant echoes, he heard the cries of his troops.

"Hey, what's this?"

"What're you doin', Vince?"

"Hey, don't desert us!"

Vince caught fragments of the slaughter. The humans dropped from Tim and Zack, then Tim, Zack, and Clem rushed the guards and tore them to shreds. It was over in seconds.

Vince set sail for Spiderweb One, hooting a silent message to Obie: *I'm coming in with the littlest Barney. My troop has been destroyed. Messiah Clem is out of control.*

There was no response.

Vince tried again.

No response.

Have they killed you, Obie?

"Captain Marcus Will ..."

It was barely a whisper. For a moment, he thought it was his imagination or a trick of the wind playing in the trees.

"Captain Will ..."

Marcus Will left the shady side of his cage and walked into patterned brightness.

"Captain ..."

He heard rustling, saw movement outside his cell. There ... A hint of a presence. Crawling. The figure froze as a big dodo passed by. Then the figure resumed crawling.

She came into view. A woman wearing a leopard-pattern dress. Marcus crouched near her.

"How—"

"Shhh …" She held a finger to her lips. "I'm Sandra."

Marcus glanced around.

"You know I wouldn't want to see the dodos harmed," he said. "Not all of them anyway, maybe these zookeepers."

"I understand."

"I'm on their side, but it won't do any good." Marcus filled her in on the doomsday objective.

"They've had that in the works before," she said, frowning.

"This time they're going to blow this world to smithereens."

He searched her face. She was looking far away. Without meeting his gaze again, she pressed her hands to his through the vines and slipped away.

Marcus rose, stepped away from the vines. Her hands had been icy cold, like touching the earth on a raw winter's morning.

"Marshall …"

It was a human whisper, sailing through the wind.

Marshall was sitting in the middle of his cell, meditating. The whisper flowed into his consciousness again.

"Marshall …"

"Yes, what is it?" Marshall stood, walked to the webbing, peered about. "Who is there?"

"Over here."

Marshall walked along the webbing until he was beside the human.

"You look familiar," he said.

"I'm Sandra."

"Oh, yes. I remember."

"What happened?" she asked.

Marshall told Sandra about the three punk dodos going after Father and Mother Barney, and of his own impromptu snatching of Chad's parents after the horrendous knowledge hits at the Garrick homestead.

"Chad's parents are in cells, Sandra, down there." He pointed. "The Spiderweb employs huge Raj now. I was captured too."

Marshall raised a razor claw, slashed at the webbing of his cell. It stretched, too springy for him to cut.

Sandra pulled out her knife.

"Later," said Marshall. He looked about. "It's not safe to be out there now."

With one word, she changed the subject.

"Doomsday."

Marshall told her of his shattering knowledge hit earlier in the day. And of Plan B.

"So, Marcus is right," said Sandra.

"Marcus is right," said Marshall. "Human wings are preparing to take to the air."

"Will Plan B work, Marshall?"

"I certainly hope so, Sandra. If not, then the promise of dodo survivability will have been just an elaborate joke."

"I will have to tell Chad about his parents, and the Barneys about theirs," said Sandra.

"Chad's parents turn the living into ghosts," said Marshall. "The one called Milky ..." His voice darkened, and he told her what he knew of Milky.

Sandra reached through the webbing and patted Marshall's chest. Her hand felt icy. Marshall shivered, backed up, looked away. He did not care for tactile interaction; his realm was the world of the mind. He looked back at Sandra, but she was gone.

Earth touched me, Sandra, through you.

The pilot walked along the flight line, scanning the surrounding territory. It was nothing like his native Kansas; it wasn't as green, wasn't as tame. There were large tracts of wilderness out there. Large tracts of something else, too. Something that stretched the imagination.

His bomber squadron had flown in from their desert base during the night. He glanced at the hangers behind him, visualized the big black aircraft behind the doors.

Bats. Their nickname. They were so secret that not even the pilot, who was the squadron commander, knew what their official name was.

Bats. To some, watching the desert night sky, they were flying saucers. Whispering. Darting. They were experimental. Now operational. Perfect for a mission such as this.

The pilot scanned the horizon, checked his watch. The afternoon was winding down; the summer sun was pouring on the heat. The pilot caught a stiff gust of punishing air, desert hot.

An attack on U.S. territory is imminent, the mission commander had said.

The pilot was in the dark. All he knew was that they were going to destroy the threat using high-yield nuclear weapons.

In the dark …

The pilot did not like to be in the dark.

His thoughts returned to Kansas. His last visit had been two years ago, for his father's retirement party.

The rented dining hall had been packed. Wall-to-wall well-wishers. He knew none of the people there, except for his father and a smattering of relatives.

Dinner had been served.

Then the pilot's father had been served—roasted.

A parade of well-wishers made their way to the podium. The pilot's father laughed his way through an hour or so of slings and arrows. The last sling had come from his son.

The pilot had enlisted a few accomplices. Waiting in the wings were well-wishers with gifts for the new retiree: a brand-new wooden stepladder, a pair of yellow jeans, a yellow shirt. The yellow garments were not just yellow—they were *vivid* yellow.

The pilot stood at the podium as a CD player played a recording of a canary singing. Meanwhile, the well-wishers trooped in one by one with the gifts. Not a word was said. Suspense soared. Then the canary sounds stopped and a voice on the CD cut in:

"That was very good, Gerald."

Gerald was the pilot's father's name.

"Thank you," said another voice on the CD. It sounded like the pilot's father, but it was just a person who was good at doing voices.

"Now," the first voice went on, "that you've had your singing lesson, Gerald, let's get those yellow jeans and shirt on and … up on the ladder … and we'll begin your first flying lesson."

The well-wishers collapsed in laughter.

The pilot's father nearly died of laughter. He had said he wanted to follow in his son's footsteps and take up flying after retirement.

Less than one year later, the pilot's father was dead. A fast-acting cancer ate him. They put him in the ground. He never flew. The pilot missed the ceremonies.

Duty calls ...

The pilot stared at the land.

He walked toward mission headquarters. The latest satellite photos would be in. He thought the mission would commence before sunset. If so, the Bats would fly in daylight. Something they seldom did.

After the last mutant was torn asunder, Clem turned to his new companions.

"Tim and Zack, I believe?"

"Yes, Clem. I'm Tim, he's Zack."

"Pleased to meet you. We have no time to waste." Clem ran to the tight cluster of humans. Tim and Zack trailed.

"Hubert," cried Clem, "how far is it to your house from here?"

"I'd say about fifteen miles. But we have to save Ralph." Hubert looked to the western sky. Vince was now a mote hanging over distant trees.

"Hubert ..." Clem told him about Roger and his two pals. Mel, Angela, and Chad crowded around to listen. Sickening horror grew on their faces.

Angela looked at her watch.

"Mom and Dad usually don't get home for another hour or so," she said.

"Could he have been bluffing?" asked Mel.

"Not likely," said Clem. He looked at Tim and Zack. "Fly or fly?" he asked. It was dodo parlance for *Do you cover that distance faster in the air or on the ground?*

"Hmm …" Tim mulled it over. "Fifteen miles … We'll take to the air. We're not quite as zippy as the Thunderdudes, but we can move out pretty well once we've built up some steam."

"Hubert," said Clem, "guide them to your house."

"I'm going to stay and save Ralph. Angela can guide them."

"If we take the brats out quickly, Hubert," said Zack, "we can be back in time for the festivities at the Spiderweb. That so, Clem?"

"Yes. But use stealth as you approach the mutant's nest. No telling how things'll be standing. Go, Hubert. It's the best thing you can do at the moment."

Hubert looked at Angela.

"Angela doesn't have the rifle, Hubert," said Clem. "You might have to beat the bush to flush them out. You might have to shoot them—they're sissies—if Tim and Zack can't reach them with their razors."

"Go, Hubert," said Mel. "I've got my cannon. Ralph will keep till you get back."

"Go, Hubert," said Angela. "What if Mom or Dad comes home early?"

"Go, Hubert," said Chad. He raised his staff. "I can violate the rules now. Those mutants don't stand a chance."

Clem raked the air with his razors, emphasizing the point.

"That's right, Hubert," said Tim. "Actually, if you guide us to your house, and if you have to enter the brush where they're hiding, *you'll* be in the biggest danger of all. Am I right, Clem?"

"Right, Tim. Ralph is safe. They want to use him in a trade. Me for him. But—"

"We can't ask you to trade yourself for Ralph," said Hubert.

"I don't intend to, Hubert. The mutants will just go back on their word anyway."

"Courage, Hubert," said Mel.

"Go, Hubert," said Angela. "Be careful."

"We've no time to waste," said Clem.

Tim crouched low, and Hubert swung up. Then Tim and Zack meditated and rose into the air. They floated like balloons for a while, then moved out, heading southeast.

Clem looked at his remaining companions. Angela and Mel looked frightened. Not for themselves—for Ralph. I fibbed, he thought. Ralph may be in great danger. He may be dead already.

He looked at the newcomer.

"Chad, I believe?"

"Yes, Clem. I'm Chad Garrick. I'm a human."

Clem chuckled.

"I'm a dodo, Chad. Welcome aboard."

Chad raised his staff. "Drakon trained me."

"If Drakon is your *sensei*," said Clem, "then you're a valuable addition to our war party. Pray that Ralph is safe. We'll discuss strategy as we travel."

They headed across the prairie, toward the nearest grove of trees.

"We'll stick to the woods as much as possible," said Clem.

"Willies!" cried Angela. "We've got to move faster."

"Slithers!" shouted Chad. "They're called slithers."

Clem looked at the two youngsters.

"Air passages, Clem," said Mel. "They mean air passages."

"Oh. Yes." He glanced around as he walked. "Watch for them. Give a howl if you see one."

"Strategy, Clem," said Mel. "What's your plan?"

"Right now our biggest ally is the innate lack of organizational skill of dodos. We've always played things by ear—or by DNA, if you prefer. By organizing, the Spiderweb mutants are bucking a powerful tide of survivability."

"Dodos always seem to zip around without apparent plan or purpose," said Mel.

"On closer examination," said Clem, "there's *always* a plan and a purpose. It's just not always apparent to the observer. And the zipping around tends to thwart bureaucratic organizers. It sends scribes into frizzies and tizzies. Disobedience of the rules is the key, friends."

"Yes, Clem," said Chad. "I've discovered that. I thought I was supposed to rescue you, and Ralph was supposed to rescue himself. I thought those were the rules."

"God, Chad, how crazy can you get?" said Angela. "And I always thought you were so level-headed."

Chad looked at her. "No, you didn't, Angela. You're just saying that so I'll help rescue Milky Barney."

"Ah ..." Angela puffed out her cheeks, looked around sheepishly. "Let's discuss it later, Chad. Let's look for a willy."

Clem chuckled. Save me? Dodos save themselves.

"Drakon is a legendary teacher, Chad," said Clem. "One of his teaching methods is to pull your leg, to see if you are truly disobedient and a thoughtful entity in your own right. So, you finally saw through his ruse?"

"Well, not quite. My staff whispered it to me."

Clem chuckled. Then he focused on Ralph. Hang on, Ralph. We're coming. We'll move mountains to save you.

He picked up the pace. They entered the woods. Like willowy ghosts, they trekked through the shadows. Pray they are in big disarray, thought Clem. Pray, everyone.

In hushed coolness, a sparkling willy opened before them. A woman stepped from it.

"Sandra," said Chad.

"The Barneys' parents are in danger," said Sandra. She told them about Roger and his two pals.

"We know," said Clem. "Hubert, Tim, and Zack are on the way to intercept them."

Sandra looked at Chad.

"The dodos have your parents, Chad," she said.

"What?"

She told him about Marshall seizing his parents.

"They're in cages, Chad." She reached out a hand to him. "Come, we must plan for their rescue."

"God, you have cold hands, Sandra." He drew away from her. "I have to rescue Milky Barney—I mean Ralph Barney—first. Now what am I going to do? There are too many people to rescue. Hoodoo!"

Clem hopped about, flapping his wings. He knew he had to take charge.

"Don't worry!" he cried. "Everybody, onto the willy—slither—fast!"

The willy winked open before them, and Clem fanned them aboard.

"Does Doomsday mean anything to you, Clem?" asked Sandra as she stepped aboard.

"Doomsday? I can't say that it does, Sandra."

He followed her onto the willy. They braced against the dazzling walls, and the willy began to move.

"Do you know about Plan B?"

"No."

She whispered to him, told him what she knew. It was sketchy; not even Marshall knew all the details.

"When it comes, it will come from inside," she said, touching him with a cold hand.

Clem grew calm. He missed Ralph. A big hollow place welled inside him.

There she is, thought Vince. He eyed the monster tree at the edge of the grove that anchored Spiderweb One. He drew close, ducked under the canopy, and floated down, scanning the rippled gray bark.

The tree bore crude markings, slashes that seemed to be the work of animals or birds that had stopped by to sharpen their claws. The markings were code. It was a message board for spies. Drakon had left a new message. It concerned Ralph. Vince read it, then landed lightly and walked toward the Spiderweb.

He eased his wing open.

Ralph popped his head out.

Vince allowed him to crawl out and ride on his back.

The Great Hall swung into view. It was surrounded by huge guards. Endocrine giants. Maurice's specialty. Youngsters without conscience, experience, or knowledge. Deadly because of their size and razors. Deadly because of their obedience to established powermongers. Mutants. Every single one of them. Nil survivability.

As Vince approached the door, a guard moved to stand in his way.

"I am your commander, son," said Vince. "Step aside."

"Maurice forbids anyone to enter without first being announced." The guard's voice was a nervous singsong. "It's a new rule."

"I announce myself. Step aside or I'll tear you in half."

The guard stood his ground for a moment, then waddled away.

"Maurice will punish me," he said.

Vince threw him a disgusted look, then whipped the door webbing aside and entered the hall.

He saw Obie's head on the table, and Obie's body on the floor. An enormous guard sat beside Maurice, a blood-encrusted ax on the table in front of him.

Vince rounded the table and looked back toward the door. Andrew stood beside it. He saw Charles seated at the table. Vince peered closer at Charles, saw the death face and rigid body.

He walked toward Maurice. The chairman had been huddling with the guard since Vince entered.

Maurice looked up.

"Vince …" He waved a wing toward Obie's head. "Our first martyr. Saint Obie." He choked back a sob. The hall shook with a gale of laughter that came from the guard.

Maurice stood.

"Lute. Charles. On your feet."

The guard pushed his chair back and stood.

Charles levered himself out of his chair and stiff-walked behind it, where he stood at rigid, death-like attention.

"Lute, prepare for the trial. Clear Saint Obie from the room. Andrew, scrub the blood away. And tidy up the sun-roofs."

Lute grabbed Obie's head and body and dragged them toward the door.

Andrew left the hall and came back with a bucket of soapy water, a brush, and clean rags.

"Step this way, Vince," said Maurice. "Let's see what you've got." Maurice, staring at Ralph, led Vince to the far end of the hall. "I didn't expect it to go according to plan," he said. "Does anything ever? But the catechism will survive these dark early days of Clemianity. It will shine its powerful light on all of Dodoland for millenniums to come. It will be a beacon in the storm."

Becoming fluid, Andrew scampered over the table, chairs, and floor, and scrubbed the blood away. Occasionally, Vince, Ralph, and Maurice strayed across his vision.

It's a trap, Vince.

He released escape advisories into Vince's mind. Treachery was afoot. Guards were ringed around the outside of the hall, brandishing axes. Andrew, after cleaning up the blood, was supposed to climb to the ceiling and adjust the sunroofs. He was then supposed to fall right beside Vince, startling him, giving the guards time to rush in and hack him to pieces. Guards were poised to lift up the wall webbing at the far end of the hall, mere feet away from where Vince stood.

To the mountains, Vince. Leave the little one. The karmic wheel spins.

Andrew did his own spinning, slopping up Obie's blood. Not all of it came clean. Stains remained. Obie had been, after all, a martyred saint.

Charles, maintaining exemplary death-like characteristics, stood near his chair. He saw Maurice and Vince. He heard Andrew splashing around.

Suddenly, Vince lowered himself, and the little boy who was on his back slid to the floor. The boy stick-walked toward the table—a miniature version of Andrew. The sight made Charles shudder.

The boy, wearing a cowboy hat, levered himself onto a chair, then onto the table. He marched about, surveying his domain, a roguish little stick-walker, then sat on the table, rigid, a corpse with the confident flames of hellfire flickering within.

Something began to happen at the far end of the hall. Charles shifted his focus.

Vince was in the air, shooting toward the ceiling.

Maurice was throwing a tantrum. He shouted something unintelligible.

Andrew streaked to the wall, made like a spider, and was on the ceiling in a flash.

With sword-like thunder, Vince ripped a hole in the ceiling with his razors. Then he flew out.

"Too late, Andrew," shouted Maurice. "Come down." Andrew landed on the floor with a thud.

The wall at the far end ruffled, as if hit by a stiff wind.

"Stay out, you idiots. He's gone."

Maurice walked back to the table. His face looked old and worn. He stamped a foot.

"Thought we had the bastard." He stamped his foot again and sat. "Charles, back to your seat. We must write another chapter in the catechism."

Charles levered himself onto his chair. He became fluid and grabbed pen and paper.

"Vince, perverter of dodo hatchlings, friend of humans, was slain by Mighty Maurice, who hath given his only begotten son ..."

Charles wrote.

Throughout all the commotion, he noted, the little cowboy seated on the table did not so much as flicker an eyelash.

They don't make people like that.

You are kin of Andrew's.

You are another god-in-residence.

The slither raced through the woods. Chad, bracing himself against the velvety walls, felt sick. Why did Marshall have to kidnap his parents?

What am I going to do?

They killed Milky.

He mused wistfully: If only his parents, in their youth, had had Drakon to guide them.

He imagined his parents, in their youth, hooking up with Drakon in a peaceful clearing by a stream, listening to his stories, meditating, training with the staff, hearing the *Elyth Skilly* verses. They'd be in touch with their souls then. They'd be resourceful. They'd never have killed Milky.

The slither lurched; Chad fell against Sandra. He looked about. Angela was holding onto Mel, her face in shadow beneath the brim of her hat. Clem was muttering silently: *We need Drakon.*

Chad glanced away. His thoughts crystallized. Drakon is an elemental. An essence. A vein of ore that runs through all of us in varying degrees of thickness and purity.

I will be Drakon, thought Chad.

He looked back at Clem. Clem's eyes met Chad's. Their minds merged for an instant, and Clem no longer looked troubled.

The slither stopped, yawned. The group ran out onto the grass.

"Look," cried Sandra. The next grove was immense, a battleship moored on the prairie sea. "That's Spiderweb One."

They walked across the open prairie, their eyes on the big trees that loomed ahead.

Something leaped into the sky from deep in the big grove

and stayed afloat in the air. It was just a speck in the distance, but they watched it with growing concern.

It seemed to lock onto them. It sped toward them, came in low over the treetops.

It was a dodo attacking them.

"Get down!" yelled Clem. "Hug the earth!"

Chad threw himself to the ground, held his staff in readiness, felt his heart beat with a strong, steady rhythm. He was ready for a fight.

They were buried in the grass, motionless, their nerves a jangling mess. All was silent, except for the wind.

Something heavy set down nearby. Chad poked his head up and saw a huge, fierce-looking dodo.

"Peace," shouted the dodo. "Clem, it's me, Vince."

Clem poked his head above the grass, stood. "You're the one who swiped Ralph," he said, his voice superheated with anger.

"He's in the Spiderweb. In the Great Hall."

"Why did you steal him?" shouted Clem.

"To protect him. It was the best way, with Spiderweb killers after you."

"You'll help us get him back, won't you?" said Angela. She stood and walked toward Vince. She seemed to float on the grass.

"Stay back, Angela!" cried Clem, waving her down. "All of you, stay back! I don't trust him!" He stared at Vince. "I don't like the smell of this!"

"I was Drakon's spy in the Spiderweb, Clem. They just tried to kill me. I had to take off fast. I'm on my way to the mountains. I stopped to warn you. The dainty ones want you there for a trial. All of you. It's a charade, of course, but if you go in, you'll be in a position to recapture the little human. It may be your only hope. Go. Try it. Maurice is the name of the chairman, but there are other dainty ones waiting in the wings. They have the hall surrounded by juvenile growth morons with axes. Have faith, Clem. So long."

He rose into the air, took off, and soon vanished.

Hoodoo! thought Chad, springing up and racing with the others toward the Spiderweb.

The savage force of the wind threatened to rip Hubert off Tim and toss him into the abyss. Clear, see-through demons of turbulence screamed in his ears, threatened his very existence.

They were flying over the bur oaks, approaching the wound in the earth. Tim and Zack dove closer to the ground, leveled out, and slowed. Tim looked over his shoulder and said to Hubert, "There's Clem's egg, right below. Which way to your house?"

Hubert spied the egg, scanned the countryside, and pointed. "That way!"

Tim and Zack picked up speed and increased altitude. They had discussed strategy earlier in the flight. On the approach, each had a sector to scan. Hubert scanned below, looking for anything that stood out against the prairie.

If only I could fly, he thought, amused at the notion. I sense the utter freedom in the air about me. I could go anywhere I wanted to, whenever I wanted.

Ah ... maybe not, he thought. We are all slaves to myriad impersonal forces. The air itself is a slave to the sun's radiation and the earth's rotation. And what bird ever took to the air except to hunt for food, escape from a predator, migrate, or perform some other chore of survival? Airplanes have flight plans, destinations, missions.

Is there any freedom at all? he wondered.

Hubert put his binoculars to his eyes, looked to the south, saw a house tucked into the woods. Chad Garrick's house.

His knowledge hits of Chad came back: Chad chained to a tree, thinking he had rabies, screaming and thrashing; Chad stalking Milky; Milky stalking Chad; Chad playing soldier; Chad playing mountain lion; Milky, a ghost distant in the woods and meadows, always moving to that other place, the place of death; mental-health providers kidnapping Chad, incarcerating Chad, drugging Chad; Chad saying *I saw you kill him, Dad. I saw you kill Milky.*

He wondered what Chad would do if three punk dodos were stalking *his* parents. Would he fly to their rescue?

His thoughts returned to Ralph, but he blanked them from his mind. He could not bear to think of Ralph now. He could not allow anything to divert his attention from the mission ahead.

He saw his house, pointed it out to Tim. Tim signaled Zack, then veered off. Zack was to come in from the south, Tim from the north.

Tim circled around. They approached.

Two horses stood side by side in the corral behind the stable, heads down, looking through the fence at thickets that lay at the outskirts of the yard. Hubert pointed at the horses.

"Something has their attention."

Tim floated downward, stopped just above the ground near the thickets. He cruised around, keeping the thickets between him and the house.

Hubert scanned the thickets. All was silent save for the twittering of birds in the meadows and trees. Tension in the air gripped him. The sun's heat poured down on his arms, hands, neck.

"I've got one in my sights, Hubert," whispered Tim. "When I land, get off fast."

Hubert saw nothing but thickets and grass.

Tim touched down and Hubert slid off. Tim slipped into the thicket. Hubert unslung his carbine and followed. He heard Tim's voice.

"Move nary a feather, mate, or I'll slice your head off and send it flying up your asshole." A pause. "What are you doing here—"

A furious flapping broke out. It tore through the thickets. Then silence.

Hubert crept farther into the thicket, expecting to see Tim standing over a dead punk. He remembered the massive guard Tim had torn apart at the Greenways. Tim came into view. There was no punk.

"Lost him," said Tim. "Had to interrogate him first. Not right to kill first, ask questions later. But now we *will* kill them. His evasion seals it."

Tim pointed at the thickets.

"He's not much bigger than Clem. Track him, Hubert. He's a sissy. Blow him away. I'll track him from the air and keep you posted. Look up now and then; I'll signal down."

Tim rose into the air.

Hubert chambered a round and took the safety off.

He scanned the circle of brush around him. It was thick, but not too thick for a young dodo to scoot around in. Tim was a giant. I'm the right size for this kind of work, he thought. At last I've found my niche in life.

He felt a biochemical rush, his body preparing him, as he tuned to the surroundings and stepped into the brush.

Charles Barbier was resting in his chair, maintaining death-like integrity, when he heard someone enter the Great Hall. The voice came from behind him.

"Chairman Maurice, I, Captain of the Guards, Lute, report a sighting of Messiah Clem and his disciples."

Faint waves of annoyance crossed Chairman Maurice's face. He set the catechism aside, shifted in his chair, and began fanning his beak.

"Lute ..." he said, then fell silent. He leaned farther and farther to the side, until he became a mere tangential awareness in Charles's frozen field of vision.

"Lute, where is he?"

"He and his assembly have just entered this very band of trees. They appear to be headed this way."

Maurice sat bolt upright.

"Lute, do we have anyone who can bring him in? I want Clem in custody."

Charles saw fear on Maurice's face, and in that moment a lightning bolt of an idea shot into his mind.

Lute's silence filled the air.

"Lute, can you yourself lead a group of guards to Clem and bring him here for trial?"

Charles sensed the terrible uncertainty in the proceedings. Maurice was afraid of Clem, physically afraid, and afraid of the magnetism of Clem's personality. To solidify his position as chairman, he needed to have Clem here for trial. And yet Maurice apparently could not rely on any of his subordinates to produce results, except ham-handed killings. Skilled, experienced guards were nowhere to be found. They'd either been hacked to death, shuttled into cells, or they'd escaped into the wild. Maurice had surrounded himself with reckless brute force. And he knew that the council members, each a rival to his throne, were awaiting the collapse of his house.

Infused with his new idea, Charles swung apelike through the branches of his mind. It would entail considerable risk. His pen moved across a fresh sheet of paper. The dead weren't supposed to do this, show initiative ...

Risky.

Charles wrote slowly. He wanted it to be precise. He hoped Maurice would not notice this breach of dead-human etiquette. He kept his zombie eyes on the paper, not daring to look up, wondering if the chairman's eyes were on him.

Done.

Charles slapped his pen down, stood, and began stick-walking the paper around to Maurice. He caught seesawing views of the little cowboy seated on the table and of Andrew standing by the door. Pray that this is right, Andrew. Charles felt a cool chuckle work its way up his spine.

Charles caught sight of Maurice. The mutant was staring

at him open-beaked. Charles slapped the paper down on the table in front of Maurice. The chairman jumped in his seat, then pawed the paper with his wings and picked it up. He read it, his beak moving silently.

Charles stood there, staring at the distant wall.

Suddenly—in a voice so un-Maurice-like that Charles at first thought it was someone else—the chairman erupted in joyful tones.

"Excellent idea, Charles, old boy." Maurice set the paper down and beat his wings against his breast, sending up a chilling wind that cut like a knife across Charles's throat.

"Excellent idea, Charles, old boy," said Maurice again, "but how can a dead human come up with an idea without first being ordered?"

Charles did not answer. He stick-walked back to his chair and climbed into it.

Maurice stood. His voice rose through the hall.

"Andrew, Charles swears that you are the only one here who can bring Clem in and hold him for trial." He paused, letting the boisterous echo fade, then barked, "Do so. Bring in Clem and his disciples. Ensure that they behave well during the trial. But first, before you go, kill Charles further. It appears that he has sprung slightly back to life with this idea of his. We must put him back to death. And this time do a more thorough job of it, Andrew."

Maurice sat.

Charles heard the sounds of stick-walking behind him, headed his way.

Feast your eyes on the festivities, mutant scum, he mentally shot to Maurice. Pray, don't kill me for real, Andrew. You, mutant scum, Maurice, one minute alone with you, away from your mutant guards ...

Charles, in his mind, was methodically ripping Maurice to shreds with his bare hands when he felt an icy touch upon his neck. Cold it was. Numbing. It wrapped around his neck—icy spiders—and gripped. An ice lock. The icy fingers drew him up and out of his chair.

They were out of the hall like a gust of wind, Andrew running maniacally. Charles was like a leaf in a storm. Flapping around, he could do nothing but follow in Andrew's wind. They spun around, bouncing off guards, receiving mighty shoves and curses, and—amidst beating wings and precipitating feathers—a few words of encouragement and direction.

"Messiah Clem's thataway." A wing pointed.

"Bring 'em back alive so's we can kill 'em," bellowed a punk.

Other wings pointed. Axes rose. Shouts issued.

Andrew sped through the grove, Charles draped on his back, facing rearward, the arctic vice of Andrew's fingers upon his neck. The sun gleamed through at intervals, blowing forth a madly racing shadow.

They took a circuitous route through the grove, and at last burst upon Clem and his disciples.

Andrew dropped Charles to the ground. Charles rose to a crouch, stared into a hatchling's eyes, then into the eyes of some shocked humans. He stood. He was alive, no longer dead.

᚜◦᚛

Chad stared into the face of death. He knew it was a homunculus—what else could it be? But even so, the sight drove icy nails through his flesh. Abe Lincoln came to mind. A scary Abe, pulled from his grave, standing stiff-frozen, with arms thrust slightly in front of him. And yet, moments ago, he'd come hauling in from the forest with a passenger on his back.

Chad looked at the passenger: a wild-eyed, wild-haired man, his clothes hanging limp and tattered on a frame in need of nourishment. The man stood uneasily, staring at them.

"Clem?" asked the man.

"Yes," said Clem.

The man tried to say something, but stumbled on the words, his voice cracking.

"It's Charles," said Sandra.

Chad remembered him now—he'd seen Charles in his cage. He rushed to him and handed him his canteen. He gave him a sack of Forest Buckle, then whipped his staff through the air, willing the fauns to come by with some more, but the woods remained silent.

The man drank and ate.

"My name is Charles Barbier," he said. He told them about the impending trial. "I've been writing the birds' catechism. Forced into it." He looked at Clem and said, almost apologetically, "They're expecting you, Clem." He looked at the others. *"All* of you."

"I'm aware of their designs on me," said Clem. "I have no intentions of cooperating. We are on our way to rescue a little human called Ralph."

"Does he wear a cowboy hat?" asked Charles.

"Yes!" cried Angela.

"He's in the Great Hall. But he is a god, not a human."

"A god?" said Angela.

"He's like Andrew." Charles pointed at the monk. "Andrew was ordered to bring you in."

"Like Andrew?" wailed Angela. "You mean he's dead?"

"No," said Charles hastily. "He's every bit as alive as Andrew."

Angela wailed again.

"I mean ..." Charles looked at Andrew. "Andrew, show them you *are* alive." Andrew remained motionless. "Go climb a tree, Andrew. Show them what I mean."

Angela wailed and wailed.

Andrew launched himself at the nearest tree, turned fluid, and made like a monkey. Seconds later, he was out of sight, hidden in the branches more than a hundred feet up.

"Look out," shouted Charles. He hustled them away from the tree.

The air whined. Andrew hit the ground with a thud, then popped up and resumed his former stance.

"He has the dodos on his stringer," said Charles. "They give him orders, he obeys, but ..." Charles looked at them.

"He's one of Drakon's spies," said Mel. "A monk."

"Exactly. Drakon. Right." Charles looked anxious. "We really have to be getting back. Any moment they could have these woods full of two-ton goons with axes looking for our heads."

"But how did Ralph get to be like Andrew?" asked Angela.

"I'll explain, Angela," said Mel. "It's best if we go along with Andrew, Clem. I think Drakon is manipulating the whole thing behind the scenes. If so, we're safe. His monk will secure passage for us."

A keening, wounded sound filled the forest. Not loud, but full. And Andrew began sinking into the earth.

Chad stared, astonished. He felt his stomach sink along with Andrew. The monk went down, blending with the ground, adding himself to the earth. The keening sound stopped. Andrew was gone. A gentle mound that once was Andrew spread out and swam to merge seamlessly with the ground all around.

Chad felt a momentary siege of helplessness.

He fought it.

I'm strong now, he reminded himself. Resourceful. Andrew's passing does not change that. Humans save themselves. They save others, too. They even save dodos, if necessary.

His staff seemed to growl. Everything was all right. You didn't need Andrew—a monk, a god—to save you.

Noises intruded. Chad broke from his reverie. Angela was running through the grove, in the direction Andrew and Charles had come from. She was screaming something awful. About Ralph. About saving him. Saving him before he melted into the ground. Clem and Mel were giving chase.

Chad was about to follow them when he felt a tight grip on his arm. It was Sandra.

"Your canteen and sack of food," she said.

He picked them up, looked around. "Where's Charles?"

"He ran that way." Sandra pointed to their backtrail. "Looks like he doesn't want to attend the trial."

"Let's go, Sandra." He began running after the others.

"Chad. Your parents."

He froze. The forest blurred before him. The sound of rushing footfalls grew dim in his ears.

Hubert scanned the shrubs, the maze of trees. He stepped from shadow to sunlight, back to shadow, crouching, peering all around, trying to make silent footfalls, carbine at the ready. He willed incongruities to come leaping at him: the red and black of bill, the gray of feathers, the odd contours, the concert of dodo that clashed with the orchestra of prairie jungle.

He glanced up. Tim had said he'd try to locate them from above and for Hubert to look up now and then for signals. Tim was not in sight.

Eerie silence met his ears.

The air around him felt like a high-tension wire.

Was there just one punk in here? All of them? They would be doubly tough to take out, now that they were alerted to danger. But there was just so much brush for them to hide in. There were no extensive thickets near the Barneys' home. It was open prairie with scattered pockets of brush, like here in the gentle draw in back of the house.

He crept along, scanned the brush.

Come out, sissies!

He glanced up. The thicket reduced the sky to a blue fragment. Tim was not in sight. He cocked an ear. Silence. He crept on.

Where the hell are those sissies?

Hubert reached the edge of the brush. It was possible a

dodo remained in there, hidden from view. He considered letting the horses out of the corral. They'd been interested in the dodos earlier. Would they be able to find them? He guessed not. The horses would probably just run away.

Hubert ran toward the house, searching the sky. The sky was empty. He looked all around.

He was getting nervous.

Where were Tim and Zack?

They couldn't stay here all day.

Hubert ran toward the corral. Approaching it, he stopped in his tracks. The most amazing sight met his eyes.

The two horses, crowded at the far end of the corral, were watching the incoming flight. Beyond the fence, in the distance across a field, was a punk dodo running pell-mell for the corral. Tim was in flight, pursuing him, reaching for him again and again with his razors. The punk zigged and zagged, but Tim stayed with him. Zack was hovering in the background with a punk dodo hanging lifeless in his razors.

The running punk came on, a life measured in seconds. Tim swooped again and again. Just when Hubert thought Tim was about to seize him, Tim peeled off. Hubert saw the reason why: the punk was heading for a row of trees near the corral. Tim swept high and came over the trees. The punk shot between the trees and hurdled the fence. He turned on a dime and shot through the open stable door. Tim pulled up and landed. There was no way he could fit through that door.

Hubert opened the corral gate and ran for the stable door. He stopped just short of the entrance, steeled his nerves, and stepped inside.

He stood in shadow, aiming his carbine around.

A shape moved in the darkness.

Four horses are all we've got, thought Hubert. Two out in the corral, and Pioneer and Cassandra penned up out on the prairie. It's the punk dodo, and nothing else.

The shape in the darkness sprang at him. Hubert fired twice, dived aside, and the punk shot out the door.

An awful ripping sound came from outside the stable. Hubert rushed out to see the punk dead in Tim's razors.

"You got him, Hubert. Neatly placed. In the chest. He'd have run off and died—the sissy."

"How many?" asked Hubert.

"Two. Third punk's unaccounted for. He's that first one we saw in the brush."

"I walked all through there—"

Hubert saw the horses. They were standing side by side, as before, at the far end of the corral. Their heads were low. They were staring at the open doorway of the stable.

He's in there, thought Hubert. He must have snuck inside when I was tracking him through the brush. Hubert, with icicles trickling through his veins, walked back toward the stable door.

The frantic footsteps of Angela, Mel, and Clem were distant echoes in Chad's mind. Frozen, staring at the forest, he heard Sandra's voice.

"Chad, let's go see your parents, but first—it's time you came face to face with Milky."

The forest spun for Chad.

"Is he here?"

"He's here."

She walked with him through the grove.

"What do you know about Milky, Chad?"

"He's the brother I never got to know."

A sparkling slither opened in front of them. Sandra and Chad hopped aboard, and it snaked through the grove. Prison cells came into view. The big web-like structures were everywhere the eye turned.

The slither meandered through the prisonland and came to a halt in dense brush. Sandra and Chad crawled from it. Crouching next to Sandra, feeling her coolness, Chad peered through foliage and stared into the eyes of Milky.

It was like looking into a mirror.

"So, you're Chad. Huh?"

Chad, for a moment, was flummoxed. Milky was not held captive in a cell. He was free.

"They-they killed you!"

"Uh ... not really. The Indignities!"

Chad found his voice. "You're bigger than I thought."

Milky laughed, shook his staff. "Yeah." He turned and crawled away.

Chad spoke to the empty spot that had held Milky. "You're stronger than I had thought. You're more resourceful than I had thought."

Silent moments passed.

He turned to Sandra. "Let's go see my parents."

They found Chad's parents together in a cell, catatonic.

"I see absolutely no family resemblance, Chad. Are you sure they're your parents?"

He knew Sandra was joking. She had led him to them. They were his parents, all right. The killers of Milky. Or were they?

"Can they rescue themselves, Sandra?" He looked at her. "It doesn't seem right, me just letting them stay here. But ..."

Chad looked around. It would be super risky getting his parents out. Guards patrolled regularly. A monstrous dodo was in the area now. And what could you do with people who were like logs? You'd have to carry them.

"Why do so many of these prisoners zonk out?" he asked Sandra.

"You zonked out too, Chad."

He remembered waking in Tim's wing.

"Yeah, I did."

"People zonk out for safety, at first. Then it becomes habit. A comfort. An escape from responsibility."

"If we could just wake Rory and Marcia, Sandra. That's their names. If we could just wake them." He gazed at his parents.

Something popped into his mind. Saturday nights, years ago, Chad's bath night as a tyke. He'd dry himself, jump into his pajamas, and run shivering to his bedroom to hide under the covers. Monsters were after him. He would wrap himself tight in his sheet and blanket and shiver to beat the band. Shivering felt good. It was fun. Comforting. An escape.

"Chad, something is going to happen later today that will wake everyone." She explained Doomsday and Plan B, as best she could, which was pretty spotty.

"Hoodoo," said Chad. He now believed his parents could rescue themselves, or at least try. He wondered what life would be like with Rory and Marcia after this was over. Would he have to use his staff on them in self-defense? He pictured himself walking through his house, staff in hand. Rory and Marcia would cower at the sound of his footsteps. His staff would growl.

They maneuvered through the brush and found Marshall in a cell.

Marshall stirred from meditation and walked to the wall of his cell.

"Mr. Garrick. Sandra." His voice was a whisper. "Chad, I'm afraid I've kidnapped your—"

"I know, Marshall. They deserved to be kidnapped."

"Uh, oh ..." He eyed Chad. "Did you see Milky?"

"Yes."

"I summoned him."

"From where?"

Marshall snapped his eyes around then bent and whispered in Chad's ear. Chad, surprised, heard Marshall intone the key *Elyth Skilly* verse.

Marshall stood upright. Chad peered into his eyes.

"I think I understand, Marshall. So, what's this about Doomsday and Plan B?"

"Human wings are preparing to take to the air, Chad. Their mission is to destroy Dodoland." Marshall glanced away. "Our saviors will come from the mountains, and"—he looked back at Chad—"from within *each* of us."

"Marshall ..." said Sandra. She held up her knife.

"Your arm ..."

"Good as new." She waved it around. The knife blade sliced the air. "Time to cut some vines."

Marshall nodded. He pointed to a row of cages down the way.

Chad and Sandra crawled away.

"Sandra, why doesn't Marshall just use his razors to cut himself out?"

"He'd probably get tangled up. The webbing is too springy for dodos to cut it easily. It's designed that way. I'll show you what I mean. Also, the guards usually know in advance who's plotting an escape, so they watch those prisoners more closely."

"Knowledge hits?"

"That and subtle clues. Like reading faces. Wanting to be free shines through the social mask, Chad. Even growth morons can see that."

They reached a row of cells. Chad peered inside.

"They're empty, Sandra."

She began cutting.

"Chad, we aren't letting anyone out; we're letting us in. You'll see."

She demonstrated how difficult it was to cut the vines.

"You have to hold them tight, Chad, or there's not enough tension."

She cut a few vines in the first cell, leaving them so they looked undisturbed. They crawled inside, then made their way down the line, cutting crawl holes into each cell.

"Remember that first cell, Chad. That's the key. Get the whole group inside, then disperse them through the cells. It's essential."

"I still don't quite understand, Sandra."

"Neither do I. Trust in Plan B."

"Oh, I do."

"Good."

"Hoodoo!"

They crawled out of the cells.

Chad thought of Plan B. He was frightened, and not just at the prospect of dying. Dying was one thing. But being your own instrument of death. Choosing it. Finding out what's deep inside.

"Sandra, if we don't make it ..."

"Hush, Chad. We will make it."

They crawled through the brush, toward the Great Hall.

Mel and Angela sat side by side in the Great Hall, sharing the same oversized chair. Angela was sobbing, touching away her tears with a hankie. Clem stood on the table a few feet down from them.

Ralph commanded their attention. A stick of death, he walked back and forth on the table, his arms and legs as stiff as the appendages of a frozen cadaver, his face a mask of staring insensibility.

Holy Jesus, thought Mel. He *is* a monk.

"But how ...?" Angela looked up at Mel with the question. It was the fourth or fifth time she had asked. Each time Mel tried to explain, she would burst into a new flood of tears.

Mel began again. This time Angela listened.

"A goulash, if you will, Angela, of the things you and Hubert need to leave behind—that is what Ralph is."

He glanced away from her and looked up at Ralph. The sight made him shiver. Then he told her about his life in Africa.

Africa had been a picture-book idyll in Malcolm Moreland's mind for several years. He wanted to go there, to be a missionary, to serve the Lord and the church, to help lift the people out of their straits, to save their damn sorry souls from the consequences of an unchristian life. Reverend Moreland applied for a missionary post, was selected, and bid goodbye to England.

"Can you imagine the arrogance of the whole works, Angela? Back then it never occurred to me—I was sold on the dogma—but can you imagine some alien with a head full of slag coming into your world and telling you that you must set aside *your* beliefs, *your* mythology, and follow *his* beliefs, *his* mythology, or else *you* will suffer eternal damnation?"

Mel reared back and laughed, catching a few odd looks from the dodos arrayed around the conference table.

"And the alien's mythology turns out to be the screwiest damn nonsense ever, Angela. Can you believe the arrogance? Well, it was me. I was that alien. One of them. Carrying on the grand Christian tradition of mocking the other guy, squashing him, and bolstering my own crumbling house in the process."

Mel paused, shook his head. Then he went on with the story.

Once faced with the reality, Mel's idyllic Africa slipped away. A corruption rose to take its place.

"Sure, we had converts. It was easy. There were already lots of good little Christians running around in Africa. Have been for hundreds of years. We lured more in. Food. Medical services. Social services. Schools. A helping hand. Who wouldn't appreciate all that?

"They traded with us. They became Christians in return for handouts. That's how I saw it. But they still practiced their superstitious beliefs at every turn, Angela. They did not cast off their paganism, yet we called them Christians. I saw them as shallow, as corrupt. They were faking it. They had no true spirituality.

"Angela, we could have been telling them to worship Satan's rump. They'd have done it. It would have been just the same to them.

"Also, the natives who preferred to have nothing to do with us, I thought of them as backward, stupid, ignorant, selfish, childish, even dangerous: dangerous to *our* cause, to *our* mythology. Dangerous to Christianity. Because they might—heaven forbid—undo our carefully laid work. Unmake our good little Christians. After we had so neatly sewn them up."

Mel, becoming disillusioned, began going on long hikes in the wild. He shirked his missionary duties, getting himself into ever increasing trouble with his superiors.

"And you know what, Angela? The defiant ones—I no longer cared about their souls. Because they had the good sense to reject my mythology and hold on to their own, I thought they were doomed. The arrogance, Angela."

Then one day, Mel saw a giant dodo. Standing in the distance, it swam in the savanna's heat waves. Moments later, it stepped out of sight. Shaken, Mel told no one but his wife. The next day, they went looking for tracks.

"To make a long story short, Angela, my wife and I had many hair-raising adventures in Dodoland. We got caught in the bubble, so to speak, couldn't get back into Africa, had to go traveling with this world.

"I was filthy with people-pleasing odors, but fortunately I was big and strong—and they had caught me at a time in my life when I was turning mean—so I survived in the *dojos*. My wife also. She fought like a wildcat.

"We earned blood shadows. We could walk safely in Dodoland. We met Drakon. We stayed around the fringes of Dodoland, but dropped out to earth occasionally. I visited libraries, did some much-needed reading on various cultural myths—including my own cultural myth, Christianity. And—voila—Angela, I became a new man. I crept closer to my soul."

Mel looked up at Ralph. The little death stick was still pacing back and forth on the conference table. Mel looked at Angela. Her face, red and swollen from crying, was buried in her hands.

"Angela," he said gently, "look at Ralph." She refused. "See him, Angela. That is your childhood. Dead. It's gone. Little Ralph serves as its shrine."

Angela looked up and broke into fresh sobbing. Mel went back to his story.

One day his wife turned up missing. He searched. He nearly went insane. He thought the dodos had killed her. He ran to Drakon.

Malcolm Moreland, Drakon had said, *that woman was not your wife. You were married to Christianity. Now she is gone. Spontaneous symbols sometimes spring fully to life here in this quasi-spirit world; in some cases, they come complete with memories to make for real illusion. You thought you'd known her for a long time, but really you didn't. You thought you knew Christianity, but really you didn't.*

Gradually, memories of her as his wife wore away. He recalled her now simply as the monk who helped him break away from Christianity.

"I'm still changing, Angela. Still creeping closer to my soul. When I think of how much I've learned just today …

"And you will too. Keep changing. Keep learning. Keep reaching for your soul." Mel paused, wiped a tear from his eye.

"We'll have to break the news to Hubert, Angela. Be strong. Help Hubert understand."

A commotion broke out at the door. Mel turned and saw Chad and Sandra enter. They scuffled with the guards, shouting that they had to attend the trial.

He heard Angela sob.

"We never should have brought him," she said. "He was too little. But he threatened to tell Mom and Dad about the egg."

"Andrew … Andrew …"

With a whispery voice, Charles Barbier called for Andrew. He saw where Andrew had stood when he sank into the earth. It was a place like any other. Nothing distinguished it.

Andrew, you have returned to dust. Come back. We need you.

He looked in the direction Clem and his disciples had run. The girl had been hysterical.

Momentarily captured by good intentions, he tramped after them, then halted. It was suicide to return.

He sat against a tree, felt a chill, shuddered. They'll think I've deserted them. It's a morbid world. None of us survive. Our deaths were preordained the moment we came into this world.

Charles got mad.

"What do you want, Charles?" he asked himself.

He framed his answer the way he'd learned to frame most everything in Dodoland, as a mission.

I want to go back to the hall and kill Maurice and the other mutants and extract Clem and his disciples and destroy the catechism.

Then his thoughts trailed off into other desires.

He thought of food.

He remembered the sack of food the boy had given him. It had been delightful. Fascinating. He wanted more of it. Where had Chad gotten it?

He popped to his feet.

Charles walked.

Andrew?

Charles felt something enter him.

Soon, he was walking like Andrew walked.

He wished for a mirror. In the mirror, he knew, he would look very much like Andrew. A whim struck him. He launched himself at a tree. Before he knew it, he was up, up, in the highest branches ...

He fell, landed smack on the ground, popped up, then Andrew-walked toward Spiderweb One's Great Hall.

Hubert stood outside the open stable door. He figured the punk was hiding in one of the four stalls inside. It would be helpful to know which one before proceeding too far. He remembered Clem's advice to use startling tactics against dodos.

He picked up four stones, leaned through the doorway, and peered into the shadowy corridor that ran between the stalls.

He tossed a stone into the closest stall on the right. It landed softly on hay. Then silence. He tossed a stone into the stall on the left. Silence.

He stepped inside the stable.

He tossed a stone into the far stall on the right. He heard it land, then heard a faint sound. *A sob.*

He tossed a stone into the far stall on the left. Silence.

He flicked the overhead lights on, looked inside the two closest stalls, found them empty, and crept farther down the corridor.

He looked into the far stall on the left. Empty.

He crouched and looked through the fencing of the last stall. He saw mounds of hay. A dirt floor. Shadows.

He made the dodo out, raised his carbine, took aim. He edged closer, saw the dodo more clearly.

The bird was sprawled out, racked with tremors, whimpering.

He's dying.

Did one of the horses stomp him?

Hubert stood, looked over the fence into the pen, kept his carbine trained on the dodo, prepared to fire a round to defend against a panic-fueled assault.

"Who's there?" A weak, rasping voice. The dodo's breaths were rapid, shallow. He squirmed, clutched his chest with his wings.

He must have been resting his injury out in the brush, thought Hubert. When Tim surprised him, he fled in panic on wings borne of fear, then crawled in here to die.

"What happened?" asked Hubert, motioning toward the dodo's chest.

"Clem. He has killed me. From a distance." The dodo's voice took on strength, blowing the words out in rasping waves. "Clem is evil. He must be killed." The dodo tried to raise himself but collapsed. He stared at Hubert with dumb, murky eyes.

This isn't the time to be antagonistic, thought Hubert. He wanted to draw the dodo out. He relaxed his grip on the carbine.

"What can be done to ease your suffering?"

"Aaaa ..." The dodo cried, then fell silent. He writhed, then said, "This is not what they taught us in school. Clem has killed me!"

"What's your name?"

The dodo had closed his eyes. Now he opened them.

"Ro-Roger," he said with much difficulty.

"My name is Hubert Barney."

The dodo closed his eyes, relaxed his head against the hay, looked peaceful.

You are dark inside, Mr. Dodo, thought Hubert. Your soul is stained with the darkest of thoughts, and now you have the darkest of conditions—death.

Hubert raised his carbine, took aim, and shot the dodo in the head.

He tied a rope around the body and ran the loose end out to Tim. Tim pulled the carcass out of the stable.

Minutes later, Tim, Zack, and Hubert were airborne, heading for the wound in the earth and Spiderweb One beyond.

Three dead punks sailed from the sky, released from Tim's and Zack's razors when the flight passed over the line into Dodoland.

They swept high and shot toward the Spiderweb.

The pilot listened to the mission commander's voice, watched the eerie special effects projected on the screen. More details about their mission were being dispensed. They wanted to safeguard the experimental aircraft.

"The Bats *will* come home." The mission commander leveled his eyes on the pilot. "If anything happens ..." He left a huge gap.

The pilot understood: He was to abort the mission if the experimental aircraft were imperiled. There would always be another day, another shot at that other world.

But the pilot was known for tenacity.

The lights came on. Everyone stood. It was time.

The bombers streamed down the runway and rose like whispers into the blue sky. They shot high and in minutes were over the target.

They sank in a lazy spiral. They had to approach the window just right. The window into that other world.

The pilot relaxed, letting the computers do the work. He stared out the windshield at that huge expanse of blue.

Cold. Deep. Earth.

Andrew chuckled as he sank into the cold, deep earth, losing his body.

He heard Charles Barbier's silent cry for help. That was expected.

He chuckled again, a cold, cold chuckle swimming up from the depths.

Where are you, Charles?

Charles was hiding in the woods, calling for help.

Lend a hand, Andrew!

You are the only god in residence!

Aye, Charles, thought Andrew. That I am.

Andrew flowed into Charles's consciousness, merged with his body, and once again took on a new illusion, a new life.

Charles stick-walked up to the door of the Great Hall. Seeing him approach, a growth moron brandishing an ax stepped in front of him, blocking his way.

"Passage is forbidden to all but Clem's executioner!" shouted the growth moron.

"Step aside!" commanded Charles. "*I* am Clem's executioner!" Charles's words were cold and musty. His jaws worked methodically on creaky hinges.

"But ... but ... you?" stammered the growth moron, continuing to block Charles's way.

"Step aside, growth moron!" commanded Charles. It was a social impropriety to call anyone a growth moron, regardless of how accurate the description was.

The growth moron looked at Charles with shocked-open beak and horror-struck eyes. He took a step backward, looked around for help. Eighty or so growth morons ringed the outside of the hall, each with an ax cradled in a wing. But they seemed to want to mind their own business.

The guard looked at Charles. "You are …?"

"I am Charles! Announce me!"

The guard ducked inside the Great Hall.

"Your Excellency, Chairman Maurice, announcing Charles-who-is-dead-but-can-speak." The guard stepped aside.

"What?"

Charles heard the hooted exclamation from Maurice. Dodos in shock often hooted their words, issuing them in birdsong inflection. It was a disgrace that cultured dodos like Maurice tried mightily to avoid.

Charles stick-walked through the door, paused, and cast his eyes about. Maurice was at the table, on his feet. They had a full house. The dodo council was all present and accounted for. Growth morons ringed the inside of the hall, each with an ax gripped in a wing. Clem and the little cowboy were standing on the conference table. Two of Clem's disciples sat on one of the big chairs.

Charles stick-walked toward the table.

"That is right, Chairman Maurice. I am Charles-who-is-dead-but-can-speak." He reached the table, became fluid for an instant, and climbed up, joining Ralph and Clem.

Charles fixed his eyes on Maurice. "You hooted, Chairman Maurice. Does that mean you are surprised to see me?"

The Chairman was staring at him. Uncertainty marked his features. It was a social impropriety to mention a dodo's hoots.

"Charles, dead humans aren't supposed to speak. They aren't supposed to purposefully look at anyone or anything either. This is a gross breach of etiquette."

"Do you believe I am not dead, Chairman Maurice?"

"You look much deader than before, Charles. But such behavior! Where is Andrew? He was a much, much better dead human than you, Charles."

"Andrew has vanished."

"We will find him. But for now, Charles, attorney from D.C., you will obey my every command. You will not speak. You will not look at anyone or anything except for objects that naturally fall before your eyes. You will do only what you are told. Is that clear?"

Charles did not respond. He turned and stick-walked off the end of the table and crashed to the floor. He levered himself up and walked to the door. He stood beside it where Andrew had always stood, looking out on the Great Hall, taking in all that happened to meet his frozen gaze.

I'm standing in Andrew's space, thought Charles, pride leaping through him. He felt a cold chuckle rise within. Then he knew.

Andrew, it was you. All along. Possessing me.

Merging with you, Charles. Not possessing you.

Good. Good. Good.

Charles, allow knowledge to come into your mind. Don't fight the creative forces that want to help.

Charles relaxed. Andrew's presence comforted him. His death pose became exquisite.

Ah ... food. Food. Each of those growth morons hates their mama. None of them ever got enough to eat. They hate their daddy also. Never mind that none of them knows who their mama and daddy are. No dodo does. But, leave it to growth morons ... Charles chuckled deep inside.

He wished for some food. For himself. And for the growth morons. He sent a silent whisper to Chad Garrick.

Chairman Maurice shouted at the top of his lungs.

"Let the trial begin!"

He took his seat, summoned Lute to his side, and handed him the portion of the catechism that described the trial.

"Read this to the assemblage, Lute, and make sure it's followed to the letter."

"Yes sir, Chairman Maurice." Lute took a seat at the end of the table.

Clem and Ralph, still standing on the table, turned to face him.

"This court is now in session." Lute smashed the blunt end of his ax against the tabletop. "The case of Malcolm Moreland, a human, versus Clem, a dodo, and Malcolm Moreland, the same, versus Ralph Barney, a human, is before the court. Let it be known that Malcolm Moreland is the judge in this trial. Also, let it be known that Malcolm Moreland must decide if Clem is to die or if Ralph Barney is to die. One or the other must die, not both."

Lute paused, cleared his throat, rattled the papers, and continued.

"Further, let it be known that Chad Garrick, a human, is counsel for the defense for Clem, and that Ralph Barney is to be his own counsel. The executioner is Charles Barbier, a dead human. The sentence to be carried out is hanging from the neck until dead-and-no-longer-walking-around."

Lute looked up.

"Clem, you have been charged with grievous capital offenses against God and man by Malcolm Moreland. By dodo standards,

Clem, you are a perfect being. By Malcolm Moreland's human standards, you should be put to death. How do you plead?"

Clem began to speak but Lute waved him off and handed him a sheet of the catechism, snarling under his breath, "Read your lines."

Clem cast the sheet aside and took up a fighting stance.

"I plead guilty to being a dodo," he said, "but innocent of having to measure up or down to anyone's standards."

Anger rose in Lute's face. He stood and smashed the blunt end of his ax on the tabletop.

"Order in this court! The defendant will answer—"

Clem slumped; the fight seemed to go out of him. Lute sat and withered Clem with a look of pure enmity.

Thanks, Clem ...

Chad had been creeping around under the table, flowing with energy and purpose. He had secretly asked Clem to set up Lute. Now, he sprang.

"Aaaaa ..."

A shriek exploded from Lute. He pawed his right eye. A jet of blood stained his wings.

Chad yanked his staff free from Lute's eye socket. And suddenly, the Great Hall was filled with the startled hoots, calls, and mad flapping wing dances of a hundred dodos, spooked into goo-goo land by Chad's wounding of Lute.

Amidst this insanity, Chad scrambled onto the table.

Lute, in agony and rage, climbed onto the table and attacked Chad with his ax.

Chad blocked Lute's ax with his staff and forced it aside, then drove the end of his staff into the dodo's exposed beak.

More screaming from Lute. More goo-goo land for all of the assembled dodos. Lute spun around like a tornado, then flew at Chad again.

The battle stormed across the tabletop, Lute launching attacks, Chad deflecting them with his staff, blocking deadly swipes of ax and razors.

Finally, Chad dislodged the ax from Lute's wing.

Lute retreated, groped for the ax, grabbed it.

Chad rammed his staff into Lute's throat, but it didn't slow the enraged dodo. He flew at Chad, the ax raised.

Chad sidestepped the streaking ax and dislodged it again from Lute's wing, sending it sailing to the floor. Its clatter upon landing was a dim echo through the insanity that still racked the hall.

Lute came at Chad, razors slashing.

Chad dodged Lute's razors and rammed his staff into Lute's throat again, this time with greater effect.

Lute retreated, his wings flying up protectively as Chad drove his staff into his chest, abdomen, and throat again—powerful blows—sending Lute reeling.

Lute's wings began flapping madly. He fell off the table and joined the other birds in goo-goo land.

When the pandemonium broke out, Mel hustled Ralph and Angela under the table. Clem quickly joined them.

"Guard them, old boy," said Mel to Clem as he unslung his rifle and crept out.

He looked for Maurice. He couldn't see him. The dodos were a sea of frothing waves. The chairman was lost in the storm. This won't last much longer, he thought. When they're back from goo-goo land ...

He trained his rifle around. He was going to kill as many of them as he could, as soon as they fell out of their dance.

Charles became fluid enough to pick up an ax. The floor was littered with them. The growth morons' frenetic wings had flung them aside.

"Hoo-ray!" shouted Charles mechanically. Stick-walking, he went looking for Maurice.

Maurice felt his wings and legs become less spasmodic. They did not trip around so much anymore. His mind became calmer, the seizures attenuating.

He knew what had happened. He did not relish falling out of his dance. He feared Lute. A vengeful one-eyed monster would be tough to handle.

Why doesn't Lute just die quickly? he thought. In return for the giant's allegiance, Maurice had promised Lute a safe working environment. That had been important to Lute—he was a mutant and couldn't regenerate, as Maurice well knew, though neither had broached the subject.

Maurice had never admitted his own mutanthood to himself. His mind was bound up in powerful denial.

Maurice, shaken from his dance, came back from goo-goo land. Tottering, he looked around. Lute! Lute! Don't blame me!

Then he saw Charles. Stuttering, Maurice's beak formed worryful words.

"Ch-Ch-Charles, d-d-dead humans ar-aren't su-supposed to-to—"

The blade sliced toward Maurice's throat. His wings flew up. He hooted madly. He turned and ran. Something tripped him. Something felt wet on his wings, on his legs. He writhed, rolled, covered up, looked—blood!

"Aaaaa ...!"

Hack!

Silence.

Chad leaped to the floor and pressed his attack against Lute. But it soon became clear that the madly spinning, blood-whirling giant was truly in goo-goo land. So Chad, warily, left him alone.

He rejoined Sandra by the table. They watched the insanity. Finally, the dodos' excursion into goo-goo land ended.

"Look!" Sandra tugged on his arm.

Chad saw Charles in a spidery dance going after Maurice with an ax.

He heard a thunderous roar and spun around. Mel had unleashed his elephant shooter. Another roar. And another. Birds, still disoriented, began falling.

He heard a scream, spun around, and saw Charles chop Maurice's head off.

Suddenly, the atmosphere in the hall changed.

Mel's gun continued to blast away, heaping deafness through the room. He was very selective in his targets. Chad knew he was going after dainty ones. The growth morons apparently sensed this also.

Unafraid, they picked up their axes and began advancing on Chad. He had harmed one of their own. Bloodlines were sizzling.

Chad stepped away from Sandra, spun around, and watched the growth morons close in. He whipped his staff in artful circles, and fauns came running in from out of nowhere, hauling sacks of Forest Buckle.

Thousands of fauns. Thousands of sacks. The aroma of Forest Buckle mingled with the gun smoke to produce a strangeness of smells.

The growth morons dropped their axes and tore into the sacks of Forest Buckle. Chad was surrounded by a circus of darting dodo beaks and chattering wee creatures. He watched as the feast moved outdoors—the fauns luring the growth morons into the forest.

Mel's gun convulsed for the last time.

"Got 'em all," he said. "Like picking doves off a power line. They never really came down from that flingin' jig o' theirs."

Chad surveyed the hall. Dodo bodies lay in scattered clumps. Axes lay everywhere.

An explosion of voices came from under the table. Laughing. Crying. Clem popped out. Ralph came running out, dragging Angela, who had him in a tight grip.

"Let go!" cried Ralph.

She let him go.

"Tell us, Ralph," said Clem. "Tell us about Drakon."

"I already told you, Clem, old boy. I was Drakon's window onto the Spiderweb."

"Ralph, is that really you?" said Angela. "We're going to take you home, and if you're fooling—"

"Angela!" said Mel sharply. "Let him go!"

Ralph broke away from Angela, turned to her, and saluted. "Cheerio," he said. And with that, he sank into the floor of the Great Hall and merged with earth.

Angela sobbed and buried her face in her hands.

"I'm so glad," she finally said, looking up, wiping her tears away. "I'm so glad we brought him with us."

Hoodoo, thought Chad.

Ten

✺ DOOMSDAY ✺

As the flight swept over Spiderweb One, Hubert sensed a rapidly changing environment below.

"Growth morons loose in the grove," said Tim.

Hubert saw swarms of giant dodos milling about, then spied Angela and the others huddled beside a monstrous web building.

Tim and Zack landed.

Hubert dismounted.

Angela, looking distraught, rushed to Hubert.

"Hubert ..." She sobbed. "I have to tell you about Ralph."

He looked around. "Is he gone?"

"Yes. He—"

"I knew, Angela."

"You knew? How?"

"Some things you just know. Don't worry. Ralph will always be a part of us."

She looked away and wiped her tears.

"The punks?" asked Mel.

"They're dead," said Zack. "What's the story here?"

Mel filled them in. He told of Chad's role and of the fight in the Great Hall, then turned it over to Sandra.

"Doomsday and Plan B," she said, searching their faces. She gave them the sketchy details.

"We'd better get into the cells," said Sandra. "There isn't much time. Chad?"

She turned and ran.

Chad, in a torrent of energy, led them to the first cell.

"Everybody in," he said.

"I don't quite understand this, Chad," said Tim, squeezing through the opening Sandra had cut.

"It's a ritual," said Chad. "The Universe requires it, I think."

"Oh, that explains it." Tim popped through the webbing and stumbled into the cell.

With everyone inside, Chad said, "Tim and Zack, stay here. Get down. Stay immobile. You're part of the variegated mass."

He led the others into the next cell. "Charles, stay here." Charles stayed behind and the others followed Chad deeper into the cells. Mel was dropped off next. Then Hubert. Then Angela and Clem were put in a cell together. Chad crawled into the last cell.

Hubert sat in the middle of his cell. Chad's instructions had been simple. *Don't move. You're hidden. Wait. You'll know what to do when it happens.* When what happens? Chad had just shrugged.

He heard a shout of alarm from Angela. Then he heard Chad's voice.

"Don't be afraid. It's just Andrew, the repairman. He'll be going through the cells, sewing up the openings we made."

Hubert heard willies escape from Angela, then saw a vague shape dart about in the next cell.

Moments later, the face of death poked its head into Hubert's cell, and Hubert's willies danced up his spine.

The pilot braced himself as his super-sleek Bat hit the window into that other world. Momentarily, his vision swam with double images: two cockpits, slightly out of sync; two worlds out there. The images twined together, creating an uncertain whole.

The Bats rose, fanned out, and flew toward their targets.

The pilot watched a bank of display screens. In one of them, a mountain caught his eye. He pushed a button and a camera zoomed in.

The mountain was jagged, peaked. It was nothing like a grave, and yet that is what came to the pilot's mind: his father's grave back in Kansas. His father was trying to break out of that mountain.

The pilot watched, transfixed. He saw the mountain quiver, as if it were trying to fly.

The pilot snapped his eyes away from the screen.

We've got to drop these bombs, he thought, and get the hell out of here.

The air inside the cockpit exploded with a loud, sizzling crack. *Oh, no! Whatever that was, it ripped open the universe,* or so the pilot thought. Stunned, he felt a red-hot lava creature pop out of his chest.

He sensed this lava creature bobbing around in the cockpit. He looked at the screen that showed the mountain. Dancing upward, the mountain split in half.

Crack! Crack!

Its halves split.

Crack! Crack! Crack! Crack!

Lava creatures, felt not seen, flew around inside the cockpit.

A million throats roared in the distance as the mountain split a million times, a billion times. The roaring faded to silence as the mountain rose. A swarming hive, it accelerated upward and became a mushroom cloud, massive against the face of the world.

The pilot relaxed. He was tenacious. Nothing would stay him from his rounds. He reached out a hand and patted a small lava creature's head. Back in Kansas, as a child, he had had a puppy.

Warm thoughts came to him.

<hr />

"Clem," said Angela, "you're the messiah, tell me what's going to happen."

"Technically, Angela, I'm no longer the messiah, my enemies are dead."

"I guess that's true."

"And I have no idea what's going to happen, but I feel something."

"So do I," said Angela.

They were hunkered down in their cell. Andrew, the scary repairman, had come and gone.

Suddenly, Angela felt soaring waves of energy course through her body. Not the willies, not quite. This was something different, like someone typing a message on her vertebrae. Maybe it was kin to the willies.

She heard footsteps outside the cell, a growth moron walking by, glancing around. They're back, she thought. Chad had warned them they might return. *Be quiet and don't move,* he had told them. *They won't notice you.*

She saw other growth morons wandering the grounds. They're probably in shock, she thought. Their leaders are dead. Their food, more than likely, is gone. And, unless they're different from us, they're feeling strange energy surge through their bodies. She almost felt sorry for them. They're like big dumb puppies—but not quite. They're mindless killers. Her compassion sank away but quickly returned. They're hunting themselves. And killing themselves. And they don't even know it.

The key *Elyth Skilly* verse swam into Angela's consciousness—the first time she had heard the words. It sent goose bumps racing all over her. She *knew* it was the key verse. It was *there* all along, locked in with all the willies, all the fear, excitement, and horror.

Again, it rose from the depths.

She sensed Clem was hearing it also. They all were.

She looked outside the cell. It was raining. A light rain. It had grown overcast.

A stone fell through the webbing and landed near Angela. She grabbed it. Examined it. It was a split stone. It had split from another stone, which had split from another. The stone split again in Angela's hand as she watched it. She dropped the two halves.

It was raining stones.

Coming down heavier.

Sharp stones.

Shadows capered. Growth morons scattered, pelted by stones. Their cries raged.

But the stones did not hit those in the cells.

Rrrr ... rip!

The falling stones tore at the Spiderweb.

All the while, the Universe sang the key *Elyth Skilly* verse:

"Are you casting a stone which if it were true would split in half and half fly back at you?"

Hubert, within the depths of his mind, heard the key *Elyth Skilly* verse.

He heard Angela singing it. He joined in. He heard Clem, Mel, Charles, Tim, and Zack. All were singing it.

The Spiderweb, disintegrating under the rain of stones, collapsed around him. He looked up and saw tunnels through the air.

Willies!

Chad, singing the key *Elyth Skilly* verse with Angela and the others, looked up.

Slithers!

The pilot saw the dark mass of rain loom closer. He knew what it was. It was the mountain, precipitating from its mushroom cloud. Split to pieces. Chips. Fragments. Traces of itself. Fear rode his spine. Pebbles rained on the Bat.

We're doomed, he thought.

He started to radio the other Bat pilots, but a stone flew into the cockpit.

Oddly, once it had punched through, it fell in slow motion.

He grabbed it, looked up; a hole in the canopy gaped at him. He looked at the stone. It split in his hand. He dropped both halves.

The pilot barked a warning into the radio.

A horrifying thought leaped into his mind: If we drop these bombs, I don't know how, but they will follow us, the bombs will ...

One of the half stones flew up and hit the pilot. It seemed to speak. *Go back to base.*

The pilot gave a gruff command to the other Bat pilots: "Abort mission. Return to base."

The Bats formed up, flew out the window.

All but one.

Caught in the storm, the lead Bat stayed.

The pilot landed on a long expanse of green grass. He gazed out the canopy at a purple hedge more than a mile long, and beyond it, at a bewildering community of purple shrubs.

As stones pelted the pilot's craft, he heard a peculiar chant, a chant that seemed to originate from somewhere inside him:

"Are you casting a stone which if it were true would split in half and half fly back at you?"

The rain of stones veered away, leaving the Bat alone.

Under clearing skies, the pilot looked out the canopy and felt his body clench.

Birds!

Giant birds were heading toward the Bat, wandering over from the maze of purple shrubs. They gawked at the aircraft, meandered closer, stepped over the hedge.

The pilot raced his eyes and hands over the Bat's systems, checking for readiness. Not all systems were go, but he had to fly it anyway, and fast, before the birds could surround him.

The pilot coaxed the Bat into the air. He flew in circles, his navigation system shot. He had no idea which way to go.

Where is home? his mind screeched.

A roar deafened Chad's ears. The rain of stones fell around him in mad, whirling sheets. The slithers were insane vortices overhead, careening their cyclone bodies in dizzying displays.

A slither dipped low. Chad leaped for it. It danced away, ghostlike.

Chad fell to the ground. He was shocked. Slithers are supposed to save you, take you away. Deliver you to your next destination.

Am I supposed to stay in this world? he thought.

Chad stood, looked up. He felt like collapsing again. He felt like crying. He whipped his staff at a clowning slither.

"Damn you!" he shouted. "Damn you! Damn you! Damn you!"

He looked at where the next cell had been. The Spiderweb

was gone; the webbing lay in pulpy tangles. Through the rain of stones, he saw Angela and Clem dancing for the slithers. Hubert and the others were also dancing, but to no avail.

"Don't give up!" shouted Chad.

He flew back into his own dance.

The pilot gazed out the canopy, stared at the distant rain, idly kept the Bat circling clear of the storm. He was holding a warm little lava creature, petting it, cooing to it.

It cooed back.

He knew the lava creature was a part of him. It had separated from him when the mountain had split. He held the creature to his chest and pushed it back inside.

The pilot saw a glittering stream of light shoot across the sky. It danced. It coiled and uncoiled. It swam toward the Bat and opened wide.

The pilot flew the Bat into the stream of light.

It became a snake and took the Bat for a ride. After a dizzying few minutes, the Bat slipped from it.

The pilot saw the window, slipped through it, and was homeward bound.

Ahead in the deep blue sky, the pilot saw his father. Yellow jeans, yellow shirt, singing canary songs. A frolic in the air.

Negative, he thought. A trick of the mind. A trick of the atmosphere.

He prodded the limping Bat back to the base, following a highway part of the way, eliciting stares of incomprehension from the humans below.

⟞⟝

The slithers danced and jabbed at Chad, and pulled away as he reached for them, then set upon him again. Chad felt like a puppet.

He stopped jumping.

"I want to go home," he whispered.

A slither descended. Chad stepped aboard. The slither became a snake and took him for a ride.

Twisting through the air, Chad saw that the others had followed his lead. *Simple desire!*

He saw Angela and Clem—each aboard a crystal-clear slither. And Hubert and Mel and Charles and Tim and Zack— aboard theirs.

The rain stopped. Stones littered the grove. The Spiderweb was an ash. Sunlight burst through.

Chad's slither rose above the treetops. He saw Marshall in a slither, and Sandra and Andrew in slithers.

Rory and Marcia?

He looked. He willed the slither to go down, to go back.

It rose.

Chad searched the sky. Slithers were everywhere. Prisoners were free. Except those, he imagined, who were stoned to death. And those who remained like puppets, exhausting themselves.

The gang flew together.

Chad and Sandra reached out through the walls of their slithers, touched hands. She was warm now. And Chad felt warm too.

The slithers danced and frolicked, twisted and twined until

the humans and birds and monks were one monstrous laughing knot, then untwined, dropped to earth, and slithered madly across the woods and meadows.

To the wound in the earth.

Eleven

～ THERE IS A LAND ～

*T*hey were going home.

Tim and Zack and Clem and their human passengers flew through the wound in the earth.

Hubert glanced below. The air did not seem a slave to myriad impersonal forces now. The air was free. Alive. The air swam with all that touched it.

A meadow below touched the air. The meadow touched Hubert's eyes. His vision swam with green and gold—millions of greens, millions of golds, shades and shadows, glints and waves, flashing sharp and rolling soft. A meadow alive. A meadow swimming in infinite rhythms. A meadow in touch with the Universe.

And in that meadow, mused Hubert, catching sign of movement below, there lived a cat. An ordinary cat. It oozed through the grass. Sleek and tawny. Sinuous.

But ...

Something was wrong.

Or was it?

The cat was hurt or suffering in some way. At least to the man who—in Hubert's imagination—now walked below in that meadow.

The man stopped. He had caught a glimpse of the cat, a jump in front of him, a bare glimmer of fur. He peered into the grass. He leaned closer. Closer. Movement. He followed the cat's trail, its furrow through the grass, the slivers of silent, cutting fur.

The cat stopped. The cat turned and faced the man. The man stepped close to the cat, then stopped.

What is the matter? asked the man, seeing the cat's upturned eyes. The cat's eyes revealed nothing.

The cat told a story to the man, a long, long story. But the man didn't understand. So the cat sat up, exposing her belly to the man.

The man reached down and stroked the soft belly. So that's it. You have little ones inside.

Yes, said the cat.

Now the man understood the long, long story.

The cat was on the hunt. It was not sick. It had to kill and eat for many. Little ones were on the way. They needed a strong foundation. The cat was their foundation. And their fountain. Some day they would flow from the cat.

The man walked through the grass.

The cat flowed through the grass.

As they went their separate ways, the story became a fountain in the man's mind:

There is a land. And somewhere in that land lives a cat. An ordinary cat. A cat who knows the Universe. And somewhere in that land is a deep, deep well. And from that well flows something very precious: Freedom.

Clem was the highest. Chad looked up. Clem wove a spell through the blue ocean.

The staff flew from Chad's hands and sailed away. He watched it land, watched it turn into a cat, watched it vanish into the tangles below.

The three dodos landed beside the birch grove that held the two horses. The three humans slid to the ground. Tim and Zack and Clem took to the air and flew back to Dodoland.

The three humans mounted Pioneer and Cassandra.

They headed across the prairie toward Chad's house. When they were close enough, Chad slipped from Pioneer.

His shadow long in the lowering sun, he watched the two Barneys disappear over a rise.

He entered his house. Empty.

Two hours later, still empty. Another three hours passed. He walked from the dark living room and went upstairs. He wanted to rummage through the attic. That picture of Milky. He wanted to see it again.

He stopped on the second floor. Shadows whispered to him. Silence.

Yes. I will go outside. He walked downstairs, went out the door, stood in the dark.

He ran toward the bur oaks. Sandra! Marshall! Drakon! Milky!

He stopped. He looked up. There …

Drakon's voice rose within him.

There are many things unknown. They swim through the sky. They fly through the depths. They traverse outer space. They float, they slip, they shelter all about. They leave planets and trace paths of fame. The art of life is written in the stars above.

Blazing across the heavens …

Chad stared at the Milky Way.